THE BOSUN by Harlow Layne

Copyright © 2021 by Harlow Layne. All rights reserved.
ISBN-13: 978-1-950044-12-2 (Ebook Edition)
ISBN-13: 978-1-950044-19-1 (Paperback Edition)

Edited by: Your Editing Lounge
Proofreading by: The Polished Author, Amira El Alam, Brittany Bailey, Fiona Larbi
Cover Design: Harlow Layne
Photographer: Armando Adajar
Cover Model: Eric Guilmette

No part of this book may be reproduced in any form or by any electronic or mechanical means, including information storage and retrieval systems, without written permission from the author, except for the use of brief quotations in a book review.

Manufactured in the United States of America.

This is a work of fiction. Names, characters, places, and incidents either are the products of the author's imagination or are use fictitiously. Any resemblance to actual persons, living or dead, businesses, companies, events, or locales is entirely coincidental.

# BOSUN

## HARLOW LAYNE

# 1

## STELLA

"I CAN'T BELIEVE I let you talk me into this," I murmured to my best friend, Pen, out of the corner of my mouth so the other girls wouldn't hear me.

"Why not? You totally deserve it after going through one of the worst divorces of this century." Pen said the last loudly, making all eyes turn toward me.

I rolled my eyes at her embellishment. "It was hardly the worst. Maybe coming from our little hometown of Oasis, but not by LA's standards. Mine was but a blip on the radar compared to some of the celebrity disaster divorces that hit the magazines and blogs."

"If you go by the water cooler talk at Brock's office, you're nothing but a gold-digging bitch. Do you remember all those nights you called me crying?" I could only nod as

I thought back to all the talk that made its way back to me and the way I broke down into tears on the phone while Pen picked me up. "You deserve this after everything that man put you through."

I wouldn't deny my ex had put me through the wringer, but I wasn't used to such splendor. My eyes grew wide the closer we got to the dock, and I saw the boat. Okay, it wasn't exactly categorized as a boat, but a yacht. It was mammoth and nicer than anything I'd experienced in my thirty-seven years on this Earth.

"Let me pamper you," Zelda smiled across from me. "It's the least I can do for a friend."

We weren't friends. We were barely acquaintances, but I wasn't going to fight her on it. Zelda was a friend of a friend who'd heard about my divorce from her friend Reagan, who was friends with Pen. Pen convinced me to let this woman take us on an all-expenses-paid trip to Spain, and I needed to show her how grateful I was to be whisked away from the stares and whispers of the people in our small town. Away from my ex and his pregnant fiancée.

Reaching forward, I placed my hand on hers and smiled. "Thank you, Zelda."

"Of course, darling. Now, what do you say we get on that boat so you can start making your ex jealous." How was I going to do that, I wondered? Zelda must have seen the confusion on my face since she answered my unspoken question. "Oh,

## THE BOSUN

we're going to get our bikinis on, take pictures, and post them on Instagram. Show your ex what he gave up."

Posting pictures of myself in a bikini for the world to see wasn't something I was comfortable with, but if I could stick it to Brock, it might be worth it.

The limo stopped in front of a row of people standing in front of the yacht that looked like it was bigger than my house.

"OMG, Z, this is going to be an epic trip," Reagan squealed loud enough to make my ears ring.

I went to roll my eyes for Pen to see and commiserate with, but as I looked around, everyone had happy smiles on their faces as they took in our new home for the next five days. Even though it was over the top, I didn't want to ruin anyone's fun with my foul mood. Brock could ruin my day even from thousands of miles away.

Ever since I found out my husband, now ex-husband, had not only cheated on me but had gotten the trollop who worked at his office pregnant, I'd been in a perpetual bad mood, which was something I wanted to change on this trip.

Brock and his floozy were no longer in my life. Thank God, I hadn't had any children with him; then I'd have had to fight with him for the next eighteen years. Nope, instead, I got a huge payout since we didn't have a prenup, and we had exactly twelve cents collectively to our names when we got married. Normally I wasn't a vindictive person, but I'd worked two jobs so we could get by while Brock went to medical school. My payout was just the interest I charged for all of those years of hard work. If it wasn't for me, Brock never would have been able to pay for medical school.

Now was my time to have fun and live free. And maybe decide what I wanted to do with the rest of my life.

Stretching my legs out of the limo and dipping my head out into the sunshine, I was immediately hit with salty air and took a deep breath in. Instantly I relaxed. Pen was right to force me on this trip. Spain was the perfect place to start over.

The girls were already in a line meeting the crew, and Zelda was eating up the way they fawned over her. Now I knew why she liked to go on these trips as often as she did. This was the life.

With each new crew member I met, I wondered how they kept getting better and better looking. Just when I thought one of the girls was the prettiest little thing I'd ever seen, up popped the next one to show off her dazzling smile and beach waves that hung down her back, who was even more beautiful than the last.

Damn, was being gorgeous a requirement for working on a yacht? I was sure it didn't hurt.

I stopped dead in my tracks when the hand of the stereotypical tall, dark, and handsome times a million was in front of me. When his large, calloused hand engulfed mine, I nearly swooned and turned into a puddle of drool right at his feet.

Pen pushed me on to the next person. Probably so she could

## THE BOSUN

have his hands on her. Maybe I should call dibs on Mr. Sexy. It was probably frowned upon to sleep with the guests, but damn would I be happy to break a few rules with him.

It was probably my hormones talking or my vagina since it had been way too long since any male had been close to seeing my lady bits. Shit, I knew I should have gotten that Brazilian when I had the chance, but I never thought I'd be around a guy I'd drop my bottoms for while I was on the boat.

I moved forward and shook the Captain's hand, and stood off to the side as I waited for my best friend to finish up. Once she was through, Pen skipped over to me with hearts in her eyes and a grin that screamed man-eater. "That boy is so fucking hot," she whisper-yelled.

Boy was the key term. He had to be at least ten years younger than the two of us. His clean-shaven face didn't help his boyish charm. Fuck, was I a cougar now? Normally I didn't have these thoughts, but I was married before, and now I was free to think whatever and ogle whoever I wanted.

"I wouldn't mind getting to know him a little better down below if you know what I mean." I waggled my eyebrows, causing Pen to throw her head back and laugh.

"Girl, you should go for it. You totally deserve it. Maybe sneak a pic and post it on social media so Brock can see what he's missing." Pen laughed through her words, thinking she was hilarious.

There was no way in hell I was posting myself in bed with

anyone, even if it would make Brock jealous. I'd make him see what he'd let go by living my best life.

"If you'll take off your shoes and follow me, I'll show you around the boat, and you can pick your rooms," the crazy gorgeous blonde stewardess, Ophelia, said with a fake smile plastered on her face.

"No shoes?" Reagan squeaked.

"To protect the boat, there are no shoes allowed." Ophelia looked down at Reagan's high-heeled feet.

Reagan's nose scrunched up in disgust. "But I don't want to see anyone's nasty feet."

"I'm sorry, but that's the rule of the boat." Ophelia gave a tight smile.

"What if someone has ape feet?" Reagan asked as she kicked off her heels.

"I'm not sure what ape feet are, but I can promise you the crew takes good care of their feet."

"You should have requested they all have pedicures before we boarded," Reagan whined to Zelda.

We all looked at each other with wide eyes. I wanted to believe she was kidding, but I knew she wasn't.

Kicking off my flip-flops, I started to pick them up when Pen whispered in my ear, "Don't look now, but I swear that hot crew guy is staring at your ass." Of course, I looked because that's what you do when someone tells you not to look.

His dark chocolate eyes were indeed settled straight on my

## THE BOSUN

ass. I wanted to shake it at him to see if I could get more of a reaction out of him but fought the urge. It was nice to feel desired, and it made my lips tip up as we followed the girls onto the boat.

I tried not to gawk as we toured the yacht, but damn, it was hard not to. It was beautiful and elegant, with every surface white and glass with gold as the accent color. We all eyed Zelda's bedroom after seeing the size of the others. She had a large bathroom with a tub you could relax in.

Zelda spun on her heels. "Alright, girls. Let's get our suits on and then reconvene on the bathing deck in twenty minutes."

"I'll have the crew bring your suitcases as quickly as possible. When would you like to have lunch?" Ophelia looked to Z.

"In an hour. You can serve us while we lay out," Zelda said as she sat on her bed.

"We can do that. Do you want something simple then?" Ophelia's tone said the answer to that should be a resounding yes.

"Something to keep us cool," Zelda replied.

"Okay," Ophelia drawled out. "I'll tell the chef you'd like something to keep you cool while you sunbathe."

Pen and I linked arms as we headed to our room.

"Maybe we should throw her overboard, and we can share her room," Pen whispered conspiratorially in my ear.

"Then who's going to pay?" I shot back, and hip-checked her.

"Good point. I don't even want to know how much she's paying. At least we're sharing a room, and it's a decent size. I can't imagine sharing a room with Reagan or Scarlett."

Me either. Reagan was too high maintenance for me, and Scarlett was too quiet. Maybe she'd break out of her shell the longer we were here and once she got to know us.

I looked around our room. There wasn't much space with our two beds and our luggage that had already been delivered scattered all over the floor as Pen started going through hers, but I didn't plan to spend much time in here. I wanted to enjoy the sun and the salty breeze as much as possible.

"Yeah, Reagan was already looking a little green, and there was no way in hell I was sharing a room with her if she's going to be sick the whole time."

"Maybe it's because she saw someone's ape feet," I giggled. Opening up my suitcase, I started to look for one of the swimsuits I'd packed, but couldn't find them. "Pen," I called as I started to unpack everything to find my swimsuits.

"Yes?" She drew out the word in a giddy tone, letting me know she was up to something.

"What did you do?" Turning around to face her, I put my hands on my hips and tried to look stern. It was impossible when I saw the red dental floss she was holding up. "That's what you're wearing?"

"No." She shook her head before she started to crack up. I could barely understand the words as they came out of her

## THE BOSUN

mouth because she was laughing so hard. "It's what you're wearing."

"I had to have heard you wrong because there's no way in hell I'm wearing that." I turned back to my suitcase, desperate to find the suits I'd packed. "Now tell me what you've done to my suits."

Pen rolled her lips to try and hide her smile. Her whiskey-colored eyes sparkled with mischief. "How mad would you be if I told you I hid them in the back of your closet so you wouldn't find them?"

"Are you saying all of my swimwear is in the States?"

"I bought you new ones." She pulled out a brown paper bag that had been hidden in her suitcase.

"Let me see," I snatched it out of her hands and started to pull out one suit after another. They ranged in colors from the red that still hung from her fingertips to black and teal. "Pen," I cried. "I can't wear any of these."

"Why?"

"You know why." My voice came out high-pitched and squeaky.

"You have a banging bod and need to get all the shit that Brock spewed to you over the years out of your head."

"I know, but it's not easy."

Brock had been the jealous type who never wanted me to dress sexy or show my body. After a while, it became easier for me to dress the way he wanted me to than to fight with him on it. Now I was used to wearing clothes that covered my body.

"Why do you care? You're never going to see these people again. Show everyone what your momma gave you." She shimmied her boobs, making me laugh.

She was right, but if I wore any of the suits, I'd be showing more skin than anyone had seen in years, and I wasn't sure I was prepared for that.

"Let's start you off with this one." Pen picked out another bag from her suitcase and pulled out something black. "Now, this is a one-piece with strategic pieces cut out of it."

It looked like strips of fabric that were somehow all connected. Still, it was more than the others. I didn't have a better option until we were someplace I could buy another that was more to my comfort level.

"When we go to shore, I'm buying one that I approve of," I said as I took the slightly less offending swimsuit from her.

"I expect nothing less," she laughed. "Now go get suited up, and I'll meet you upstairs."

I lifted a brow at her order. "And what are you going to do?"

Penelope let out a sigh as she sat on her bed. "I've got to check in at work. There's this new band they want to sign and—" She clapped her hands, ending her train of thought. "It doesn't matter. It's just something I need to take care of before I can enjoy the next few days."

Giving her some privacy, I stepped into our tiny bathroom

## THE BOSUN

and let Pen do what she needed to do. Pen loved her job and had recently been promoted. I knew it was hard for her to leave right now, but she'd made it work, wanting me to be able to celebrate my divorce with this luxurious trip.

Back up on deck, I searched for the girls but couldn't find them anywhere. How long did it take to put on a swimsuit? Even with all my procrastinating, I was the first one out?

"Stella?" Pen yelled from behind me as Ophelia stepped up to me with a tray of flutes filled with Champagne. "Would you like another glass of Champagne, or would you like something different to drink?" Ophelia asked.

"Champagne's fine for now. Thank you," I responded as I took a flute before I turned around to find Pen walking toward me.

Ophelia offered her a drink as well, but my eyes were stuck on the hot guy who greeted us before we came aboard. He slowly started to pull his shirt over his head to reveal golden washboard abs, unlike anything I'd ever seen before.

My body started to overheat as more skin was revealed. Leaning back, I tried to catch my breath, but I must have miscalculated because one second, I was experiencing the joys of ogling the crew, and the next, I was falling.

My mouth had barely opened to scream when I hit the water. Warmth surrounded me as I tried to use my arms and legs to surface, but no matter how hard I struggled to the surface, the light kept getting further and further away, making me panic.

I couldn't believe I was going to die when I'd been on the boat for less than an hour. It served me right for doing something so extravagant when I could have just gone to the spa for a day to celebrate my divorce.

Just when I started to run out of breath and things were starting to become dark, strong arms wrapped around me and started to move me back toward the light.

Coming to the surface, I coughed and spluttered as I was dragged toward a smaller boat where two of the crew were pulling us by a rope. I tried to turn in the arms of my savior but was held too tightly to move. Instead, I lay back and let them do their job. I was never going to live down falling over the edge of the boat. I was already embarrassed enough I didn't want to see the girls when I got on board or face the crew, all because a guy took off his shirt. It wasn't like he was taking off his pants and let me see the graciousness that hung between his legs.

Now that would be a dream, wouldn't it?

Maybe I could hide in my room until we docked, and I wouldn't have to face anyone. Yeah, I was delusional. Maybe I drank more ocean water than I thought.

One of the guys picked me up from under the arms and dragged me onto the boat. Wrapping a towel around my shoulders, he stepped out of the way as the person who saved me, and the reason why I fell in the water, pulled himself out of the

## THE BOSUN

water.

"Her lips are blue. Give her your damn shirt," my savior barked out as he squatted down in front of me. "Are you okay?" When I only nodded as my teeth chattered, he grabbed another towel from the seat next to me and wrapped it around me. "We'll be back on board in a few minutes, and we'll get you warm, I promise."

"Thank you…" Fuck, I still didn't know his name.

"Remy, ma'am. I'm just doing my job."

"Do you often have to save women who fall overboard?" I asked with my teeth still chattering. When did the wind pick up?

Remy shook his head and gave a signal that seemed to mean to hurry up. The wind picked up, and the water misted my face. Moving to sit beside me, he looked toward the boat as we quickly came upon it.

"I have to say you're the first, and hopefully the last person I have to save from going overboard." His jaw ticked as he looked straight ahead.

Was that a reprimand? It wasn't like I meant to fall over. Maybe Mister Body of a God should keep his clothes on while on deck, so no accidents would happen.

In a matter of minutes, I was helped off the little dinghy and back aboard the yacht, where I was met by the waiting crew and my friends. Penelope immediately wrapped me in her arms. "I'm so glad you're okay. One minute we were sipping our Champs, and the next, you were gone."

I didn't need my best friend to remind me of my folly. I would have done anything in that moment for none of them to know what happened to me and to be able to hide it from them. They'd likely keep an extra set of eyes on me for the rest of the trip since I was now a liability.

Leaning into Pen as we walked to my cabin, I asked. "How many people saw that catastrophe?"

"Do you want the truth or—"

It was bad, I knew it, but I still interrupted her. "The whole truth."

"Everyone but one of the stewardesses." Penelope's face was a hopeful grimace as she looked at me.

Kill me now.

# THE BOSUN

# 2

## REMY

"REMY, REMY, OPHELIA, can you come to the galley?" I hear through my earpiece.

I groaned as I helped Scout and Owen load the boat they'd taken out earlier when we had to save one of the guests.

"What's that about?" Scout asked on a grunt.

"No idea," I answered back as we finished. "Are you guys good from here?"

"We're always good." Owen smiled and pulled out a cigarette. "Especially if we can take a ten-minute break."

"Take a break, but then be ready if the ladies need any help serving dinner." The wind had picked up, and it was a little choppy. Not enough to cause us to dock, but enough to knock you off your balance if you weren't careful. And climbing stairs with multiple plates in your hands while the boat sways could be difficult.

"Roger that," Owen saluted me.

I looked heavenward. I'd told him multiple times I was no longer a Marine, but he continued. Maybe if I told him why I was no longer in the military, he'd understand and stop, but I couldn't talk about that time in my life. If I did, my mind went to bad places, and I couldn't let myself go there and be in charge of this boat. I wouldn't—couldn't put anyone's life in danger ever again.

Heading inside, I made my way down to the galley to find all the stewardesses' eyes on me along with Dean, our chef. "You need me?"

Ophelia gave me the once-over and smirked. We'd hooked up once a couple of years ago when I got trashed. Since then, she'd been looking for our next hookup and hadn't caught on that it wasn't going to happen, much to her dismay.

"The primary has requested that you eat dinner with them." I went to object, but she held her hand up and smirked. "You have to since you saved her friend's life." Ophelia finished the last like it was the funniest thing she'd ever heard.

"You can't say no," Kylie, the second stew, said as she sat plates down for Dean to start plating.

I knew I couldn't say no since we were required to do anything the guests and especially the primary asked of us, but I'd still try to talk my way out of it.

## THE BOSUN

"I'll go change," I murmured as I turned on my heel and headed to the room I shared with Dean. We had the only room that didn't have a bunk bed. Our beds were on each side of the tiny room with a walkway between that was about a foot wide.

After pulling my formal black uniform out of the closet and slipping it on, I sat down on my bed and took in a deep breath. It was hard to find private time when everyone shared a room, so I took it when I could. I had a feeling it would do me good to help center myself before I had dinner with the guests.

Since I didn't have time for a shower and knowing I didn't have long before someone would come looking for me if I didn't get to the aft deck soon, I slicked my black hair back and applied another layer of deodorant and a splash of cologne.

"Scout, Scout, Remy," I called through the walkie-talkie.

"Scout here," he said.

"I've been asked to have dinner with the guest, so you're in charge until I relieve you."

"I won't let you down," Scout said.

I knew he wouldn't. He was a great senior deckhand, and Owen would listen to him. They were a dream crew.

Heading upstairs, I squared my shoulders and put a smile on my face as I stepped through the door to outside, where all the ladies were laughing loudly. The moment their eyes landed on me, they quieted—all except the primary whose eyes were glassy from drinking all day.

"There's the man of the hour," she stood and clapped. The

rest of the ladies followed. Stella blushed as she stood and lightly clapped. "Please have a seat." Zelda motioned to the chair that was across from Stella.

Moving to stand at the head of the table, I tried to persuade them to let me go. "Ladies, I appreciate the offer, but surely you don't want lame ol' me to join you."

"Of course, we want you. You saved our sweet Stella," the primary said a little too loudly. She was buzzed, going on drunk. I had a feeling O was making the drinks tonight. She liked to pour them strong in the hopes that the charter guests would go to sleep early. "Right, Stell?"

The woman of the hour bit her bottom lip as she hid behind a curtain of long, shiny black hair. "Please join us," she finally said as quietly as a mouse.

It was obvious she was embarrassed about what happened earlier. I mean, it wasn't often you heard of people falling overboard while drinking their second glass of Champagne.

Not wanting to humiliate her further, I pulled the seat out across from her and sat down. Looking down the table at everyone, I gave them my best smile. "Thank you for having me. I have to admit, this is my first time being asked to join any guests for dinner."

"I can hardly believe that with looks like yours," Zelda purred. I held the urge to cringe and back away. She had one too many rounds of plastic surgery, and she was actually hard to look at.

## THE BOSUN

"You'll be fine as long as you have good table manners," the one I thought was named Reagan said.

Stella swung her head toward her friend with narrowed eyes. The woman next to her with caramel-colored hair turned to Stella with her mouth in an 'O.'

"That was rude. I'm sorry," Stella apologized for her friend.

I waved it away. It was, but I'd heard worse. All I could do was grin and bear it.

The girls at the other end of the table went back to chatting with each other while our end stayed silent.

Luckily, the stews brought out our dinner plates. I was grateful I hadn't been invited to a seven-course meal. I planned to gracefully bow out after the dessert and get back to work. Scout was supposed to work late tonight and would need a break before he was up almost all night.

"How long have you been working on yachts?" The caramel colored haired woman asked across from me.

"Only a couple of years," I answered back as I took a bite of my steak. It melted in my mouth, and I let out a little hum of delight.

"Do you eat like this every night?" Penelope asked before Stella glared at her. "What?" She mouthed to her friend beside her.

When Stella saw me watching them, she smiled and went back to eating. Was she so shy because I saved her?

"Not usually, but I never pass up a meal made by our chef."

Guests didn't understand how busy chefs were. I swear I never saw Dean not cooking.

"You might not have him for long. If he keeps serving us food like this, I'm going to snatch him up and hire him as my own personal chef." Zelda smiled wide.

I couldn't imagine having enough money to be able to do that. Although most of the people who chartered yachts for vacations probably already had maids, butlers, and chefs on the daily, I didn't like it when they flaunted wealth like Zelda did a moment ago.

"I'd be happy for someone to cook a can of soup for me every once in a while," Stella told Penelope out of the corner of her mouth.

"You've got to find yourself a good man. Maybe a chef," Scarlett spoke up. She seemed pretty quiet, and it was easy to forget she was here. I had a feeling she liked it that way. She probably knew everyone's secrets.

I looked at Stella's left hand and found it ringless. All the women seemed to be single if their naked ring fingers were any indication.

"I don't need a man, but I would be happy to get laid by someone who knows what they're doing," Stella practically yelled.

I nearly spit my food out at her declaration. Even though it was strictly against the rules, I wouldn't mind showing her a good time.

## THE BOSUN

Ophelia was definitely making the drinks tonight. Halfway through her margarita and Stella was finally starting to let loose. Her cheeks were flushed from alcohol, and she couldn't stop her deep brown eyes from landing on me every few seconds, only to then look away.

Even though it wasn't smart, I couldn't take my gaze off Stella. She was gorgeous with her big brown eyes with long eyelashes that fanned her freckled cheeks. Plush pink lips that I couldn't stop imagining wrapped around my thick cock.

There was an uncomfortable silence when everyone was done with their plate and was waiting for dessert. Wanting to give the stew girls a little more time before the guests started to complain, I asked. "Where do you all live?"

"We all live in LA, well, Stella doesn't live there yet, but will soon," Zelda answered for all of them.

"If you don't live in LA, where do you live?" I asked Stella.

She rolled her lips before she answered. "In Oasis."

Was I supposed to know where that was?

"It's a small town in the desert a couple of hours away from LA. It's where I grew up, but as soon as I find a place to live in LA, I'm getting away from there. Where do you live?"

I shrugged because I didn't really live anywhere. "On boats."

"Do you work year-round?" she asked sweetly.

"No, but close. When I'm not working, which isn't often, I stay with family or friends. There's no point in me paying rent or a mortgage on someplace I'm never at."

Sitting up taller in her chair, Stella nodded. "Makes sense. If you could live anywhere, where would it be?"

"As crazy as it might seem since I'm on the water so much, I'd want to live by the ocean. I don't mean to be picky. I'd live by any water. A lake, the gulf, or the ocean."

With each word I spoke, Stella's face lit up. "I love the water. Maybe I should live on the beach."

"Yes!" Penelope clapped. "That would be perfect. When I need a break from the city, I'll come and stay with you."

"It's decided." Stella jumped in her seat.

Maybe making life-changing decisions while drinking wasn't the best idea, but what did I know about their lives.

"Oh, I have the best real estate agent. When we get back, I'll hook you up." Zelda wagged her eyebrows at Stella, and for some reason, I didn't like the implication of Zelda trying to hook up Stella with that guy.

"Have you ever thought about living in California?" Penelope asked me with a smirk on her face.

"I'm not opposed to it." I couldn't be a bosun for the rest of my life, and I didn't see ever wanting to be a captain, so eventually, I needed to decide what I wanted to do with the rest of my life. Until then, I wanted something to keep my mind off my days of being a Marine, and to make some good money, so once I decided on what I wanted to do with my life, I could find a place to rest my head.

## THE BOSUN

"You should think about it." Penelope nodded like it was a done deal. Was she crazy? I guess she loved living in California, but I hadn't even visited the state. "Where do you come from?"

Stella nudged her with her elbow. "Geez, Pen, what's with all the questions?"

"I'm just trying to get to know our very good-looking dinner guest."

I could feel my cheeks heat up with all their eyes on me. "It's okay, I don't mind. If I don't want to answer, I won't." Like about my days in the military. "I grew up in a small town in Florida. We lived about two hours away from the gulf."

I missed my dad waking me up early. We'd arrive at the water right as the sun started to rise over the water and fish until noon. Those were the days.

"Did everyone know everyone's business where you grew up?" Stella asked with a bite. I wondered what had happened to her to make her want to leave where she'd always lived.

"You can't sneeze without the people on the other side of town saying, 'bless you.'" Everyone knowing everything that happened every second of your life was what made me not want to go home.

"Stell and I know all about small towns." Penelope frowned at her friend.

"Let's not go there." Stella threw back the rest of her margarita and slammed down her glass. "Remember, we're celebrating and putting the past behind us."

I knew that was easier said than done.

Stella raised her glass. "More margs!"

The stews walked out at that moment with dessert in their hands. There were many times when I helped serve, so it was strange being on this side of the table.

"Tonight, the chef has bad for you a chocolate lava cake with a salted caramel sauce," O said as she plated the dessert in front of the primary. She always made sure the primary was served first since they were responsible for our tip.

Zelda held it to her nose and took a long, drawn-out sniff. "This looks to die for."

"I'll be sure to let the chef know. Would anyone like another drink?" she asked as she circled the table and collected the empty drink glasses.

"Yes," Stella held her glass in the air, "I'll have a glass of white wine. Whatever you've got. I'm not picky."

"Are you sure you should be switching to wine?" her friend asked her. "You don't want to get sick."

"I can't drink a margarita with a lava cake. *That* would make me sick." Stella scrunched her nose up as if the thought was disgusting.

It wasn't appetizing by any means.

"I am not holding your hair back later if you get sick." Pen raised her glass to Ophelia. "I'll take another glass of Champagne."

## THE BOSUN

"I'll be right back with your drinks," O said with what I knew was a fake smile on her face. She didn't like that she wasn't mixing up drinks and getting them drunk. I would never understand O. If the guests were plastered the entire time, they weren't going to leave us with a great tip. They needed to enjoy the experience as a whole.

"So Remy, is it?" Penelope asked.

"Yes, ma'am."

"Is that short for something?"

"No, just Remy." All my life, everyone thought my name was short for Remington, but my mom only ever planned to call me Remy, so she said there was no point in naming me something different. There was logic there.

"Do you have a girlfriend or a significant other?"

I almost choked on my bite of cake. Did she think I might be gay or married? I don't have a ring on my finger. While there's nothing wrong with being gay, I didn't think I put off those vibes.

"No, my lifestyle isn't conducive to having a girlfriend." I caught Stella relax at my words. Did she like that I didn't have a girlfriend or that I didn't want one?

Stella and Penelope seemed to have a wordless conversation that I enjoyed watching as they stared each other down. Every so often, one of their brows would raise, or a lip would twitch, but that was the only sign of movement. After that, they remained quiet, and I was disappointed they were done with me.

With everyone eating the amazing dessert, it wasn't long before everyone's plate was left without a crumb. While I wanted to leave earlier, now I wished I could stay. I knew I couldn't, though. I had to give Scout a break.

"Thank you for having me, ladies. It was a delight, but now I must get back to work. Have a good night." I bowed to them, then taking a step away, I caught out of the corner of my eye as my dinner companion stood on wobbly legs.

"Whoa there," I grabbed her arm to keep Stella from falling on her face. "Are you okay?"

She ducked her head and hid behind her shiny veil of hair. "I drank more than I realized, and it all just caught up to me. Would you walk me to my room? I really don't want to fall overboard again."

I'd probably be fired if she fell over again. Especially if it was because I wouldn't walk her to her room.

"We can't have that, can we?" I answered her, holding my elbow out for her to take.

"Where are you going?" Reagan asked with an arched brow.

"I'll be back as soon as I use the restroom. Remy here is helping me, so I don't fall off the boat again."

"You don't have to come back if you don't want to. If you need privacy, put something on the door handle."

Stella sent a murderous glare to her friend, making Penelo-

## THE BOSUN

pe laugh. She fell over and leaned on Scarlett's shoulder.

"Let's get out of here," Stella huffed.

Her warm hand wrapped around my bicep, and she leaned into me. She smelled of the sun and coconut. "Thank you, and I'm sorry for Pen grilling you and her insinuation. She loves to embarrass me."

"Really, I didn't mind. If she had asked anything too personal, I wouldn't have answered." I tried to reassure her. It had been cute watching Stella get all flushed and embarrassed because of her friend.

"Still, she doesn't know when to stop, so if you ever get cornered again by her, you can tell her to mind her own shit."

I probably wouldn't use those words.

"I might just do that," I said to placate her.

We stepped inside, and the air instantly felt stale compared to the ocean breeze that was continuous on the aft deck.

Her hand moved up my arm and back down again. "You look very handsome in your uniform."

Women did like a man in uniform. I wondered what she'd think of me in my dress blues.

"Thank you."

"You guys seem to change an awful lot. Why is that?" She looked up at me with her big brown eyes, and I wanted to drown in them.

"We have different uniforms for different activities. You probably won't see as many changes for the rest of your stay."

"Mmm." She hummed and let me lead her toward her room.

"How are you liking your stay on the Seas the Day?" I asked to make small talk.

"It's over the top. I'm not used to this kind of luxury. Don't get me wrong, I'm loving every minute of it except for the incident earlier and you having to save me. Well," she hummed as we rounded the corner to her room. "You saving me wasn't bad. That probably makes me sound desperate, doesn't it?"

We stopped in front of her door, but she didn't seem to realize where we were. Instead, Stella continued to hold on to my arm and leaned into me, warming up the left side of my body.

"Why would it make you sound desperate?" I asked to spend a little extra time with only her.

"Because it's the most action I've gotten in almost two years. That's a long time to go without a man's touch."

It was a hell of a long time. It had been five months for me, and I felt like a walking hard-on most times when I was around a good-looking woman. I shifted my stance to hide the semi I was sporting due to Stella's proximity.

"I find it hard to believe there exists a guy who wouldn't want to touch you." It took everything in me not to growl the last part of my sentence. I didn't like the idea of others touching her.

"Well, the one man I had didn't want me," she said sadly. "But it doesn't matter now; I'm a free woman."

## THE BOSUN

I wasn't sure what she was talking about, but I did like the idea that she wasn't with anyone.

Standing up straight, Stella looked up at me and blinked with wonder in her eyes. "Thank you for helping me down here." Lifting up on her toes, I thought she was going to kiss me on the cheek, but at the last moment, Stella turned her head and brushed her lips to mine.

It was such a simple gesture, yet it set an electric current through my body. I stood stunned for a moment before my wits came back to me. "You're welcome. Let me know if there's anything else I can do for you."

Her eyes lit up, and I realized how what I said sounded.

"Goodnight, Remy. I'll see you tomorrow."

Or in my fantasies, because there was no way I wouldn't be thinking about her tonight while I beat off in the shower.

# 3

## STELLA

MY HEAD POUNDED AS I cracked open my eyes, and the bright light coming through the porthole drilled into my brain. Why did I drink so much yesterday? I swore there was a drink in my hand from the moment we stepped foot onto the boat.

I vowed to myself in that moment, I wouldn't drink today. I wasn't sure my head and body could take another drop.

Looking over to the bed on the other side of the room I shared with Pen, I found it empty. The sheets were thrown all over the place, so I assumed she'd slept in it. I hadn't made my way back to the group after I came down to my room. Instead, after I used the bathroom, I fell onto my bed and promptly fell asleep.

My need for coffee had me climbing out of bed despite how miserable I felt. Slipping out of my dress from last night because I couldn't even bother to get undressed, I put on a pair of Capri yoga pants and a t-shirt, and pulled my hair up into a low ponytail. I didn't care what everyone else was wearing. All I wanted was to be comfortable while I was miserable.

Finding my darkest pair of sunglasses, I slid them on and headed out to find my friends. Keeping my head low, I trudged out to where we seemed to spend most of our time. All the girls were already eating breakfast and having mimosas when I stumbled out into the daylight t ocean breeze.

A round of cheers erupted as I took my seat beside Pen, making me cringe. "Please," I held my hands up, "I have the worst hangover."

"We were worried about you when you didn't come back last night," Scarlett said quietly.

That was sweet. I didn't think they'd notice me gone.

"We sent Pen here to make sure Remy hadn't taken advantage of you, and she found you sound asleep." Reagan wrinkled her nose at me like I was going to make or break their night. I was sure they did just fine without me.

"Sorry, once I got to my room and got all warm, exhaustion hit me, and I just wanted to go to bed."

Pen leaned over with her lips curled up at the ends. "Did anything happen with tall, dark, and handsome last night after he walked you to our room?"

## THE BOSUN

I wanted to tell her of my stupidity, but I kept quiet since I knew the rest of the table would hear me. Instead, I only shook my head.

"I thought for sure something would happen when you pretended to stumble," Reagan laughed.

"I wasn't pretending," I practically growled at her. "All the alcohol from the day rushed to my head. I probably would have fallen down the stairs if he hadn't escorted me down."

I was not in the mood to deal with Reagan's shit this morning.

A flash of me rising up on my tippy-toes and brushing my lips across Remy's last night hit me. Ugh! How embarrassing. Now I'll never be able to face him.

Pen pretended to drop her napkin and then whispered from underneath the table. "I think you're holding something back, but I'll wait until we're alone to get it out of you."

My only response was to give her big eyes.

Ophelia came out then with a steaming cup of coffee. It was like she read my mind, or maybe she saw the way I cringed at the sunlight.

"Thank you. You're a godsend," I said over the rim of my coffee before I took a long sip.

"Would you like anything for breakfast?" she asked as she started to pick up the plates from everyone else.

With everyone already finished, I wanted something fast. "If it wouldn't be too much trouble, I'll have a spinach omelet."

"No problem at all. I'll let the chef know." Ophelia smiled at me before she asked. "What do you want to do today?"

"We want to play on the toys," Zelda answered. "I want to ride one of those jet skis and hit the waves."

"We can do that. I'll have the crew get them out. Would you like the slide as well?"

I could picture myself going down the slide and then losing my bottoms, only to never find them again.

"That sounds like fun," the rest of the girls chimed in.

I guess I should have put on one of the tiny bikinis Pen had gotten me to be ready for today.

With every sip I took, my head pounded a little less, and by the time I was done with my second cup of coffee, the world was tolerable again. Relaxing back in my seat, I let out a contented sigh.

"Are you back with the living?" Scarlett joked with me.

"Finally. I can't remember the last time I drank that much. How do the rest of you not have hangovers?" I asked as I looked around the table at each of them. They all seemed too happy and wide awake.

"That's what the mimosas are for." Zelda held hers up in a cheers gesture. "When you're finished with breakfast, why don't you join us out on the water?"

"Sounds perfect."

All the girls got up except for Pen. She sat lazily finishing

## THE BOSUN

off her drink. "Are you coming, Pen?"

"I'll be there in a moment. I'm going to finish my drink and check my emails first."

"You work too hard," Zelda told her, shaking her head.

"And you don't work at all," Pen said under her breath. "Unless you count giving blowjobs."

"Pen," I scolded with a laugh because it was true. I didn't think Zelda had ever worked a day in her life unless it was under a man to get his money.

Her only response was to give me a knowing look before we both started cackling like two old ladies gossiping.

She looked around us to make sure we were alone before she leaned back with one arched brow. I knew I couldn't get out of telling her what happened, and she knew me too well for me to keep what happened a secret.

"You're impossible, you know that," I laughed with a roll of my eyes.

"Spill," she looked around as if at any second someone was going to pop out from the shadows and hear.

"Fine," I huffed. "I sort of kissed Remy last night."

"What? When?" she whisper-yelled.

Leaning in close, I looked around to make sure no one would hear. "After he walked me to our room, I leaned up and kissed him."

Pen squealed with a big smile on her face. "Was it good?"

Okay, maybe I'd over-embellished a little bit since there

weren't any details to give.

"It wasn't so much of a kiss as it was our lips touched." I could feel my face heat up at making what happened sound like more than it was. Maybe it was because I was wishing it was more.

With furrowed brows, she asked quietly. "He didn't, like, push you away or anything, did he?"

"No, nothing like that. I said goodnight...I should have tried for more even though I'm pretty sure it's frowned upon to hook up with the crew."

"I don't know. They said to ask for whatever we wanted. I say you ask for the hottie and see if they serve him up on a silver platter. Hmm," she hummed to herself and tapped her chin with her manicured fingernail. "I think we need to find more opportunities for you to spend time with him. Just the two of you."

"That's probably not a good idea. I don't want to get him fired. I would never forgive myself if I was the cause of him losing his job."

Pen's hands flew in the air as she stood. "Don't worry about that. Let me see what I can come up with while you eat your breakfast. In the meantime, I'm going to see if I can convince all the guys to take off their shirts while they help us with the water toys."

"Good idea," I laughed. Pen never had a problem getting guys to do what she wanted, and I, for one, wouldn't mind

## THE BOSUN

some eye candy for the day.

⚓

Stepping down onto the inflated platform, the ground underneath me rippled, causing my arms to shoot out for balance. That was unexpected. How the hell did everyone else make it look so easy?

Luckily, everyone already did the slide and was tired of it by the time I ate my breakfast and changed into my bathing suit, so I didn't have to worry about it.

One of the other crew members stepped out from a cove in the back of the boat and over to me; I thought his name was Owen. "What would you like to do? All the personal watercraft are being used, but you could paddleboard or just lay out if you want. Whatever you want."

I'd never tried to paddleboard. It looked like it could be fun. With the other girls out doing their thing, I could get some exercise in and enjoy exploring the cove we were in.

"I think I'll try the paddle board. Owen, right?"

"Yes, ma'am. It's Owen."

"Sorry, I'm not a hundred percent yet after yesterday." I hated not knowing his name. I was sure it was a common occurrence for them, but I wasn't some elite snob who thought she was better than everyone else. I was far from it.

"That's alright. Believe it or not, it happens quite frequently here. Especially when Ophelia is making the drinks." He said the last quietly and then winked.

Got it. Watch out for drinks from Ophelia.

"I got it from here, Owen. You can take your break," Remy said as he went over to the few paddleboards that were leaning against the side of the boat and then bent down to grab a paddle. I watched as his tight shorts showcased his ass. He still had his shirt on, so I guess Pen didn't get her wish, but damn, was he fine. "Have you done this before?"

"Nope, I live in the desert and haven't seen the ocean in..." I shrugged because I couldn't remember, "I don't know how long, but it's definitely been too long. Is it hard?"

"Do you have good balance?" He promptly covered his mouth with his hand. He must have been remembering my grand entrance to the yachting world and his subsequent need to save me.

"Normally, it's not too bad. I do yoga regularly." But I obviously didn't have my sea legs because I had problems since boarding.

"Then you should be fine. We do require you to wear a lifejacket in case you do fall in. I told the others they were to slow down when they were close to the boat, but if I were you, I'd head inward just in case they forget. You don't want a rogue wave taking you down."

"So a wave could make me fall in?" I asked, unsure if this was the right activity for me. I didn't love getting my hair wet.

"It could, but I wouldn't worry about it." He smiled, trying

## THE BOSUN

to reassure me, and a dimple popped out—a freaking dimple. I was done for. He probably had women throwing themselves at his feet just because of his looks.

"Maybe I should wait until one of the jet skis is available. There's probably less of a chance for me to fall in the water that way." Plus, it wouldn't be so bad if I could hang out here with Remy alone for a while.

"Have you ever driven one?"

"No," I drew out the word in frustration, annoyed at all the things I'd missed out on because I was too busy working to support my husband over the years.

He looked out toward where the girls were zipping along the water. "You might want to either ride with one of the girls, or one of the crew can show you how."

That sounded promising. "Can you show me?"

"If you want me to...or one of the other guys can show you," he added a few seconds later.

Now would be my chance to have my body plastered against his. I could wrap my arms around his trim waist, and... hell yeah, I wanted Remy to show me how to drive one of those things.

"I'd love it if you could show me." Now all I needed was the girls to be done so I could have my turn.

"While we wait, I need to inform my senior deckhand that I'll be going out with you and that he'll be in charge." Remy turned and started up the steps. Once he was halfway up, he looked over his shoulder. "Don't fall in while I'm gone." He winked and then continued to walk away.

Ugh! I was never going to live down falling overboard. With him saying that, I almost wanted to try my hand at driving the jet ski without him, but I also didn't want to die just because I was embarrassed.

One watercraft was headed back toward the boat when Scout, who was short with shaggy brown hair, brown eyes, and a megawatt smile, came down the steps. He looked like a mix of young and now Zac Efron.

"I hear you're going to give it a go," Scout said with an Australian accent that nearly took me to my knees. I was a sucker for an accent, add on good looks, and hot damn, he was a winner.

Sitting on the edge of the platform, I let my legs drift in the water. Looking over my shoulder, I found Scout staring down at me. "I'm going to give it my best. It's not too hard, is it?"

"I have faith in you."

"Even after I had to be rescued yesterday?"

"Even if," he smiled. "Don't let Remy give you a hard time. I think it scared him that someone could have drowned on his first season of being the bosun."

"What's a Bosun?" It sounded super official and kind of hot. It made me think of Remy last night in his tight black uniform and how hot he looked in it.

Scout looked over his shoulder before he sat next to me

# THE BOSUN

with his feet dangling in the water. "It's the ship's officer who's in charge of equipment and the crew."

"So he's important." Scout nodded. "And having someone fall overboard or drown would be bad."

"It's bad anytime someone drowns."

"Of course, I didn't mean…"

"I know, but it would be for everyone in general, not just Remy."

Sitting side by side, his gaze scanned my face. "You like him, don't you?"

Speak of the devil. Remy walked down the steps to join us on the platform. I watched as his jaw tensed as he looked back and forth between us. Was he jealous? Jealousy was hot on the officer in charge.

"What's not to like?" I smirked up at Remy.

Keeping his eyes on the horizon, Remy asked. "It looks like your friends are coming back. Do you still want to drive the PWV?"

"I'm going to be driving?"

"What did you think was going to happen?"

"That you'd drive, and I'd be behind you." I gave him my best I'm not nervous, but I really am, smile.

A mischievous smile spread across his rugged face. "How would you learn if I'm doing all the work?"

"Oh, I'm a visual learner. I promise I can learn from behind you." The moment it came out of my mouth, I heard how it sounded.

When Remy and Scout smirked, I couldn't help but laugh at myself.

"I still think it's best if you're up front. That way, if you want to ride tomorrow, you'll have firsthand experience."

I didn't know why I was fighting it. How bad could it be to have Remy's arms around me? In fact, it might be better.

"Let's do it," I said as I stood watching Zelda and Reagan zip up to the boat with wide smiles on their faces.

"Stella, darling," Zelda called as she dismounted the jet ski as if she did it every day, "I'm glad you could join us. "Why don't you go for a ride while we get another drink?"

She turned to Remy and Scout. "Maybe in an hour or two, we could find a place to snorkel. Something we can all do together."

"I'll ask the Captain where a good place is. We may need to set it for tomorrow if it's too far."

Zelda stuck her bottom lip out like doing that was actually going to get her what she wanted.

Reagan stepped onto the platform, and her eyes went wide. Her cheeks puffed out, and her hand went over her mouth as if she was holding back from throwing up.

"What's wrong? Are you seasick?"

Her lips curled up in a sneer at Scout before she let out a shriek. "His feet are the ugliest things I've ever seen."

All eyes zeroed in on poor Scout's feet. They weren't the most horrendous thing I'd ever seen, but they also weren't the

## THE BOSUN

prettiest either.

Scout held his ground as we all stared at him, so I tried to lighten the mood. "Maybe I can paint your toenails later and pretty them up," I suggested.

"Yes, you can give all the guys pedicures," Reagan eagerly nodded her head. "Maybe you can do it right now."

"Actually, I've been waiting for you to get back so I can get out on the waves. Why don't you give them pedicures?"

Reagan gagged and started to shuffle backward in disgust. "There's no way in hell I'm touching anyone's feet. I don't even touch my own, let alone others."

The more she shuffled, the closer she got to the edge and falling into the water.

"Stop, Reagan," I held my hands up as I stepped toward her.

"No, you can't make me," she shouted, taking another step back.

Before I could try to warn her again, Reagan stepped back. With her feet no longer finding purchase on the platform, her entire face blanched right before she fell back into the water.

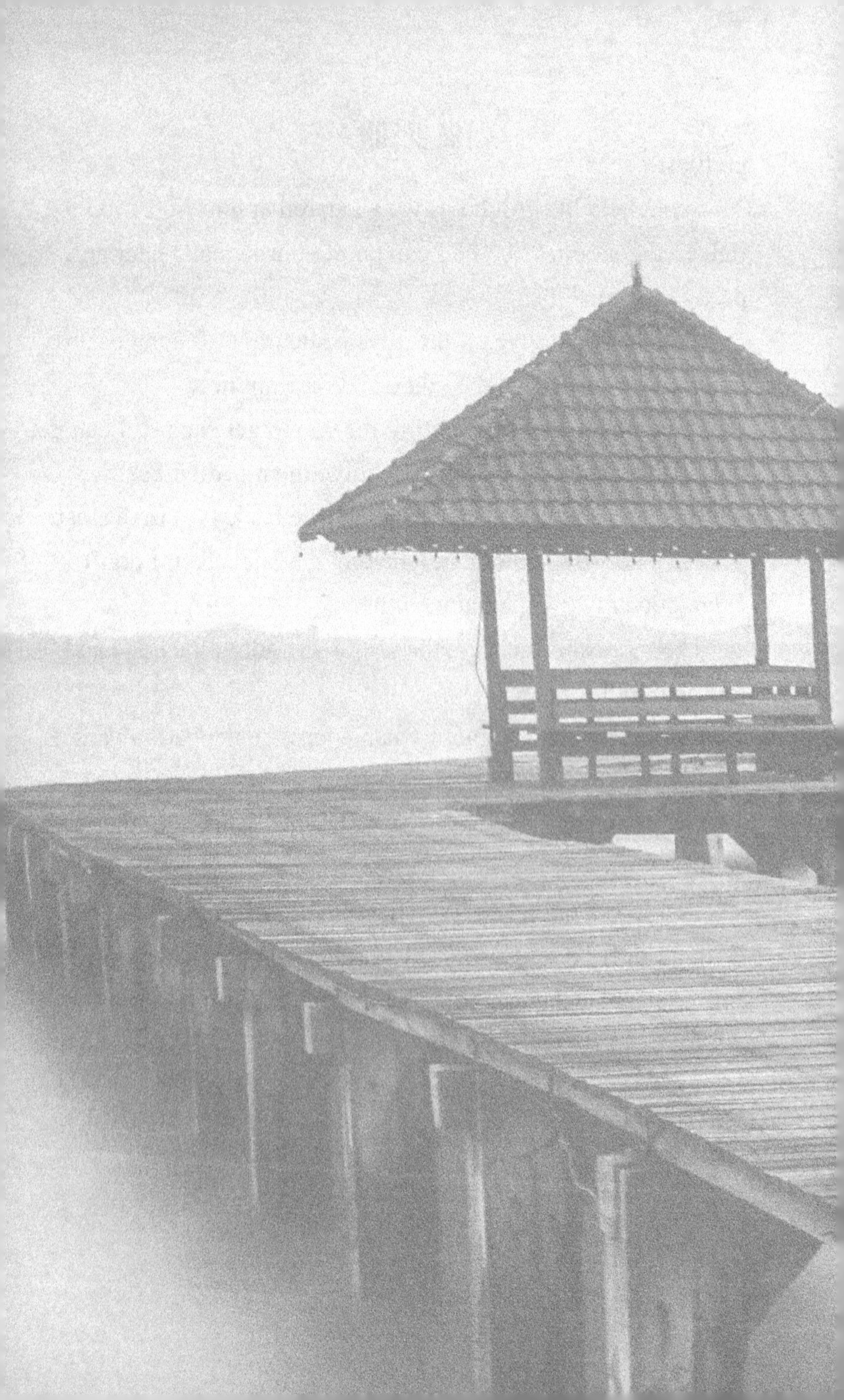

# 4

## REMY

"LIKE THIS?" STELLA gunned it, and then the watercraft promptly died. She was giving me whiplash, literally, with the stop and go.

Leaning forward but keeping my hard-on away from Stella's supple ass, I spoke in her ear. "You need to be a little more gentle on the throttle."

She threw her hands up in the air, her ponytail whipping me in the face as she turned and looked at me over her shoulder. "I give up. I look like an idiot out here. Why don't you just drive, and I'll enjoy it while you make us zip around and jump the waves?"

It was probably for the best if I drove. If her ass snuggled back against my dick one more time, I wasn't sure if I'd be able to hide the way she was affecting me.

"Are you sure you want to give up?"

She frowned and then looked back in the direction of the boat. "The girls are waiting on me, but maybe I can try again tomorrow if you're up for another lesson."

"Of course, I'm happy to teach you anytime." Holding my hand out to her, Stella placed her hand in mine. "Put your other hand on my shoulder and step around me."

Her eyes roamed from me to the water and back again. "Don't let me fall in."

"I won't. If it comes down to it, I'll fall in instead of you," I promised. If she didn't like water, this wasn't exactly the best vacation for her.

She narrowed her eyes at me but also smiled. "I'll trust you." Her warm hand seared through my shirt and into my skin as she stepped around me. There was some strange pull to her I couldn't explain. I was sure Captain Dan was going to call me onto the bridge once the guests departed to tell me how I can't let this happen again. Even though I knew he'd probably ream my ass, I couldn't stop.

Once she was fully settled behind me, I reached behind me and grabbed one of her hands, and wrapped it around me. "Hang on tight," I yelled over the engine of the watercraft as I started it up.

"What?" she yelled over the roar of the engine.

"Hang on," I laughed and pressed on the gas lightly enough to have us start to glide across the turquoise water.

## THE BOSUN

Thin arms wrapped around my waist as she clasped her hands together. Her fingers brushed along the top of my shorts, making my dick twitch.

Setting her hands higher on my waist, I took off. Not as fast as I normally would—I wasn't trying to throw her off the back—but fast enough to make her hold on me tighten.

It had been too long since I had a woman touch me that I was desperate to move her hands back to where they'd been or lower, but I fought against the urge.

Stella squealed with happiness. Her legs tightened around mine as she lifted one hand in the air. "This is so fun! I need to get one of these."

I didn't want to argue with her that she needed water to use it and ruin her fun.

"Let's never go back." It was quiet, as if she was whispering in my ear even though I knew she was more than likely saying it in her regular voice.

Why was it that for the first time in years, I had hope for a life with someone? And why did it have to be with one of our guests?

Slowing down, I turned to her. "We don't have to go back yet."

Her tiny arms squeezed around my middle. "Let's go further out for a little while. I know the girls are waiting, but I don't care. This is too much fun." Stella was quiet for a minute as I went further away from the boat and then asked. "Can we jump some waves?"

Nodding, I steered us toward some small waves. There was no way I was hitting the big ones with her behind me. Stella would likely go flying off and drown even with a lifejacket on.

Hitting our first wave, I felt Stella's body slide back and almost let go of me. I couldn't easily hold on to her hands and jump, so I moved them up until she was clutching the top of my lifejacket, giving her something more to hold on to. With this new position, we were so close, I could feel the heat from her pussy against my ass.

I imagined her lush tits pressed to my back, making my already stiff cock turn to steel. We couldn't head back with my raging hard-on, but I couldn't make her move away from me either. I needed to stop imagining what Stella would feel like up against me with no clothes on and start thinking of gross things to deflate my dick like someone killing puppies and naked old ladies. It was nearly impossible with her body flush against mine and her sounds of delight in my ear. I wanted to hear them when she was underneath me or as I took her from behind.

A hand waving from Seas the Day caught my attention, and I knew we needed to go back no matter how much I didn't want to.

"I guess our time is up," she said sadly from behind me.

Placing one hand on her knee, I patted it and kept it on her leg until someone on the boat would be able to see if they were

## THE BOSUN

looking our way where my hand was sitting.

As we idled up the boat, Stella's hands slid down my front and rested on my hips for a moment before she completely pulled away. Scout was holding his hand out for her to take the moment we stopped.

Scout winked down at me once Stella was securely on the platform, making me want to punch him. With a raised brow, he asked. "Have fun?"

"Oh my god, that was the most fun I've had in a long time. I want to do that every day."

"Well, maybe tomorrow I can take you out, and we'll hit some big waves." The smirk on his face let me know Scout knew what he was saying was meant to bother me.

"Oh, I...I think I'd rather have Remy take me out if it's okay."

"Whatever the guest wants, the guest gets, right, Rem?"

"Right," I gritted out. I just knew he was going to give me so much shit when we were alone.

"Good," she looked back at me. "I'm going to see what the girls are up to. Find out if we're going snorkeling or not."

My eyes stayed on her retreating form. Stella's perky ass swayed, giving me a show she didn't know she was giving.

"Do you want to tell me what you're thinking?" Scout asked from beside me. When I looked over at him, I found him watching Stella walk away as well.

Scout was a good guy. He worked on the same boat as I did

my first season, and I felt like I could open up to him. "I don't know, but for the first time in my life, I feel this strange pull toward her." He opened his mouth but closed it when I held my hand up. "I know this is the worst timing, but I can't help it. What do I do?"

"Well, while you were out there letting one of our guests feel you up—"

"That is not what was happening," I interrupted him with a bark.

"Dude, don't get your panties all up in a bunch. Just listen to me, okay?"

"Fine, what happened while I was out on the water?"

"The Captain was checking the weather, and there's a big storm system coming in. We're going to have to dock for at least a day, so that will give you time to spend with your lady if you want."

It would. My work would be very little, and if the guests asked for me to do something with them, I had to comply.

"Since the weather is going to get bad, we're going to take them snorkeling today, and then tonight during their sunset dinner, we'll inform them of what's going to happen tomorrow."

I clapped him on the shoulder. "You guys got it all planned out, didn't you?"

"What do you expect? The inside crew is freaking out about all the work they're going to have to do. Owen and I agreed they could stay back while we take them snorkeling to

## THE BOSUN

give them some time off if you said it was okay."

"Like I want to deal with the wrath of Ophelia if she doesn't get her break," I laughed out. She would be a horrible bitch if I didn't agree.

"I thought you'd see it that way."

Slapping him on the back, I pushed him toward the stairs. "Thanks, now let's get all this put up and something to eat before we have to head out."

"Fuck, I hate it when we have to put out the slide. We should say it's got a hole in it, so we don't have to deal with it for the rest of the season."

"If anything happened to that damn slide, they'd want to know who was responsible, and then they'd take it out of our paycheck." I, for one, wasn't giving up that money just so I don't have to haul that damn slide up the side of the boat.

"Ugh! Stop being reasonable."

"Sure, when you stop being a pain in my ass. Let's get to work. I want to make sure we have time for some lunch."

"Dean, Dean, Remy," I called into my walkie to our chef.

"Dean, here," he answered.

"Can you please whip up the crew something to eat before we have to leave?"

"When do you need it?"

"In about an hour. If you can't…"

"No, I can make you guys something. It won't be anything grand." He loved to make every meal the best it could be, and I knew he hated he didn't have more time. That's why we rarely asked him to make us any meals because we never knew when we'd have time to eat and couldn't give him the time he needed to make something spectacular.

"That's fine with us. Thank you, Dean."

"Anytime," he replied.

"Cool, let's get to work. Can you believe we're only halfway through the charter season?"

"Don't remind me," I groaned.

⚓

An hour and a half later, we'd put all the water toys away, along with the heavier than shit slide, and ate our lunch of chicken sandwiches and homemade fries Dean had made for us.

"Is everyone ready?" They all looked at me from across the table. "I have a feeling some of the women are going to be difficult, so be prepared, especially since none of the girls will be joining us to help out."

They groaned but didn't say anything.

"Just remember to keep your smiles on your faces at all times," I ordered. "Do what you have to do, and I'll see you on the aft deck in ten minutes."

Owen smoked, and I knew he'd need a cigarette before he was stuck without his vice for the next couple of hours, if not more.

## THE BOSUN

I found the ladies looking down at me over the side of the boat and giggling as I stepped outside. The small boat we'd take to the snorkeling area was ready for everyone to board once my crew arrived from their break.

Scout showed up first like I knew he would. Owen would wait until the last minute, smoking as much as possible during his break. It was annoying, but there was nothing I could do about it when there were others who smoked on the boat as well.

The ladies ooh'd and ahh'd when Scout bent over to check the gear once more. Two of us would be in the water with them while one stayed aboard to keep a lookout for any signs of distress, boats, weather, or hell, even sharks.

Scout's lips quirked at their enjoyment as he stood up and gave them a wave. "Should we let them on while we wait for Owen?"

It would be better than all of us standing around.

"Let's do it. It feels strange having them looking down at us while we wait. They're probably wondering what the hell we're waiting on."

"I don't think they'd mind so much if we gave them a little show," he said but changed his tune once he saw my narrowed gaze on him. "But we're not the entertainment."

Only we were. At least to this group of guests. It wasn't often we only had a group of women on board without any men accompanying them, but when we did, the crewmen were most definitely part of their entertainment. We just never knew how much until they arrived.

"Ladies, if you'd like to come down, we'll help you on, and then we'll be off to take you snorkeling." Even though I was talking to the group as a whole, I kept my eyes on Stella. I couldn't stop even if I tried, which I hadn't bothered doing. It would be different if my gaze on her made her uncomfortable, but going by the way her cheeks pinked up every time I looked at her longer than a few seconds, I would say Stella liked the attention.

Zelda was the first down. Her eyes trailing our bodies with hunger. I was surprised she kept her hands to herself. She seemed the type to take what she wanted no matter what. Stella trailed behind her friends with her head down and her hands clasped together as if she didn't want to come.

Taking her hand after Owen helped her step down, I looked down; the sun highlighted the light sprinkle of freckles along her nose and cheeks, making her look more girl next door at that moment instead of a knockout. Maybe it was because she was hiding her body underneath a knee-length skirt and life-jacket, obscuring her plentiful tits.

"Are you okay? You seem nervous," I said into the top of her dark hair.

"I...I'll be fine," she stammered, not giving me great confidence.

"I can assure you I know what I'm doing," I tried to reas-

## THE BOSUN

sure her.

All the women laughed at my words, but it was Reagan who spoke. "In all aspects of life?"

I wouldn't have known what she was talking about if she wasn't looking straight at my dick. Damn, she was brutal.

"There've been no complaints," I shot back. It was the most neutral thing I could think of in the moment. There was something about Reagan I didn't like, not that it mattered, but it made it hard not to say something unkind to her.

Out of the corner of my eye, I saw Penelope grab onto Stella's arm and laugh. "I think you need to take him for a spin and find out."

"Pen, you're crazy. He doesn't think of me like that. He's only being nice because it's his job."

I moved so I could watch them. The boat was small enough that it didn't matter where I was; I'd be able to hear them unless they were whispering. They were talking quietly enough that it was difficult to hear them over the voices of their friends.

"You must be blind if you can't see the way he looks at you." Stella shook her head and looked out at the water. "Stell, you're a fucking knockout, and everyone in the world can see it except you," Pen said, this time loud enough for everyone to hear.

"You're only saying that because you're my friend. I know I'm not horrible to look at, but I'm not *that*. There's no way in hell someone with a body of a God and with looks like that is interested in me."

Her quiet words stung my heart. Pen was right. Stella was a knockout. What I wanted to know was who made her think she wasn't? I was the one who was shocked that Stella wanted anything to do with me. I didn't have the status or money she had to be accustomed to.

"Who's ready to see some fish?" Owen shouted, breaking me out of my thoughts. It was probably a good thing since I couldn't stand all day staring at Stella while trying to probe her thoughts on why she felt the way she did.

The girls all perked up at Owen's question and started talking excitedly to each other.

I waited until Owen had on his lifejacket before I started up the boat and set off to our destination. Keeping my gaze on the horizon, I missed Stella getting up and moving to stand beside me. Her soft words and light touch filled me with a feeling I hadn't felt since I was in the war. Purpose. "How do you know where we're going?"

"I have a GPS that I put in the coordinates to where we're going." I pointed to the dash.

"But you haven't even looked down to see."

Had she been watching me the whole time?

"I know my way for the most part, but I put it in just in case. Once we get closer, I'll be using it more," I explained, looking down at her. "If you want, you can stay here, and I'll show you."

## THE BOSUN

Breaking our gaze, Stella looked away and then ducked her head. Everyone was watching us— even the guys.

"I better not. I don't want to be the reason we get lost and stranded out at sea." She laughed her comment off.

"That would never happen. All the watercraft have tracking locators on them, and if we're gone too long without reporting in, the Captain will send out a search party." I wasn't sure why I told her that, but I felt the need to reassure her. "You're safe with me."

Raising her hand, one finger trailed down my forearm until it reached my hand. The tip of her finger traced the veins in my hand. I wasn't sure how a simple move could be so seductive, but it was. "For some reason, I believe you." She spoke the words in a breathy whisper. Clearing her throat, Stella shook her head. "I'm going to go back over there before I do something that...yeah, I'm going over there."

Even though I wanted to tell her she could do whatever she wanted, I kept my thoughts to myself. I knew Scout and Owen would keep their mouths closed, but no matter how crazy attracted I was to Stella, I didn't know her or her friends. All I could do was watch her walk away and remember she was going to be gone just as quickly as she came. I couldn't let my feelings get me in trouble and fuck up my life.

Half an hour later, we arrived at the perfect spot for snorkeling. The water was clear and not too deep. Whoever stayed back would be able to see us.

Owen stepped to me as I set the anchor with a shit-eating grin on his face. "Do you want me to stay back?"

Unconsciously, my gaze went to Stella as she leaned over the side with Penelope and ran her hand through the water. "I can stay if you want." Owen wanted to stay back, likely to smoke, and so he didn't have to deal with the ladies. They were more than likely going to be a handful going by the shrieks.

"I'll let you be with your lady love," Owen said quietly but then started to crack up. While I was happy to have crew members who weren't serious all the time, sometimes it got old. Like now.

"Don't make it into something it's not," I growled.

Owen rolled his eyes and shrugged it off. "Dude, I'm just giving you shit because I've never seen you like this. Take advantage while we're not on the boat and the girls aren't around. You know if Ophelia gets word you've got the hots for one of the guests, she's going to freak."

"She was a mistake. One I don't plan to make again and a good reminder as to why I shouldn't fuck anyone on the boat." My tone suggested he take it as law for himself as well.

Turning his back on the guests, he leaned close. "So maybe you can get a room tomorrow night when we're docked."

Of course, Owen wouldn't take what I said seriously.

"That's not going to happen, and you know it. We can't stay off the boat when we have guests. What's wrong with you?" I furrowed my brows as I looked him over. Owen was acting a

## THE BOSUN

little strange, and I wasn't sure why. Did he want to dock so he could hook up? Because that so wasn't happening.

"Nothing," he said defensively. "Is it wrong that I like seeing you happy for once?"

I tried to decide if what he was saying was all there was to it, but I couldn't get a read on Owen. Maybe it was just that I'd been less of a hard-ass the last two days. Whatever it was, I didn't have time for it.

"Put the ladder down in case anyone wants to use it instead of jumping in," I ordered. Pushing past him, I walked to where the ladies all stood with their snorkels in hand. Scout had given them out while I was listening to Owen's bullshit.

"Are you ready?"

"More than ready," Zelda said as she eyed Scout up and down. He'd taken off his shirt and was putting his lifejacket back on.

"Great, you can either jump in, or there's a ladder in the back that you can take to get into the water."

Stella looked toward the back.

"Come on, Stella, don't be the stereotypical black woman who doesn't want to get her hair wet. Jump in," Reagan said in the snottiest tone I'd ever heard.

I looked to Stella at the comment. She was black? Not that I cared, but I had no idea.

"You can fuck off right now, Reagan. Don't bring up my race ever again, or I'll bring up what a slut you are." Her voice was hard with what sounded like hurt in her words.

Stella stepped onto the seat, looked back at Reagan, and flipped her off before she jumped.

# THE BOSUN

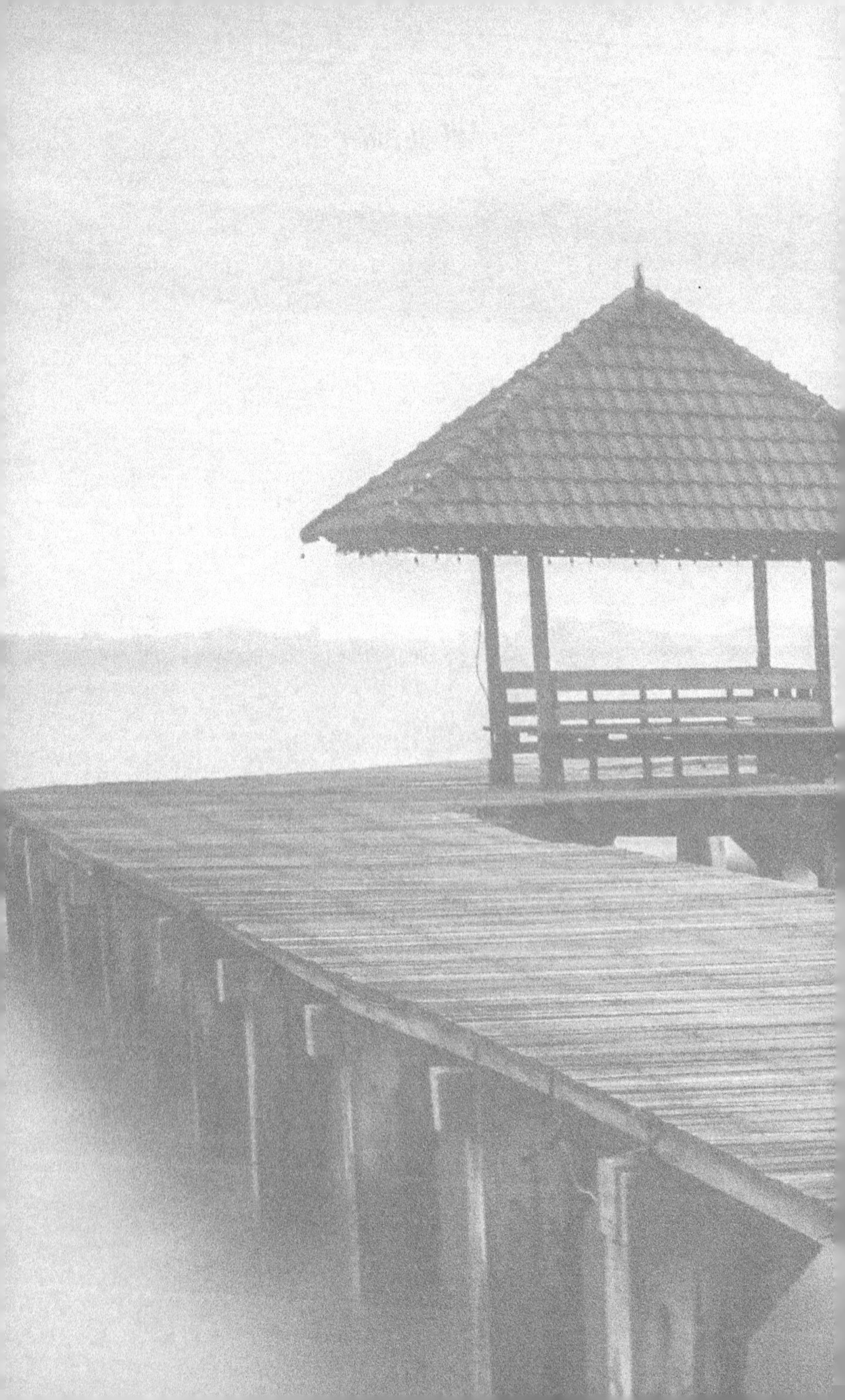

# 5

## STELLA

THAT FUCKING BITCH. Reagan knew that I didn't love to get my hair wet, but who the hell did? I hated spending the time washing and drying it only to then either have to straighten it or curl it. It was a waste of time. Plus, with three hot guys around, I didn't want to look like a wet dog when I came out of the water. It had nothing to do with being black.

"Hey, are you okay?" Pen asked, panting after she made it over to me.

I'd swum a good distance from the boat and everyone on it. I hoped Reagan got the hint to stay the fuck away from me, or I might push her under and hold her there.

"Why is she trying to push my buttons?" I asked, not

taking my eyes off the boat where Scarlett and Zelda looked to be chewing her out. At least, I hoped so.

"Probably because she doesn't have any of the crew members drooling over her, and she knows she'll never live up to your beauty."

I loved the way Pen tried to build me up, but it was also annoying. There was no way in hell Reagan was jealous of me. She went from sugar daddy to sugar daddy to support her and her plastic surgery addiction.

Scarlett, Zelda, and Reagan turned to look our way, but they were too far for me to see the expressions on their faces. "She needs to stay the fuck away from me, or I'm either going to drown her or push her overboard."

Pen's hand came up out of the water and landed on my shoulder. "I agree, and if you need an accomplice or an alibi, I'm here for you." Pen always knew what to say to get me out of my funk and to start laughing. Now was no different. We laughed and talked until our group was in the water and started to make their way toward us. "Ignore her and enjoy the day. When else are you going to be on vacation in Spain on a chartered yacht for free?"

She made a good point.

"Never. I'm going to hang back, so I don't do or say something stupid."

Pen's eyes creased at the corners. "Do you want me to hang back with you?"

## THE BOSUN

"I'll be okay. I think I need this time to myself, you know."

"If you want any company, you know where to find me." Pen swam their way, leaving me to myself. I watched as she talked to them for a moment before all eyes were back on me, and then the guys helped them adjust their masks on their faces so they could go underwater.

Putting my mask on, I placed the mouthpiece in and immediately felt like I could barely breathe. My breath picked up until it sounded like I was about to hyperventilate or Darth Vader, but at least I was breathing. Not about to let Reagan ruin my vacation, I dipped underwater and tried to make sure I kept the tip of my snorkel above water. I didn't need to be saved a second time this week.

The moment I saw all the tiny fish swimming along the rocks, all my troubles drifted away. There was a sense of peace floating along in the warm water. When I spotted a tiny octopus hiding in the swaying grass, I popped up to find I was alone. Where the hell did everyone go? Looking around, I found the boat with Owen on it, so I wasn't lost. As far as I could see, there was only the cove we were in and the beautiful blue water.

Unsure of how long we'd be here, I went back to exploring my surroundings. I swam up to the beach, noticing there looked to be a natural walkway that went up to overlook the area. Taking my mask off, I walked along the beach and up the stairs, letting my toes dig into the sand as I went. The sun warmed my slightly chilled skin from the breeze. At the top, I found there was another cove on the other side. The white crests on the waves indicated it was rougher over on that side, so I decided to stay on the side where it was nice and chill.

After a few minutes, I headed back down. I wanted to spend my time in the water and see if I could find any more octopi or maybe a colorful fish. I didn't think we were in the right location for anything colorful, especially since I hadn't seen any yet, but it didn't hurt to keep my eyes peeled.

Once in the water, I moved a little further away from the boat. I loved the way water always made me feel so weightless. Floating along, I noticed a dark shape moving my way. Lifting my head above the water, I saw it was Remy. The tattoos on his left arm stood out in the clear water, with the sun making them shine.

Treading water, I watched his body glide along the surface with grace. The way the muscles in his back rippled with each movement of his sculpted arms. Damn, he was fine. Too bad I'd be gone in a couple of days, and I'd never see him again.

"Hey, are you okay?" Remy asked once he made his way over to me.

"I'm pissed, but I'm fine. I've lived with the stereotypes all my life, so it's nothing new."

Cocking his head to the side, he gave me a tight smile. "I'm sensing there's more."

There was always more. Taking in a much-needed breath,

## THE BOSUN

I decided to open up to this gorgeous stranger. "I've never belonged. With my dad's side of the family, I'm too light-skinned to be a proud black woman. Do you know what it's like to have your family treat you like an outcast?"

I hadn't spoken to my dad or his side of my family since I graduated high school. When they didn't bother to show up to my graduation but had gone to every single one of my cousins and half-siblings, I was done letting them make me feel like shit about the way I looked. Something I had no control over.

"Not that way, no." His hand found mine underneath the water and linked our fingers together. His dark brown eyes looked me over.

"I know I don't look like I'm half black. Not unless I spend a decent amount of time in the sun. Most would probably think I'm Italian or something," I laughed humorlessly. "I'm the product of a one-night stand that never should have happened."

Moving closer, Remy took the hand he'd linked his finger with and placed it on his shoulder. "I, for one, am glad it happened. There's no one I'd rather be here with."

"Do you say that to all your guests?" I moved closer until our lips were only an inch apart. I could feel his minty breath skate across my face. His hands moved to my hips and held firm.

Remy shook his head as one hand skated up my ribs until his thumb rested underneath one breast. My breath caught at the move. I craved the soft touch more than I knew. It had been too long since someone had touched me like this.

"Believe it or not, I don't interact with guests all that much. Especially not to this level. You're the exception, Stella." Dipping his head down, the long hair on top fell into his eyes. "I want to kiss you."

"What's stopping you?" I asked breathlessly, moving a fraction of an inch closer.

The hand on my hip moved to cup the side of my face. "The fact that anyone could come around the corner at any second and catch us. I don't want to lose my job."

I didn't want that either.

"Maybe we should go back to the boat and wait for the others," I suggested.

"Owen's on the boat. We won't be alone."

"Exactly. It will keep us from doing anything that will get you fired." I tilted my head back to look into his dark eyes.

"I like being alone with you," he said on a soft exhale. "And I'm not sure I can hold back much longer."

"Then don't. Kiss me, Remy. Show me how much you want me with only your lips," I dared him.

With a brief quirk of his mouth, Remy captured my lips with his. At first, it was soft and slow as we got to know the other's touch. Our bodies fused together as he moved us to where he could stand underneath a little bluff with an overhang to shield us from prying eyes.

Strong arms held me to his muscular body as his mouth de-

## THE BOSUN

manded more from me. Remy's tongue slipped inside, tasting me, and I did the same to him. He tasted of mint and honey, a strangely alluring combination. I groaned into his mouth that seemed to spur him on. Wrapping my ponytail in his fist, Remy moved my head to the side to give him better access.

The way he took control sent a shock wave through my system. I loved it and the slight bite of pain that accompanied the tight hold he had on my hair.

My legs wrapped around his waist, and I started to grind my slick heat against the bulge in his swim trunks. One hand found purchase in the long, dark strands of his hair while the other ran along the muscles of his back.

Remy broke the kiss and leaned his forehead against mine. "Fuck, Stella, you make me forget where I am."

"Don't stop," I whined, even though I knew we couldn't go any further.

"We have to. At any moment, we could be spotted. Tonight, I'll find a way to be alone with you and finish this, but we have to stop now."

My lower lip stuck out in a pout. I knew he was right, but that didn't mean I liked it.

"Fine, but you better figure out a way for that big dick of yours to give me one epic release." My lips brushed his before I disengaged my legs from around him and was standing on my own two very wobbly feet.

A sexy smirk spread across his face before he said, "Challenge accepted."

⚓

"I think we should ask all the crew guys to eat dinner with us. What do you think?" Scarlett, our normally quiet friend, spoke up.

"Yes, then there will be a guy for each of us," Reagan looked to me as she spoke. I only ground my molars together. I'd decided I wasn't going to speak to her unless it was absolutely necessary. It may have been childish, but it was better than me saying something I *might* regret later.

"Who's getting the Captain then?" Zelda cackled.

Captain Dan wasn't bad, but he was quite a few years older than the rest of the guys. He looked like Richard Gere when he was in Pretty Woman. Swoon. It took everything in me not to say she should take him, but I kept quiet since I still wanted my free vacation.

"I'll take him," Pen piped up from beside me. I had no idea what expression was on my face when I turned to look at her besides shock, but one look at me, and they all started to laugh, with me right along with them. "What? We all know you've claimed Remy and he, you, so I'll take the Captain. Maybe he can teach me a thing or two."

I knew without a shadow of a doubt, Pen had zero interest in Captain Dan. In fact, she didn't seem to be interested in any men lately, making me wonder what was going on with her.

## THE BOSUN

Had Pen taken a vow of celibacy, or did she have a guy on the side I didn't know about?

'What?' she mouthed.

"When we get back home, we're going to have a little chat," I said, only loud enough for her to hear me.

Crossing her arms, Pen tilted her head in my direction. "About what?"

"Oh, I think you have some idea, but we'll discuss it then." I didn't want to get the whole group involved, especially if Pen was hiding something from me.

"Fine," she shot back. Turning to look at the rest of our group, Pen asked. "Now, who's going to demand their presence?"

"I will." Zelda pushed her chair back and stood quickly. She was too excited by this idea. She was gone before anyone could talk her out of it.

I wasn't sure if I'd be able to sit across from Remy at dinner after the heavy make-out session we'd had earlier while snorkeling.

A few minutes later, Zelda came back with a cat that ate the canary smile on her overly Botoxed face. "All set," she chirped.

"Yes," Reagan cheered. She was too much. Did she really think she was going to get lucky with one of the guys?

Reagan's gaze caught mine. "If you frown anymore, you're going to get wrinkles."

"Then I'll wear them with pride," I shot back. I wasn't going to be like her and Zelda and get some new procedure or ten done to my body every year. No how, no way. I was going to let my body grow old gracefully and not look like a freak show. Did they really think no one knew they were getting facelifts? They were starting to look like something out of a horror movie.

"Is that how you want it to be? Because if so, I won't hold back, Stella."

She said my name as if it left a bad taste in her mouth. What had I ever done to her? Maybe Pen was right, and she was jealous of me.

Instead of answering her, I stood and looked at the table as a whole. "I'm going to go get freshened up for dinner. I'll see you when it's time."

I thought Pen might ask to join me, but she kept her mouth shut and her ass firmly in her seat. She knew if we were alone right now, I'd be asking about why she was so eager to take Captain Dan.

Turning on my heel, I went inside, but instead of immediately heading to my room, I took the scenic way in the hopes I might see Remy. With my luck, I didn't see him, but I did find the chef in a panic, having to now cook for four extra people without much notice. He was banging everything around while he said every swear word in the dictionary and made up a few while he was at it. Damn, I'd have to mention it to Zelda, so

## THE BOSUN

she gave them all a good tip.

"Do you need anything?" Kylie, one of the stewardesses, asked as I walked past her.

"No, thank you. I was just trying to get away from the girls and decided to take the long way to my room. I hope that's okay," I tried to explain. There was no way I was going to say how I was on the lookout for Remy. It made sense he was working. It wasn't like he was sitting idle all of the time.

"Of course, it's okay. If you need anything, just let me or anyone else know, and we'll get it right away." She smiled, and it seemed genuine. I was sure it couldn't be easy waiting on spoiled rich people day in and day out, but Kylie seemed like she genuinely enjoyed her job.

Back in my room, I threw myself down on my bed and groaned. How had I thought vacationing with these ladies would be fun and relaxing? Actually, if it wasn't for Reagan, it would be, or at least it mostly would be. Even though Zelda could be a bit much, she was fun.

I needed to find a way to ignore Reagan without her trying to ruin what was left of our vacation. I wasn't sure how that was possible, but I was going to try.

A knock sounded on my door, breaking me out of my thoughts. "Miss Stella, it's time for dinner if you're ready," a soft voice said.

Already? How long had I been down here?

Standing from the bed, I smoothed the wrinkles out of my

sundress before I answered the door. Standing there in all her cuteness was Jolene. She had these round cheeks that made you want to squeeze them with sparkling green eyes. But it was her soft-spoken voice that instantly put me at ease. From the moment I heard her speak, I wanted to pick her up and tuck her away to keep with me forever.

Stepping outside the door, I turned to Jolene. "Time must have slipped away from me. I didn't realize it was time for dinner already."

"It happens if you're not too careful. The lull of the ship can make you fall asleep even when you don't mean to."

Had I fallen asleep, or did she just assume that going by my now frumpy state? As we walked up to the top deck, I ran my fingers through my hair that I'd curled earlier after we'd gotten back. I'd tried to look my best without making it look like I was trying too hard for when I saw Remy later tonight. At the time, I had no idea he'd be joining us for dinner.

My skin broke out into goosebumps, just thinking about seeing him again. Damn, what was that boy doing to me? The way my body reacted to him was unlike anything I'd ever experienced.

I was shocked to find all the guys from the crew as well as the Captain standing on deck with their hands on the top of the chairs I assumed they would be sitting in.

One look out at the horizon, and I knew I'd been downstairs for longer than I thought. The sun was setting, and I'd

## THE BOSUN

almost messed up dinner. I stood for a minute, taking in the pink and purples of the sky as the sun slowly set.

"I hope you weren't waiting on me," I said as I went to sit at the only chair unoccupied. Remy moved around and pulled it out for me and then pushed it in before he went back to where he'd been previously standing.

Heat ran up from my chest to my cheeks and then to my ears. "Thank you. It's hard to find a true gentleman nowadays," I said quietly.

Remy nodded but kept stoically quiet. As one, all the guys sat down and placed their napkins in their laps.

It was so in sync it made me wonder if they trained for that very scenario.

Captain Dan cleared his throat, getting everyone's attention. "Thank you for inviting us to have dinner with you. It's an honor. I do have some bad news to share with you, though."

"Oh, no! What is it?" Reagan swayed in her seat, being overly dramatic as usual. As if the unknown news was going to make her faint. I wanted to roll my eyes at her, but I also didn't want to start a fight in front of the Captain. Unfortunately, the crew had already heard and seen what happened earlier.

"I'll only be able to join you for the dinner portion of the evening. We are unfortunately going to have to dock tonight because a storm front is moving in and will hit early in the morning. It will be unsafe for us to be out on the water. Don't worry, though. There's plenty to do onboard, but you can always go into town to eat and shop or do whatever you'd like."

"Well, that's no fun," Zelda pouted. "Can we have the guys escort us if we go into town?"

"Of course. Whatever you'd like. They'll be at your beck and call from the moment we dock. We normally have someone go with you in case you need something." Captain Dan seemed to love saying that, going by the smirk that crossed his face before he hid it with a cough.

I swore I heard one of the guys groan, but I didn't catch who it was. My eyes were only on Remy as he sat across from me in his dress blacks, looking good enough to eat. What was it about a man in uniform? Whatever it was, I'd take him over food any day of the week.

Remy broke eye contact with me so he could speak to the rest of the table. "Let us know whatever we can do for you to make your stay on the Seas the Day more pleasant."

Was sleeping with the guests part of making the trip more satisfying?

"Oh, we most definitely will," Zelda purred, her eyes on Scout. The poor guy. I saw his smile falter for a moment before he put it back into place. I didn't blame him. I wouldn't want to be on Zelda's radar either. She screamed man-eater.

One by one, the stewardesses appeared, balancing three plates on their arms. I had no idea how they did that. I was always grateful when carrying my own food to not drop it, let alone have three plates to have to keep steady.

## THE BOSUN

With a grace I'd never know, they set our plates down in front of us. It didn't go unnoticed the way Ophelia's eyes narrowed, and her nostrils flared when she set Remy's plate down in front of him.

Ophelia moved off to the side and announced. "Tonight, the chef wanted to give you a taste of Spain, so for the main course, we have paella with seasonal vegetables. Enjoy."

One whiff of the food and I had to close my eyes. It smelled absolutely heavenly. My stomach rumbled at the aroma. I wasn't sure how I was going to be able to eat without looking like I'd been starved for a week straight.

"Oh my god," Zelda moaned as she took her first bite. "I wasn't kidding when I said I might steal your chef, and after tasting this Paella, I'm going to offer him to come back to the States with us and cook for me every night. I don't even care if I gain a hundred pounds. It would be worth it."

The Captain smiled, and his eyes crinkled at the corners. It lit his entire face, making him seem more youthful. "You'd leave me without a chef?" he asked, his tone light.

Zelda tapped her index finger to her chin for a moment. "I guess I could let you have him until the end of the season. I'm not a heartless bitch."

The Captain laughed and then took a drink of his water. "We'd very much appreciate it if you left us our chef until the end of the season. It would be next to impossible for us to find another one that's as good as Dean in the middle of a season."

If the chef was smart, he'd stay working on the boat and stay far away from Zelda. I couldn't imagine working for her demanding ass.

A smirk came across her face. "I'm still going to offer him a job before we depart."

Scarlett jumped in her seat and shouted as she pointed. "Is that a dolphin?"

All heads turned to see if there was a dolphin swimming by our boat.

"Or a shark?" Reagan's face paled.

Pen tensed beside me. "Are there sharks in the water?"

"There are sharks pretty much everywhere there's water," Owen said.

"Well, I'm not getting in the water ever again," Pen stated. I knew it was a lie because she loved being in the water and was in it every chance she got.

"If we weren't stuck at the dock tomorrow, I'd bet you'd be in it tomorrow," Reagan said while still looking out into the water.

"I don't see anything," I finally added. The sky had turned into a darker shade of pink with it reflecting off the water, making it the perfect sunset dinner. I only wished there were a few less people here. Okay, who was I kidding? In an ideal world, it would only be Remy and me, and not a table full of half-friends and his crew.

Pen stood and pulled me over to the railing with her. "I

## THE BOSUN

want to see a damn dolphin. It will be the highlight of the day."

I could think of something else that would be the highlight of my day, night, and week. Hell, it might be the highlight of the year if Remy knew what he was doing, and I got a chance to be alone with him tonight.

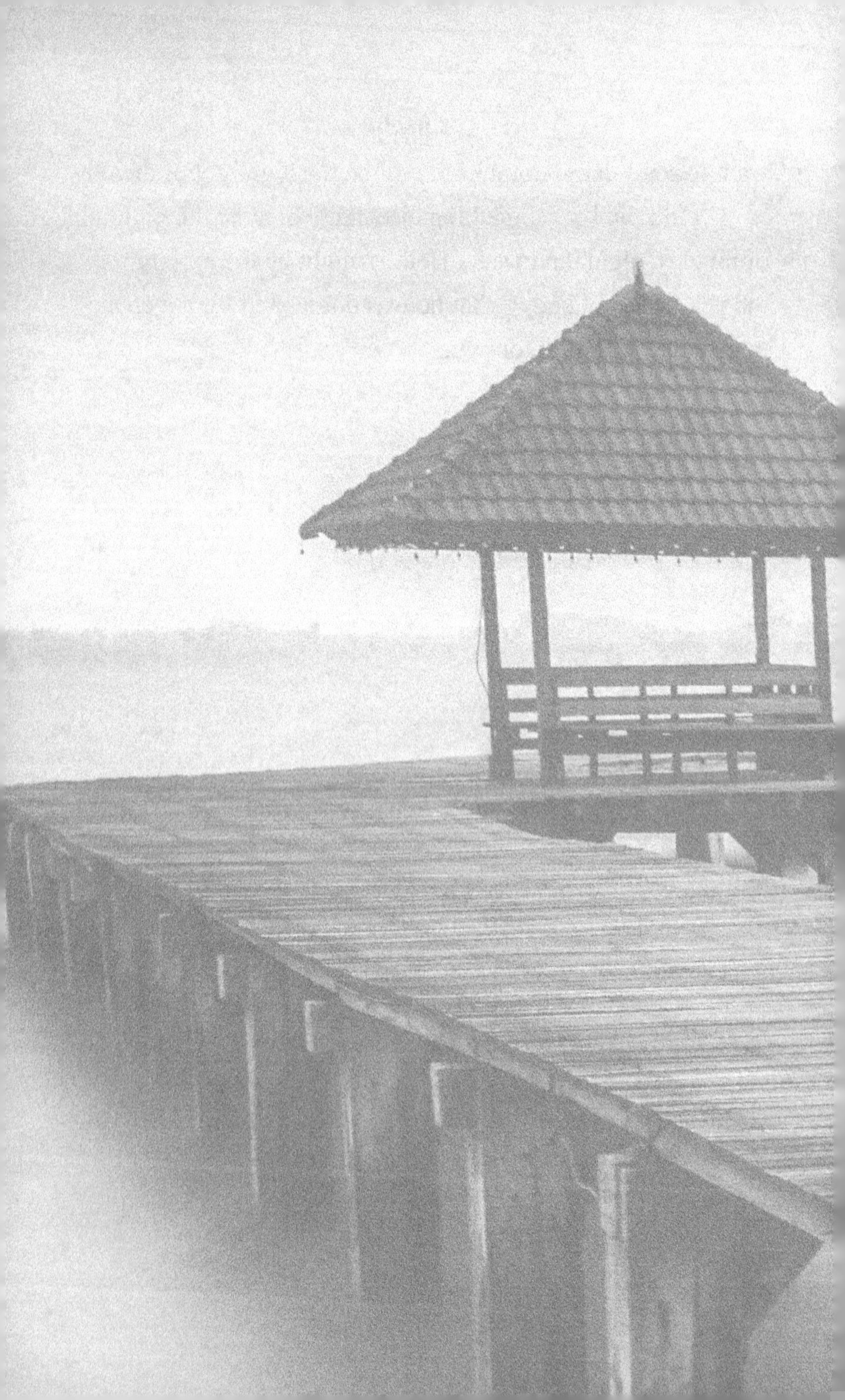

# 6

## REMY

"I CAN'T BELIEVE Captain told them we'd pretty much be their manservants for the day," Scout groaned. "What do you think they'll have us do?"

Internally I groaned at the thought. "With these ladies?" He nodded for me to continue. "A whole lot of stuff we don't want to do. I think we'll be getting off lucky if we only have to escort them around town."

"We should have slept in then," he said before taking a sip of his coffee.

"You know that couldn't happen." Looking over my own cup of coffee, I spoke. "Maybe you'll get lucky, and they won't request you."

Scout and I both knew that wouldn't be the case, though. It would be Owen who'd be working with the Captain today. While the women seemed to like him just fine, they didn't flirt with him the way they did with us.

Setting his cup down, he sighed. "I'm sure O will be pushing for them to get off the boat at some point."

"Oh, I'm sure." My jaw tensed, remembering last night. It was like Ophelia had a sixth sense about her and knew I was going to hook up with Stella. She was around every corner last night cleaning and pretending to do whatever to keep us away from each other. If it wasn't O, then it was Stella's friends.

At around two in the morning, I gave up trying to find some alone time with Stella. Now that I thought about it, maybe she changed her mind and told them to keep me at bay.

Scout stood with his plate in hand. "Well, if you don't need me, I'm going to hide out in my room until they request our presence."

"Enjoy, beating off," I laughed at the scowl he sent my way. It wasn't uncommon for Owen to walk into their room to find Scout jacking off. I'd heard Owen complain about it enough times to know.

"Fuck you, asshole. I'm going to think of you next time I do it."

I cringed back against the booth's seating at the thought before I shot back. "Whatever floats your boat."

An hour later, while I was scrubbing the deck clean, O's voice came through my earpiece. "Remy, Remy, Ophelia. Can you please meet me in the salon?"

## THE BOSUN

Placing the mop back into the bucket, I sighed. It was about to begin.

"Remy, here. I'll be there in five." I walked as slowly as possible to put my cleaning gear away and then to the salon, where I found O with her hands on her hips and her foot tapping. She was pissed, and I secretly loved it.

"Captain Dan said you were to help us with the guests today and do whatever they want. I'm not sure how you got so lucky, but whatever." The last word was said with so much disdain in it I had to chuckle.

"I wouldn't call us lucky. He basically fed us to the sharks. And you know it wouldn't be this way if we weren't docked. In fact, you should be grateful we're taking some of the load off of you guys. It's not like we're going to be enjoying ourselves."

"Oh, I think you will," O laughed humorlessly. "I saw the way you were looking at Stella. What were you thinking? Do you want to lose your job?"

She was jealous because I wasn't looking at her the way I had looked at Stella even though I'd tried to hide it. "Jealous?" I taunted.

"You…" Her cheeks turned a bright shade of red as she stomped in place. For a moment there, I thought steam might actually come out of her ears; O was so pissed off.

"I'm what? I'm a warm-blooded male who can't help but notice a beautiful woman. I haven't acted on it, so what does it matter?" I lied.

"It's unprofessional to look at paying customers that way. It could affect our tip. That's money you're taking away from all of us."

*Or it could give us more of a tip.* I didn't say it, though, because I didn't want to argue with O. She could do it until the end of time if she wanted to.

"Have the guests requested one of the other crew or me?" I asked instead of fighting.

"They want you without your shirt serving them drinks upstairs in the sky lounge. Later I think they're planning on having lunch in town and then shopping if it stops raining."

I hoped they weren't planning on me making said drinks because all I could do was pull the cap off a beer.

Turning on my heel, I made it to the stairs before I looked over my shoulder at O. "I'll be upstairs for the foreseeable future if you need me."

O narrowed her eyes but didn't utter a word before I walked up the circular staircase to the sky lounge, where I found the women all doing exactly what the name said, lounging around with their phones and chatting amongst themselves.

Walking to the middle of the room, I lifted my shirt over my head. "I heard you'd like for me to serve you drinks this morning."

"Oh yes," Zelda said with a clap. "I'm thinking now that we've got you in front of us with all that skin showing, we should oil you up."

## THE BOSUN

I looked at Stella to see her reaction, but there was none. Last night, I never told her I couldn't make it to her room or meet her anywhere else, and she had every right to be mad. She probably thought I stood her up.

"I'm sure I can find some oil around here," Kylie said with a giggle from behind the bar.

"That would be perfect," Stella exclaimed. "Do that after you make my Bloody Mary."

"Of course," Kylie tipped her head.

I was happy to see it wasn't O making their drinks today. Otherwise, they'd be drunk and unruly before lunch.

Making my way to the bar, I rested my arms on it and leaned toward Kylie. "I hope you have a light hand."

Her cheeks pinked up, and she ducked her head. What was this? I'd talked to her plenty of times over the course of the season and never once had Kylie blushed around me.

"Very light. Especially this morning. While a couple of them are more laid back, there are a few of them that are a lot to handle after they've been drinking."

I knew exactly who she was talking about: Zelda and Reagan. They were a handful without drinking, so I didn't want to imagine having to deal with them drunk for the day. Especially if I couldn't be drinking.

"They've been coming up with all kinds of things for you to do today." Kylie leaned closer and dropped her voice. "Did the Captain say you were to be their manservant?"

"Not in those exact words, but yeah, we're to do anything they want today."

"I bet you're hoping this weather system moves through quickly then, huh?"

She had no idea. If we were docked, I could spend time with Stella if O wasn't trying to prevent it from happening. Now I only needed to get Stella alone for a few minutes, so I could explain to her what happened.

Kylie set two drinks on the bar. "For Reagan and Zelda. I'll be back after I find that oil."

"Thanks," I said in a tone that let her know I wasn't thankful at all. I didn't mind the ladies having fun, but lubing me up wasn't my idea of fun. The water pressure in our cabins wasn't the greatest, and it would take me forever to get it off, but I'd do whatever they wanted with the hope it would bring us a bigger tip.

It wasn't until then that I realized I was basically whoring myself out for money.

"Here's your drink." I handed Zelda hers first since she was the primary and then Reagan's.

"Did Kylie go to find the oil?" Zelda asked as her green eyes took in every inch of my chest.

"Yes, she did."

"Good, good. Can you radio for some fruit to be delivered? Things that are easily fed to others."

"Sure," I said with my best fake smile.

## THE BOSUN

Hitting the button for my earpiece, I said. "Dean, Dean, Remy."

"Oh, how very double-oh-seven," Reagan purred.

Every instinct in my body told me to back away from her, but I knew if I did, it would be seen as a slight toward her. Instead, I stayed where I stood and waited for Dean to answer me back.

"Dean here," he called.

"The guests would like some fruit."

"Okay, I can do that."

"And they also request that it be fruit that can be fed to others." I held back my groan. Maybe they'd ask Scout to join in on the feeding.

"Okay," he drew the word out. "I'll see what I can come up with, and have fun with that," he added with a laugh. "I'll have someone bring it in a few minutes."

"Thanks." Putting on my best smile, I looked at the women. "He said it will be a few minutes. Is there anything I can do for you in the meantime?"

"Oh, I think we can think of something." Zelda clasped her hands underneath her chin and tapped her fingernails together. "For now, why don't you go talk to our Stella. She looks lonely over there all by herself."

Stella was now sitting off by herself with a glass of orange juice in her tiny hands. She was holding onto it so tight, the knuckles of her fingers were white.

"Really, I'm fine."

"I insist. Maybe Remy here can give you a foot massage."

Oh God, would they all want foot massages?

"No feet," Reagan yelled and tucked her feet under herself on one of the couches.

As if I wanted to touch her feet or any feet.

"Maybe we could get a couple of people on the boat to do massages. Wouldn't that be nice? After we get back from shopping and lunch."

"That does sound nice. Especially if we're stuck here," Scarlett agreed.

"It's settled then. Kylie, can you get some masseuses to give us massages after we come back?"

I hadn't noticed Kylie had walked in behind me. Looking over my shoulder at her, I found her standing in the doorway with a bottle of baby oil in her hands.

"Yes, I'll have Ophelia arrange it for you." She waved the hand with the oil in it. "Look what I found."

"Oh, perfect, we'll have you all oiled up in time to feed us. Please be a dear and retrieve the oil so we can watch you walk away." Zelda bit on her bottom lip as her eyes flared.

Damn, I was nothing more than a piece of meat to these women.

Walking over to Kylie, I held my hand out for the offending oil. I was sure I had a scowl on my face as I stood before her.

"I'm sorry, Remy. You know the mantra." She actually did

## THE BOSUN

look sorry, but I was also sure she'd enjoy them torturing me throughout the day as well.

"Do whatever the guests want. I know, but it doesn't mean I have to like it," I said for only her ears to hear but noticed Stella stiffen out of the corner of my eye. Had she heard me?

It wasn't Stella who was a chore. In fact, she was my reward for all the bad shit that had gone down in my life and for putting up with her friends.

"Nope, just do it with a smile on your face." Kylie patted my bare shoulder. "You know, if you guys did all your work shirtless, I bet we'd get much better tips."

"Just as if you did all your work in skimpy bikinis," I shot back with a big smile.

But we weren't meant to be seen as meat while we worked, rather with a semblance of respect as the help.

"Point made. Now go get oiled up for the ladies to enjoy you better," she cackled as she went behind the bar.

My feet felt like they were in quicksand as I made my way toward the women.

"Why don't you start, Stella? You look like you could use a good time." Reagan gave her a nasty smile. What the hell was wrong with that woman?

I didn't mind having Stella's hands on me. Since she was sitting away from the rest, it might give me the chance to try to explain to her about last night.

"Where would you like me?" I asked as I stood in front of

the dark-haired beauty.

A sly smirk replaced the sullen set to her plump pink lips. "Get on your knees."

Liking where this was going, I did as I was ordered and got down on my knees in front of Stella.

Plucking the oil out of my hands, she coated her palms before she leaned forward and placed her hands on my shoulders. Her fingers dug into the muscles a moment before she started to coat my skin while her eyes following her movements.

"Stella," I called her name quietly. Her gaze flicked up to mine before she looked back at what she was doing. "I'm sorry about last night. After I got done with my work, I tried to make it to find you, but at every turn, I was stopped. I couldn't very well send you a note saying I couldn't meet up for our rendezvous."

"I fell asleep waiting for you. Do you know what it feels like to be stood up on a boat?" Tears filled her eyes that she tried to quickly blink away, making me feel like an even bigger asshole.

I wanted nothing more than to be able to take her hands in mine or to be able to hold her in my arms, but that wasn't a possibility with everyone around. "I can't imagine it felt good. I'm sorry. I truly am. If I could have gotten away without being caught, I would have. Please don't doubt that."

"Alright, you hogged him enough. Now it's our turn," Reagan said, breaking our moment.

## THE BOSUN

Closing the cap on the oil, Stella's sad brown eyes met mine. "Is it crazy that I hate the thought of them touching you?"

"Not at all. Believe me when I say I don't want them touching me either. I wish I could hold you right now and kiss you until you knew how sorry I am for standing you up last night," I admitted, hoping Stella could read the sincerity in my words.

"Me too, but you need to go before Kylie becomes suspicious." Handing me back the oil, Stella's fingers brushed against mine and held for only a moment before they were gone.

What the hell was this woman doing to me? I barely knew her, and yet the pull to her was too strong to deny.

"Who's next," I asked as I turned away from her.

Reagan's hand shot up quicker than lightning, "That would be me."

I wanted so badly to turn and look at Stella, but I knew I couldn't.

"I'll join you. Two is always better than one," Zelda added.

Handing over the oil, I said. "You can each do an arm."

"Only an arm?" Reagan pouted, and it wasn't cute like when Stella had done it.

I shrugged, not knowing how to answer her. Personally, I didn't want her hands on me at all. I knew Zelda was doing it all in good fun, but I had a feeling Reagan only wanted to touch me to piss off Stella.

"We want to go into Mallorca to shop and have lunch, and the Captain said you and Scout would escort us."

"We'd be happy to escort you. When would you like to go?" I tried to keep my mind on the conversation and not on how Reagan's hand kept 'accidentally' slipping from my arm and touching my chest, and then how her fingers would linger around the waistband of my pants until I picked her hand up and removed it.

"Hmm," Zelda hummed. "I'm thinking in an hour or so."

"We can make that work. Is there anything special you're looking for? I can have one of the girls come along who knows the shops."

"We won't need them. Just you and Scout will be fine. But no, we just want to explore the city and do a little shopping. I know Stella is looking for some new bathing suits." She waggled her eyebrows at me.

That caught my attention. I was all for seeing Stella in more barely-there bikinis that showed off her tanned skin and lush curves.

A throat cleared from behind me. "If we're going to be leaving the boat in an hour, I'm going to get ready. That way, Pen can get ready after me."

"I guess we all should start getting ready. It will take me at least an hour to get presentable." In all actuality, Zelda looked better the way she was than without makeup, but I wasn't going to say anything if it would get her to take her hands off me.

## THE BOSUN

"I'm sad you didn't get a chance to feed me my fruit." Snapping her fingers, Zelda ordered. "Kylie, please bring the fruit tray that was prepared to my room."

My stomach fell to the floor. What if she wanted me to come into her room to feed her while she got ready? There was no way in hell that was happening.

"Yes, ma'am." Kylie picked it up off the bar and promptly left.

I took a step back away from the women. "I should let Scout know we'll be leaving soon and make sure the Captain doesn't need anything either."

"Aww, but Pen didn't get to put oil on you," Zelda frowned.

"That's okay. I'm sure I'll get another chance to have my hands on a hot guy." Pen stood and walked quickly from the room.

"What's up with her? Normally she'd be all over a hot guy."

Looking off in the direction Penelope fled, Reagan said, "She's so up Stella's ass, I bet it has something to do with her."

With friends like Reagan, who needed enemies?

Before anyone could change their minds, I left the room as quickly as possible without it looking like I wanted to escape. As I was rounding the corner to go down the stairs, I ran into Stella in the hallway. My hands went around her waist to keep her from falling.

"Shit, I'm sorry. I was...escaping from your friends and

wasn't watching where I was going. I shouldn't have been so distracted while walking the halls."

"Shh." She placed her index finger over my mouth and looked up at me with a soft expression on her face. "Don't apologize when you have your hands on me."

"I like that rule." I kissed the finger she still had pressed to my lips. "I'm sorry about you having to watch as your friends touched me." I laughed at my words. "I never thought I'd say that to a girl before."

"I never thought I'd hear them, and if it was under different circumstances, it would be totally unacceptable, but I can't make waves when Zelda is paying for all of this."

With Stella's words, I wanted to know more about her and hoped I'd get a chance today and tonight. It would only be another day before I'd have to watch her walk away and likely never see her again.

"We should separate before we're caught, but first, can I kiss you?" My hands tightened their hold on her.

Lifting up on her toes, Stella cupped my face with both hands and licked along the seam of my mouth. It was hot as fuck and made me groan deep in my chest.

Opening to her, I sucked on her tongue until I felt her leg wrap around my hip and knew we needed to stop before we got caught. If O saw me, she'd have no problem telling Captain Dan about my indiscretion.

Pulling away from her was one of the hardest things I had

## THE BOSUN

to do. I hoped once I fucked her, Stella would be out of my system. It shouldn't have already been so difficult to part with her, especially knowing I'd be seeing her in an hour.

Moving my hands to her shoulders, I kissed her on the nose. "Go get ready, and I'll see you soon."

Stella had a dreamy look in her eyes when I left her standing in the hallway.

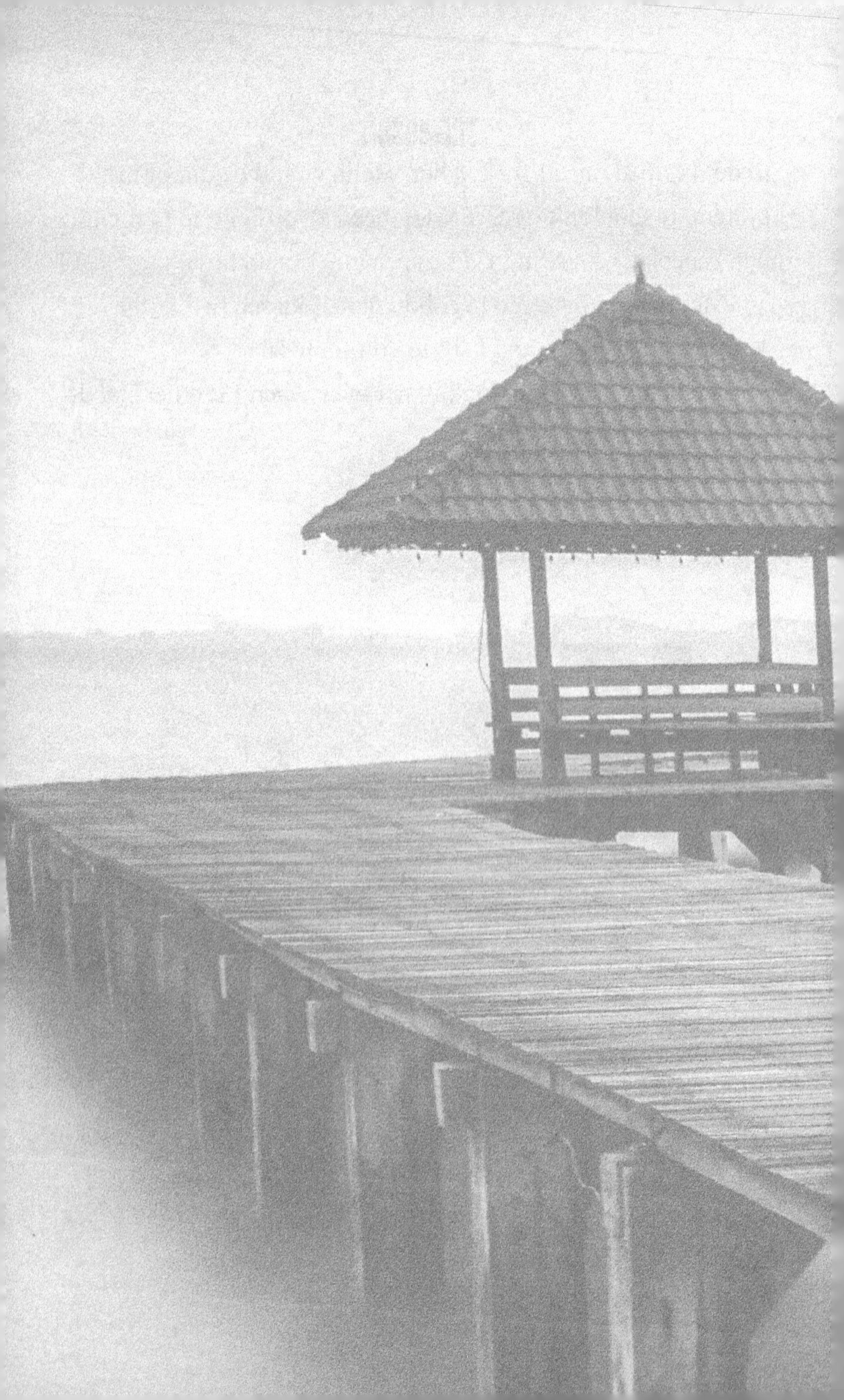

# 7

## REMY

"LET'S SPLIT UP. Scout can take Zelda and me, and Remy can go with you two," Reagan pointed at Pen and Stella.

"Sounds good to me," Stella said and started to walk in the opposite direction from the other two. "I swear they are trying to make a sport out of shopping. There's only so much you can do in a town this size."

"I'm glad they wanted to split up. I wasn't sure I could go into another little store and act interested in everything they thought was cute. Now, Remy," Pen hooked her arm through mine, "show us something, anything that isn't related to shopping."

I was on the same wavelength as both Pen and Stella. We'd been in and out of shops for the last two hours and had to listen to them squeal at every little thing they saw.

I wasn't sure they actually thought the items were cute, or they were doing it because Scout and I were with them. Either way, I was happy to be with Stella and her friend.

"Do you think they'd be mad if we ate lunch without them? I mean, we can say we tried to find them and couldn't," Stella asked hopefully.

"Scout can call me on the walkie at any time, so I don't think we can play that."

"We should have told him to pretend like he was trying to get ahold of us and just met us on the ship at a certain time."

"These are your friends." I laughed at them.

"Ones I'm ready to not see for a year at least," Pen huffed. "All except Stella, here. I can't wait to get her moved up by me."

"I'm surprised you haven't offered to move me into your house until I find something of my own," Stella laughed.

"Sometimes a girl needs her privacy," Pen stated.

"I knew you were hiding something from me," Stella yelled, causing everyone around us to stop and stare.

"And you said we'd talk about it later."

"Fine." This time it was Stella's turn to huff.

They were fun to watch, and I could tell they loved each other.

"We can grab something to eat, and if Scout radios me, it will be up to them to decide if they want to join you for lunch or not."

"I hope or not, is what they pick. I need a break from Reagan

## THE BOSUN

with her ugly looks and jabs." She turned to Pen. "This is the last vacation I go on with her. You'll be lucky to find me in the same room as her after this."

"And I don't blame you. She's being a huge bitch to you, but really I think she's just jealous."

"Of what?" Stella threw her arms in the air. "That I'm thirty-seven, divorced, and starting my life over?"

*Thirty-seven?*

It was hard to believe the woman who stood in front of me was eleven years older than me. If I was to guess, I'd say we were the same age.

"She's jealous because she's in a shit marriage to a man who cheats on her all the time and doesn't have the guts to divorce his sorry ass. Plus, you've got this young hottie drooling all over you."

"Hey! I am not drooling," I defended myself.

"Whatever you want to tell yourself," Pen laughed at me. "Now, take us to lunch before we get hangry and turn on you."

"We can't have that now, can we?" Instead of giving Stella my other elbow, I reached down and laced our fingers together. Her fingers were stiff in mine for a couple of seconds before they relaxed and folded around mine.

"What are you ladies in the mood for?"

"You pick. We'll trust your judgment," Pen said and started walking off.

I looked down at Stella to see if that was okay with her. She gave me a small nod.

Giving her hand a squeeze, I decided on something a little different to eat. I wasn't sure if the chef was only planning to serve Spanish food while they were on the boat, but I was going to take them to this little cafe that served the best French food.

"This island is beautiful. I wish we could stay longer and explore," Stella commented as she looked up at one of the old buildings. It was beautiful here. That was why we ported here for a vast majority of the chartered clients.

"Are you headed back to California immediately?" I asked, thinking of getting away from the boat for a night and staying in a hotel with her. Someplace where we could truly be alone.

"Unfortunately. If I would have known the beauty here," she peeked up at me with a smile, letting me know she didn't only mean the island with its architecture and water. "I would have booked a hotel for an extra day or two, but…" She shrugged and looked down at the sidewalk we were traveling on.

"It was kind of last-minute," Pen added. "Zelda didn't give us much time to prepare. Otherwise, one of us would have looked up where we were going and probably wanted to live here."

"Maybe I'll move here instead of LA," Stella laughed when Pen stopped in her tracks and began to stare her down.

"Don't even joke about it. I'd never see you then. We're finally free to see each other as much as we want, and you want

## THE BOSUN

to move halfway across the world. I don't think so. We'll find you a beach house not far from me, and you'll be perfectly content."

Penelope started walking as if she hadn't spoken.

"Don't you just love how bossy she is? I guess I won't be moving here." She winked.

"Why couldn't you see each other before?" I asked, unable to push down my curiosity to know more about Stella, even knowing she was leaving in a matter of days.

"Because of her asshole ex-husband. He said I was a bad influence on her when in reality, it was because I saw through his shit excuses and tried to wake her up to the man she was married to. In the end, it didn't matter, he got caught with his pants down, and now Stella can finally live her life."

With them talking, we arrived at the café quickly, and luckily for us, they weren't too busy. I spotted a table outside that was tucked away so we'd be safe from the wind and would be perfect for us to sit and afford them the luxury of seeing the water and the city.

"Let's sit here, ladies." I guided them over to the table.

Only a few seconds later, a busy worker dropped off waters and menus for us to peruse. Since I'd been here before, it didn't take me long to decide on what I wanted to eat. It gave me plenty of time to digest what I'd heard on our walk here.

I wasn't sure how Stella couldn't have a life while she was married and was afraid to ask. I was merely a stranger who had an intense attraction to her. What right did I have to ask her all the personal questions that were burning inside of me? One thing I did know was Stella's husband sounded like an asshole, and whatever he'd done to her, I was sure she still had to be raw over it. I needed to keep that in mind when dealing with her.

"Once I find a new place, I can start to live, that is." Stella set her menu down and stared across the table at her friend. "I have a feeling if I take too long, Pen will find me the house and furnish it for me, which doesn't sound too bad now that I think about it."

"I might have to if you never finish writing your book, but seriously, don't test me. I think if you have some new scenery, it will get your writing juices flowing."

"Ew," Stella scrunched up her nose. "Please don't ever refer to my stalled writing as juices again." She paused for a minute while looking out at the water. "But I think you're right. I need to get out of Oasis, away from all the pitiful looks and whispers and Brock. Most definitely away from him. Although he's a great villain muse."

They both laughed, making me smile at the two of them. I enjoyed the way they talked to each other. They gave each other a hard time, but also in a way that they knew it was done out of love.

"So, you're an author?"

"Not really," Stella said at the same time as Pen gave a

## THE BOSUN

resounding yes. "It's my first book."

"She's always written, though. Since she was a little girl."

"This will be my first time publishing."

"I convinced her to send the first five chapters of something she'd been writing for years to a few publishers."

"She's not telling you the truth." Stella narrowed her eyes at her friend. "Pen here went and sent them herself without my knowledge."

"Only because I know how good her writing is and knew she'd never send it on her own," Pen shot back with a smug look on her face. "They loved it and gave her a big advance. Now she only needs to finish writing it."

A sense of pride filled me for Stella. Getting published wasn't easy. "What's the book about?"

Tucking a loose strand of hair behind her ear, Stella answered with a slight duck of her head and not meeting my eyes. "About a wife who starts to suspect her husband of the murders happening in their small town."

Wait. Was her ex a murderer?

Both Stella and Pen started laughing hysterically. Pen was doubled over while Stella practically laid the top half of her body on the table as she cackled.

After a minute of them losing it, Stella straightened herself up and cleared her throat. "Brock, my ex, isn't a killer. He may be a total douche and asshole, but not that. He is the inspiration, and some of what he's done to me has been translated into the book. It's been cathartic. A way for me to deal with what he's put me through."

"And there was a serial killer in our town. It gave her the idea to combine the two. She's an amazing writer, and I can't wait for the world to finally be able to read her words."

Stella's pinked up before she covered her face with her hands. "You only say that because we've been friends since middle school."

"I say it because it's true. Once you're away from that asshole always putting you down, you'll start to believe in yourself once again. You'll be the girl who you were before you married him."

"I'll never be her." Stella's eyes turned glassy. "At best, I'll be a combination of the two with my younger self winning more often than not."

"Oh, Stell," Pen's chin trembled, "I'll take you any way you come. You know that, right?"

Stella nodded shakily as one lone tear escaped.

"Buenos días señoritas, señor," the waiter tips his head. "What may I get for you today?"

Their emotional confession was interrupted by our waiter. I, for one, was happy to have it come to an end. I'd never been able to deal with women's tears. They were my downfall.

We all ordered and then sat quietly staring off in different directions until our food came. I couldn't help but glance at Stella every few minutes. I wanted to get my fill of her before

## THE BOSUN

she was gone and out of my life.

Our silence was broken when Stella let out a sinful moan as she took a bite of her croissant.

"Oh my god, you sound like you're having sex with your food," Pen laughed but then let out a moan of her own. "Damn, these are almost as good as sex. I'd request these be brought on the boat if I wanted to gain twenty pounds." Her eyes landed on me. "Thank you for bringing us here. It's perfect."

"I agree," Stella leaned against my side with a serene smile on her lips. "Thank you," she murmured before she kissed my cheek.

"It's my pleasure, ladies." Reaching under the table, I held Stella's hand in mine. "It really is. It's not often I get to be surrounded by two beautiful women making those kinds of noises."

Penelope's eyes narrowed on me, letting me know I'd said something wrong. "Oh, do you often hear those noises by multiple women at a time?"

"What?" I laughed at the awkward way our day had turned. "No, it's not like that. I chose my words wrong. I was merely stating how I was enjoying spending my time with you and—"

"The enjoyment of our noises. Yeah, we got that. Watch out for him," Pen interrupted and nodded at me. "He may be young, but he's got experience."

Stella bit her lip with a smirk on her face.

There was no way in hell I was going to admit to a threesome. Stella would probably run for the hills or think I wanted to include her friend when there was no way in hell I would share her with another.

My walkie-talkie beeped, letting me know someone was trying to get in touch with me. "Remy, Remy, Scout. The women are ready to head back to the boat." Each word was said with a bite. What the hell had happened?

"Scout, Remy here. We're finishing up our lunch and can meet you in twenty," I replied back.

"No need since we're docked. Enjoy your time on the island."

I heard the implication that wouldn't be the case on the boat. I wished I had an international plan. Instead, I used the boat's Wi-Fi and an app when I needed to contact anyone, but if I wanted to message Scout, I'd need to find somewhere with Wi-Fi.

"Sounds like it was smart of us to break apart. Do you think Zelda and Reagan got into a fight?" Pen's eyes lit up with excitement.

"It wouldn't surprise me. Reagan has been a bitch the entire trip, and I'm just glad it wasn't me this time. If we don't have to go back, I say we enjoy ourselves. I doubt we'll ever be on this beautiful island again."

My chest felt heavy with the thought that I wouldn't see Stella walk along these streets again.

"Yes, let's enjoy our orgasmic food and the company of our

## THE BOSUN

young escort." She could barely say the words without a smile splitting her lips.

"Why don't you stop reminding me how young he is. I'd ask, but I don't want to know. I like being blissfully ignorant in this instance."

"I'm not that young." She made it sound like I was barely legal, or I was a secret to keep.

"I know." She tightened her grip on my hand. "We're just having fun at your expense, and that's not kind of us. I'm sorry. It's been a long time since we could do this."

Her words put me at ease—a little. Still, I had a feeling she felt it was wrong to be with me for some reason. Was it some residual effect her ex had on her?

"I don't mind," I lied to make her feel better. They weren't trying to hurt me in any way, and I understood that. Still, it hurt, feeling like she was ashamed of me. I already had enough people ashamed of me for the actions of my life. I couldn't imagine what Stella would think if she knew about my time in the military.

"We're being mean and shouldn't take it out on you. Sorry," Pen gave me a half smile, half frown. "Where should we go after lunch?"

"Let me think," I hummed. "The Catedral de Mallorca is a must. If we had time, I'd take you to all the little towns around here, but we'd need either scooters or a car to get to most of them. You need to come back so I can show you more."

Stella placed her elbow on the table and rested her head in her hand. "Is that an invitation?"

"Yeah, I mean, it would have to be once the season's over, but I'd love to show you around."

"Well, if I get my life together by then, I might take you up on your offer." She took the last bite of her croissant sandwich and closed her eyes. A dreamy smile filled her face.

"I hope you do."

"And I have a feeling I should have left you two alone today. Maybe you could have gotten a hotel for a few hours."

"While that would have been nice, I couldn't have you wandering around by yourself." Stella reached across the table and held Penelope's hand for a moment. "If we're meant to spend time together, we will. Hopefully, there won't be interference by the crew tonight."

"If you need the room, just let me know. I can sleep on a lounger." Pen waggled her eyebrows at us.

"I'm sure we can find someplace else, so you're not displaced from your bed." I laughed. It was hilarious her friend was trying to get us to hook up.

"This is getting embarrassing," Stella groaned.

"It's all good," I leaned over and kissed her cheek. "I think it's cute."

"It looks like it's going to rain. Maybe we should start to head back to the boat." Stella's tone stated she wanted to do anything but go back.

## THE BOSUN

"What's a few sprinkles?" Pen blew her off.

"She's probably right. The wind has steadily been increasing, and it might get nasty."

"Fine," Pen huffed. "You two are no fun, which means you're perfect for each other."

"Yes, that's exactly what it means when two people have common sense." Stella bumped her hip with her friend.

Linking her arm with mine, Pen winked up at me. "Thank you for being our tour guide, even if it was only for a short while. You made the day most enjoyable, and tonight you'll make Stella's night."

"Pen!" Stella shouted, her eyes narrowing as she gave her the evil eye.

"What?" She laughed, nearly tripping over her feet. "I'm just stating the obvious."

"You're putting way too much pressure on something that might not happen. Look at what happened last night."

"Well, I won't let anyone interrupt you two. I'll make sure to keep them all busy. I'll get Zelda and Scarlet on it as well. They're team Stella needs to get laid."

My body shook from the laughter I was trying to hold back.

"I feel like some teenage boy whose father takes him to a brothel to lose his virginity. Thank you, but I don't need your help."

Stella pulled on my arm until I looked down at her. "Please don't think I'm desperate or that there's something wrong with me. Yes, it's been a while, but I'm not going to die if I have to wait. It's not your job to break my celibacy streak."

Wrapping my arm around her shoulders, I pulled her closer as we walked. "How long has it been?" I asked quietly. That way, it was easier to pretend Penelope wasn't alongside us.

"Two years, but it's not like I've been actively trying to have sex. One year of it was while I was married." Stella wrapped her arm around my waist and leaned into me. The simple movement felt so right that it scared me. "If you're ever married, and your spouse doesn't have sex with you, let me tell you right now she's getting it from somewhere else."

"Either that or you were never doing it right in the first place, and she's giving it to herself." Pen broke out into a laugh and slapped her leg. "Can you imagine?"

No, I couldn't imagine going a year without sex, let alone two. I needed to make tonight good for Stella. Better than good. I wanted to ruin her for all other men. I wanted her to think of me every time she was with any man in the future.

"Anyway, the next year was our divorce, and I didn't want to give our town another reason to talk about me. It's bad enough they all know he cheated on me and is having a child with another woman."

"That can't be easy. I'm sorry." I hugged her to me.

"That's why I'm moving away. I want a fresh start in my life."

"I don't blame you. I did something similar when I started

## THE BOSUN

to work on the boats. I wanted to forget about my old life and focus on the future." I tensed at giving away too much, afraid they'd ask questions, but they must have sensed it was something I didn't want to talk about.

We were silent as we walked toward the marina. I was surprised I'd had a fun time with them. I'd been dreading the whole day for no reason.

The marina came into view the second the first drop of water hit.

"Did you feel that?" Stella asked, her pace quickening.

"No, what was it?" Pen asked.

"Rain," Stella said in a 'you're stupid' tone.

"Or bird piss," Pen shot back with a cackle.

"Ugh, that's all I need to think about is a bird taking a piss on me. Thanks, Pen."

A few more drops landed on my skin, but I kept quiet since the two of them were so amusing.

"Okay, I felt something," Pen admitted.

"It's probably a bird circling and pissing all over us," Stella started to laugh, and we soon followed after her.

"That's so gross." Pen faked gagged.

"You're the one who brought it up, not me. You deserve a little bird pee on you," Stella threw back.

Droplets landed on the surface all around us, but I didn't think any of us felt them as we laughed. Pen started to spin in circles and shouted. "Pee on me all you want."

I could only stand as I watched Stella join in. Her arms spread wide, with her head tipped back.

After all she'd revealed to me today, it was nice to see her let loose and have fun.

"We should run," I yelled as the rain started to fall harder. We'd be drenched by the time we made it to the boat.

The wind swept by, and the temperature dropped just as quickly, causing Stella to break out in goosebumps.

"This is our punishment for having fun without the others," Pen yelled from behind me. I could hear her flip-flop feet slapping the ground as she ran.

"It doesn't matter because we had fun," Stella shouted over her shoulder. "Run faster."

"I'm trying," Pen laughed from behind us. "You're too damn fast."

"That's because we don't want to get wet."

I didn't mind getting wet. If I did, working on a boat would be the worst job ever.

Our steps slowed as we arrived to board the boat. Bending over, we quickly took off our shoes, and my gaze met Stella's. Electricity connected us for a brief second in time.

"Go get warmed up, and I'll see you upstairs later." Her mouth opened, but I didn't want to hear her say it was a bad idea now that we were back. "I promise to find you, even if we have to kick Pen out of her own bed."

"Let's go," Pen said, breaking our moment as she pulled

## THE BOSUN

Stella away.

I slowly walked around the boat, making sure everything was as it was supposed to be before I headed downstairs to take a shower and put on a clean set of clothes while trying to avoid Ophelia as much as possible. I knew she'd question why we split up and why we hadn't come back together.

I made it for the most part. Only running into Dean as he stepped out of our shared space at the same time I walked in.

"You look a mess," he said as he slipped by me.

"We got caught out in it. It's really coming down now. I'll bet dinner has to be served inside."

He shrugged as if it made no difference to him, and I guess it didn't. Only the girls. "Will there be extra guests tonight?"

One thing I knew all chefs hated was finding out at the last minute that they'd be expected to serve more people than they were counting on, and that had happened the last two nights.

"Not that I know of, but you can never tell with this group of guests."

Bumping my shoulder to get by, he grumbled. "Well, if you weren't so damn personable and handsome, they wouldn't want you to join them every night."

"Not something I can help. Don't act like if you weren't the one cooking food, they wouldn't have invited you because you know that's the truth." He shook his head in denial. "I know it to be true. I heard a couple of the girls going on about how hot you are, and the primary said she was going to offer you a job."

"Oh dear god, I hope she doesn't offer me a job. I don't want to have to decline." He looked down at his toes and wiggled them.

"Are you sure you don't want to be her personal chef and get off the boat? You'd make some sick money."

One shoulder lifted. "I haven't been offered, so I can't say."

That's what I thought. "Stay cool, dude. I'm going to grab a shower."

"See you on the flip side." Dean ducked around the corner headed for the kitchen.

Stripping out of my wet clothes, I turned on the water and set it as hot as I could stand it. After hours of being hard over Stella, I needed to relieve some of the pressure from my straining cock.

Pumping soap into my hand, I rubbed them together, creating a thick amount of suds, and ran them down my chest, over my abs, and straight to my stiff cock.

I let out a moan as I squeezed my tip. Knowing I didn't have much time, I leaned my other arm against the wall of the shower and fisted my cock, stroking faster with each pump, all the while thinking of Stella in the bikini she wore yesterday. With her body playing behind my eyes, it didn't take me long to explode. My forehead connected to the cool wall as streams of cum shot all over the shower wall.

Now that my head was slightly clearer, I dressed in my t-shirt and shorts uniform, ready for anything that might come

## THE BOSUN

my way. I slicked my hair back with some gel and sprayed on some cologne, making sure I smelled good for her later.

With pep in my step, I left my bedroom and went up the stairs two at a time. Hitting the landing, I saw Ophelia and Stella talking by her room, and my gut told me it wasn't good.

Ophelia put her hand to her ample chest and gave a fake look of shock. "Oh, Remy was with me last night."

Stella's face went pale for a moment before it flushed with color when her eyes met mine.

Fuck my life.

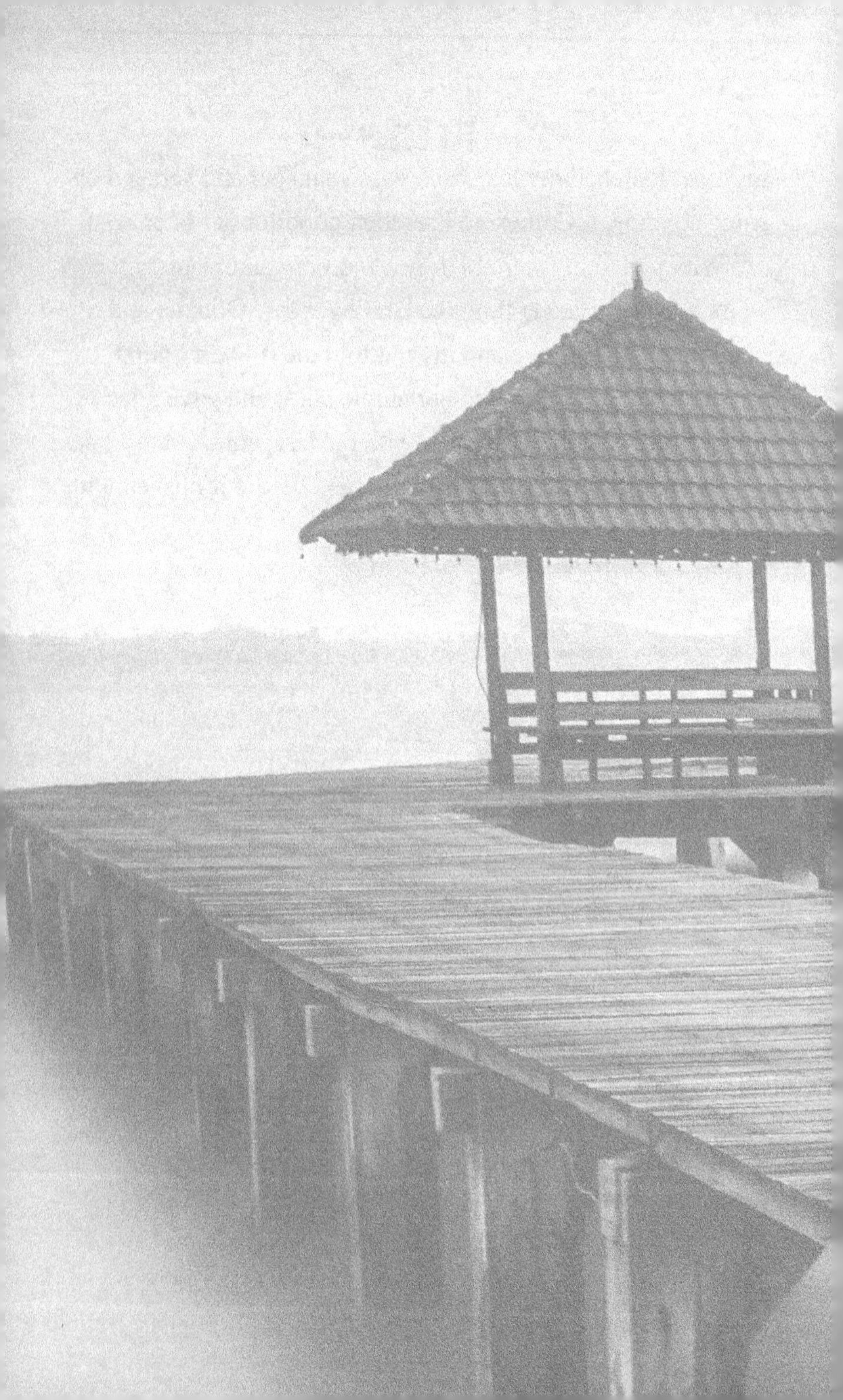

# 8

## STELLA

UNSURE HOW TO take Ophelia's words, I acted shocked as I ran into my room before she could say anymore or before Remy could interrupt. I'd seen the way she looked at him from the moment we stepped on board. And I knew they'd probably slept together, but I didn't think they were a thing. All I could do was keep my questions to myself until I could get Remy alone tonight. If he didn't say the right words, I knew I'd be disappointed about not getting to fuck him, but I wasn't going to be with him if he was with someone else.

Remy didn't seem to be the type, but I didn't actually know him. I couldn't judge his character after a few short conversations, but in my gut, something I liked to pride myself on said that Remy was a good man. He was hiding something, but it wasn't for me to ask him. I had a feeling it was something that wounded him deeply.

Not ready to talk, I bypassed Pen as she left the bathroom. I should have known I wouldn't get to avoid her twice. Pen was sitting on my bed when I came out of the bathroom wrapped in a towel with another in my hand, trying to get the moisture out.

"Dinner is going to be ready in twenty minutes. I was told to tell you not to be late, so that means no stopping by to see Remy."

I rolled my eyes at her. She could be so immature sometimes.

"I can promise you I'm not going to see him. In fact, I'm not sure what will happen tonight."

"Why?" She furrowed her brows.

"Ophelia stopped me before I came inside and felt the need to tell me the reason why Remy didn't meet me last night is because he was with her. Why did she feel the need to tell me that? Were you guys talking about it around her?"

"No," she held her hands up. "We always made sure to shut up when they were around. Maybe she was lurking around a corner and heard us. She was acting strange when she saw me after we got back. I think she's jealous. I think we've all noticed her checking him out, especially at our dinners."

Clasping my hands together, I held them in front of me. "Please don't tell me Zelda invited Remy to dinner again."

"I don't think so, but you never know with her. Anyway, we

## THE BOSUN

could talk about this all night, but you need to hurry up and get ready and looking extra sexy for Remy tonight."

"Ugh." I slumped down on the bed. "I don't need all this pressure to get laid. Why does the one guy I'm finally interested in have to work in Spain of all places?"

Pen leaned into my side and rested her head alongside mine. "Because life isn't fair, but think of it this way; that boat hottie is going to get you out of your funk, and then maybe once you move to LA, you'll be ready to date."

"I hope you're right. Now leave me to get ready, so I don't hold up dinner. I don't want to piss off Chef Dean."

Rolling off the bed, Pen grabbed her phone off the bed. "I'll see you up there."

I couldn't decide what to wear and since I hadn't unpacked, and all of my clothes were wrinkled. I knew I should have taken them up on their offer to unpack for me. Luckily, one of my colorful skirts had ruffles on it, which I paired with a cute white button-down shirt over the red bikini set Pen bought for me. I hadn't packed any sexy lingerie for our trip because I didn't think I'd want to jump anyone's bones. Too bad shoes weren't allowed onboard because I would have worn a pair of sexy high heels.

Normally I wasn't late in my real life, but somehow, I was the late girl on this trip, and I hated it. All the girls were waiting with drinks in hand when I got upstairs.

"Nice of you to join us," Reagan sneered the second her

eyes landed on me.

"I think I did pretty well for only having twenty minutes to get ready. Some of us don't have rooms all to ourselves." It took everything in me not to flip her off.

I'd barely sat down when Ophelia came floating into the room with a crazy smile on her face. "Would you like anything to drink?"

I didn't want a repeat of our first night, so I decided wine would be best for the night. That way, I could control how intoxicated I got.

"Do you have Moscato?" I asked hopefully.

"Of course, it was on your preference sheet." She gave me a fake smile before she walked off.

The crew guys helped serve our dinner, and every time Remy even looked my way, Ophelia was rushing him away or glaring at him. If she was trying to make dinner awkward, she succeeded. The chef outdid himself, making the best food I'd ever had in my life. The Langoustine marinated in mango and passion fruit was my favorite dinner of the charter, and the chocolate soufflé was to die for. If I had the money, I'd probably want to hire the chef like Zelda did so I could eat like that every day. I was sure my waistline wouldn't be happy with me either.

I swore we all waddled away from the table and moved up to the sky lounge to let our food digest.

"Jolene dear," Zelda called her over, "do you think you

## THE BOSUN

could set up a movie in here for us to watch and maybe make us some truffle popcorn?"

Dear God, how could she think of eating another bite? And did she really need some type of truffle on or in all her food?

"I'll see what we can do. You may have to switch to a different room, but I'm not sure." Jolene bowed her head and wrung her hands. "What would you like to watch?"

"I'm not sure yet, but we'll figure one out." Zelda smiled big and fake, making her face look like it was about to split in two. Seriously, stop with the plastic surgery and implants.

"Okay," she answered shakily. "Let me go speak with Ophelia. This is more her realm than mine."

Jolene scurried out of the room. We could hear her feet pounding on the stairs as she went downstairs. The moment we couldn't hear her any longer, Zelda hopped up and came toward me.

"Now's your chance to go. We'll keep the girls occupied."

"What's going on?" I looked to Pen and back to Zelda and back again in confusion.

"We're distracting the crew members while you go spend some time with Remy. Now go before someone comes back," Zelda pushed me by the shoulders.

"I don't know if this will work. Won't they wonder where I am?" There was always at least one crew member around us at all times unless we were in our rooms.

"We'll say you have a headache and want to be left alone.

It will be perfect." She clapped her hands. Her face glowed with excitement, or maybe it was all she'd had to drink during dinner. Either way, Zelda seemed proud of her plan.

"Thank you." I kissed her on her cheek.

Next was Pen with a hug. "I'll see you later."

Leaving through the sliding door, I had no idea where I was supposed to find Remy. Since most of the places we'd been were in the back of the boat, I headed to the front. Something told me I'd find him there, and I wasn't wrong.

Remy was shirtless in a pair of shorts that hung ridiculously low on his hips while he looked to be shining the railing. The way his muscles rippled with each movement had me hypnotized. My hands itched to get acquainted with each and every one of them.

He cleared his throat, breaking me out of my lustful thoughts and reminded me of what Ophelia had mentioned earlier. "Are you going to stand there and stare all night?"

I crossed my arms over my chest in anticipation of what he might say. "Perhaps. It depends on what your answer is when I ask you a very important question."

He stopped what he was doing and stood facing me. "Okay, what do you want to ask me?"

I was surprised my voice was steady as I asked. "Did you spend last night with Ophelia?"

Stepping closer, he stopped with only a foot between us. "Not even close. If you'd like, you can ask the guys and the

## THE BOSUN

chef since he's my roommate."

"There's no need. I believe you. I couldn't in good conscience spend any more time with you if you were with her." I had to ask even though I didn't want the answer. "Have you slept with her?"

His eyes closed, and his face fell. I had my answer, but I wanted to hear it from his mouth.

"I have, but it wasn't recent. It was on the first boat I worked on. I knew immediately it was a mistake and one I didn't plan to repeat. O can't seem to get the message no matter how many times I've told her it's not going to happen again."

"Maybe it's because you're so damn good." And damn, did I want him to show me just how good he could be.

A lazy smirk crossed his sexy face. "I'd happily show you. Would you like a sample or full service?"

"Full service, please."

⚓

Slamming my back against the wall, Remy's lips continued to ravage every inch of my neck and jaw. "Fuck, you taste good. I want to dip my tongue between your legs and see if you taste as sweet."

The thin fabric that covered my sex was drenched, and I couldn't decide if I wanted him down on his knees before me or if I wanted him to fill me with his thick cock.

My fingers tugged on his hair, moving his mouth to mine. I

bit on his bottom lip and tugged. Breaking away, I nibbled on his jaw as I spoke. "You need to do something before I combust."

A sexy smirk broke across his face right before he gripped my shirt and, in one smooth move, tore it open. The buttons went flying in every direction. "We can't have that, can we?" Slowly he started kissing down my neck and moved on to sucking on the tender flesh of one breast and then the other. Using his teeth, Remy pulled the red triangle of fabric to the side, so he could lave my nipple with his tongue.

His hot tongue, along with the cool breeze on my overly sensitive flesh, sent shivers down my spine. As his scorching mouth moved further south and met the fabric of my skirt, Remy kneeled and ducked underneath. His nose swept along the fabric of my swim bottoms once before he moved it aside, giving him unhindered access to my dripping core.

"Your smell is driving me wild," he moaned out. "Now I'm going to sample your sweet pussy."

The moment his soft, hot tongue met my folds, my back arched off the wall, and my knees nearly buckled. Bracing one hand against the wall and the other on his head, I bucked my hips up until his nose met my clit. "Yes," I whimpered at the sensation.

It had been too long since my body had been touched this way. It wasn't long before my toes started to curl, and my bundle of nerves started to pulse. "I'm close," I breathed out.

## THE BOSUN

"Whatever you do, don't stop."

At that point, I didn't care if someone came down to the back of the boat where we were and saw us. It wouldn't matter as long as I got the release I was desperate for.

Plunging two fingers into my sleek heat, Remy began to suck on my lips and moved to my nub. With his lips and tongue doing devilish work sucking and then biting down, I exploded into a million pieces. Thousands of fireworks went off behind my eyelids, and tingles erupted underneath my skin. Particles of my being would forever be left in Spain after the way he brought me to release.

My back slumped against the wall, even with Remy's hands on my hips to steady me as he stood.

With his hair a sexy mess from my fingers running through it and tugging on it, Remy licked his lips. "I knew you'd taste divine. I would happily stay between your legs if we had the time." I hated we had to leave after tomorrow, but there was nothing I could do about it. I'd known from the first moment I saw him whatever we had would be fleeting. "I wish I had someplace to lay you down so I could properly ravage your body. I guess I'll have to make do with what we have here."

"You seem like a resourceful guy. Show me what you're made of." I pushed off the wall and draped one leg around his waist. Even after the amazing orgasm he'd just given me, I was hungry for more. I rubbed my core against the bulge in his swim trunks as I snaked my arms around his neck. "I want to feel you inside of me."

"And I want to sink deep inside of you. Pull my dick out, Stella." My name on his lips was the most delectable sound I'd ever heard. My pulse hummed at the command while my hands went to the drawstring of his trunks and untied it, keeping them riding low on his hips.

With one final slip of the string, Remy's bottoms fell to his knees, and all I could do was stare. He was magnificent and bigger than big. Not only was he long, but he was thick with a vein that ran the length of his massive erection that had my mouth drooling. I wanted to lick and suck on the beast he kept hidden in his pants.

"Fuck, Stella, the way you're looking at me has my cock weeping to be inside of you. I can't wait any longer. The last few days have been torture trying to stay away from you."

Looking around, Remy pulled me behind him until we came upon one of the platforms they put out into the water for us to lie out and walk around on. "This will have to do."

Remy threw his trunks to the side before he pulled me down with him on the soft surface until I straddled his hips. The apex between my thighs rubbed along his stiff erection as I settled my hands on his shoulders and looked into his dark eyes that were full of lust for me.

Keeping one hand on his shoulder, I pushed my bikini bottoms to the side and then hesitated. My hand ran up his taut stomach and over his pecs that jumped from my touch. "Do

# THE BOSUN

you have a condom?"

I hated to spoil the moment, but I hadn't been on birth control for a few years. Before Brock and I stopped having sex, we'd been trying to have a baby, and when that didn't work, I never went back on it and saw no point since I wasn't having sex.

His hands sitting firmly on my hips gave me a squeeze before he leaned over and grabbed his trunks. "I...I was caught up, but I did bring one."

I sat, watching enthralled as he sheathed himself and then as he gripped my hips and placed me over his waiting erection.

With my hands back on his shoulders, I slowly lowered myself inch by inch onto his massive cock. I'd barely gotten more than the tip in when I had to stop and let my body get accustomed to his size. Remy's jaw tensed but had no other outward sign that it was hard for him to hold back.

"I don't know if it's because it's been so long or if it's because you're the biggest guy who's ever been inside me, but I'm sorry."

"You never have to tell a guy sorry because he's too big, but maybe I can help you get there faster."

I was about to ask him how he'd do that when his lips captured mine. His tongue swept inside as his thumb connected to my bundle of nerves.

"Stop thinking and just feel, and when you can, fill yourself fully with me."

With both his mouth and thumb distracting me, it was easier to slide the rest of the way down. The burn as I became accustomed to him heightened all my senses making the way his hands moved up my stomach and rib cage tantalizing. Slowly I started to rock back and forth and moving up and down.

Dipping his head, Remy bit and sucked on my breasts as I rode him. The only sounds were our panting breaths and the water slapping against the side of the boat, giving me the perfect rhythm to move to until neither one of us could hold back any longer.

Wrapping my arm around his shoulders, my pace quickened. When the tip was about to slip out, I would slam down and circle my hips only to do it again.

"Fucking hell woman, you're tight. I can feel your pussy squeeze me every time you slam down on my shaft." Closing his eyes, he moaned deep in his throat. His hand on my waist moved underneath the skirt I'd kept on. One finger ran through my juices before it circled my tight ring and slipped inside.

Having his finger in my ass, one on my clit, and his thick cock inside me, I was overtaken with sensation. I let out a low moan before I bit down on his shoulder and tried to stifle the noises I was making.

"Keep squeezing me like that, and I'm going to go off," he groaned into the shell of my ear. His words spurred me on. I wanted to see what Remy looked like when he came more than I wanted my next breath.

## THE BOSUN

I knew it would only be a matter of seconds before I detonated all around him. The way our bodies connected felt more divine than the finest dessert. I'd never have another sweet in my life if I could fuck Remy until the end of time.

When my walls began to flutter, I bore down on his finger, loving the feel of being so full of him and felt him swell inside of me. I didn't think it was possible for him to get bigger, but somehow, he managed to.

Arching back, I erupted with this new angle. My body seized up as pleasure wrapped itself around me. Holding onto me, Remy pumped two more times when he stilled underneath me and buried his head into my shoulder before letting out a groan that came from deep inside.

After a few moments, he rolled his head to the side and kissed my neck. I was a puddle of happy goo in his arms as I rested my head on his shoulder with my eyes closed.

Was boat sex always that good, or was it all Remy?

A cold shiver wracked my body at the thought that after tonight I would never feel him fill me so completely.

Wrapping his big, strong arms around me, Remy stood as if I weighed as light as a feather and pulled me flush to him. His hands rubbed up and down my back as he whispered against my lips. "Let's get you warmed up."

"I'm not ready to go inside yet," I whined. It wasn't so much because of me being cold as it was that I knew once we parted ways things would be different between us.

Pulling away, he righted my bikini top and slipped his shorts on before he grabbed my hand and started us up the stairs. "As far as I know, no one is using the hot tub."

At least we'd get to spend more time together. Only I wasn't sure I'd be able to keep myself under control with him wet and sexy sitting across from me; I agreed, nonetheless.

I was surprised we didn't see or hear the girls as we walked along in the shadows until we slipped inside the hot tub. Pen needed a reward for making that possible.

Water bubbled up from the jets tickling my back and making me squirm across the way from Remy.

"It seems silly to ask this now, but what did you do for a living before you started to write your book?"

Leaning back further, I let my legs float in the water. "I've had a few jobs, but the last was a receptionist at my ex's medical practice. Before, to support him through medical school, I worked two jobs. One as a hostess at a restaurant and the other, I was a manager at a bookstore."

Grabbing one of my feet that was floating, Remy dug his thumbs into the arch. "And he repaid you by cheating on you?"

"And getting her pregnant. That was the hardest part. Brock is a pediatrician who loves kids, and we tried for years with it amounting to nothing. He said it made him look bad, like I was purposely not getting pregnant. One day we gave up, and that seemed to be the end of our marriage. Now he's this

## THE BOSUN

renowned doctor with a baby on the way, and I'm stuck trying to start a new life."

"It sounds like you're not stuck for what little I know. You're writing a book, something most people only dream of doing, and you're moving away from all the negativity in your life." He switched to my other foot. "I bet in a year; you won't remember feeling like this. It will all be a distant memory."

I hoped so. It was draining to hate Brock for what he did to me and to us. Cheating never made sense to me. If he wanted to be with other people, then why hadn't he ended our relationship first?

After what Brock put me through, would I ever be able to trust another man not to cheat on me? I wasn't sure. Not that it mattered since I didn't have any men on the horizon except for the one in front of me, and he'd be out of my life in the blink of an eye.

Not wanting the memories of my past life to ruin the night, I changed the subject off of me. "You said you've only been doing this for two years. What did you do before this?"

His thumb dug into a particularly tender spot making my foot jerk back in response. "Sorry, um…" He cleared his throat, and his hands stopped moving. His long fingers wrapped around my foot, and then his thumbs started to caress the top. "I was a Marine. Joined when I was eighteen, and when I got out, I needed a change of scenery."

I eyed one of the many tattoos he had on his arms. It was

of an eagle standing on a globe with stars around it. There was more, but it was hard to make out all the details from this far away.

"Is that a tattoo from your military days?" I pointed to his left arm.

His Adam's apple bobbed before he answered. "My entire team got one, one drunken night before we were deployed."

"Do you want to talk about something else?" I sensed he wasn't comfortable talking about that time in his life.

"Anything else," he rushed out a relieved breath.

"Okay, is this something you want to continue to do, or do you want to do something else eventually?"

Sitting up straighter, his hands started to work my foot once again. "I actually want to be a fireman."

"Really? Wow, that's awesome and kind of scary."

He laughed. "Lots of jobs are scary. Sometimes the most rewarding things in life have the direst of consequences."

"Those are very poignant words. If you ever make the change, you should come to California. We're always having fires that are out of control, and I know they could use the help."

Cocking his head to the side, Remy studied me for a moment with a curious look. "I'll keep that in mind. I've been saving money and hope to make the move to training in a year or two."

It dawned on me, he probably thought I wanted to hook up

## THE BOSUN

with him or something if he moved to California. Not that I would be opposed because I wouldn't, but I wasn't desperate enough to ask someone to move there for a hookup.

"The area where I'm thinking of moving has fires all the time. I'm not sure I want to move someplace where my home is in danger so often. I guess that's the tradeoff for living in that area." I didn't even want to think about how much fire insurance would cost.

"What area is that?" Pulling on my foot, Remy dislodged me from where I'd been sitting and guided me to straddle him.

"Oh," I squeaked before I wrapped my arm around his neck. "Are you sure this is okay? I'd hate to be the reason you're fired."

"I think we're safe. Besides, I couldn't have you sitting across from me any longer. I need to touch you."

"I'm not opposed to you touching me." My words came out sexy and breathy, and the effect of them had Remy's dark eyes turning into the blackest of nights.

"Good. While I touch you, tell me where you're going to move." His hand cupped one breast as his thumb circled my already hard nipple.

"Malibu or somewhere around there. I can't say for certain since I haven't looked at any houses, but I want to live on the beach. It will be a nice change after living my entire life in the desert."

"And what's living in the desert like?" His other hand slid

down my ribcage to my hip and rubbed lazy circles there.

"Hot," I laughed. "No, it's not that bad most of the time. The summers are unbearable, but the rest of the year makes up for it."

Leaning down, his lips traced along the column of my neck. "Then why move?"

"Because I love the ocean and the beach, and I want to get away from an entire town talking about me when I walk by. I hate being the talk of the town."

"That's understandable, but if you love it there, don't run away from them. Stand up and show them what they say about you doesn't bother you."

"Easier said than done, but I agree."

The hand on my hip moved until he slipped two fingers under the fabric of my bottoms. Finding my center, he slid his long, thick fingers inside me and started to pump.

"You're so incredibly tight."

My arms wrapped around his head, giving him perfect access to my breasts that were begging for his mouth.

Sucking along the skin, he bit into the fabric that covered my stiff peaks hard enough it would likely leave a mark. "I love your tits. They're so full and perky."

My hips swiveled as I rode his fingers. I was close, but I needed more. "More," I murmured into the top of his head.

Bringing his head up, he nipped at my bottom lip. "I love a woman who isn't afraid to ask for what she wants. Now, I want

# THE BOSUN

you to come all over my fingers.

I started to protest, but as his thumb connected to my clit and rubbed fast circles, I clenched around him. Taking my mouth in the hottest kiss of my life, I moaned down his throat as I came apart. Fingers tangled and pulled on his hair as I soared above the stratosphere for one brief second before I started to come down. Panting, my body sagged against his, unused to three orgasms in such rapid succession.

"Watching you come undone is the hottest thing I've ever seen. I wish I could do that all night."

I was sure I'd be a pile of goo somewhere on the ship, but I was okay with that.

"Fuck, I wish I had another condom on me."

"Why don't you?" I murmured as I nuzzled into his neck.

"I didn't think I'd be meeting anyone I'd want to hook up with. Usually, I have better restraint, but one look at you, and I couldn't hold back. It's like you've put a spell on me that broke down my usual iron-clad self-restraint."

"If I said I was sorry, I'd be lying. What you did to my body brought me to heights I've never experienced. But what about this?" I asked as I rubbed over the bulge that felt as if it was about ready to break through the fabric of his shorts.

"I'm fine. I can take care of myself once I get back to my room. That was all for you."

Thinking of Remy jerking himself off because of me had me ready to go again. It said something about a man when he was a giver. I wanted to reciprocate what he'd given me.

Why hadn't we bought condoms while we were in town?

"Come on, beautiful. As much as I hate to end our night, I have to get up early. We're going to try and take you out once more before you have to leave."

And just like that, our time was over.

# THE BOSUN

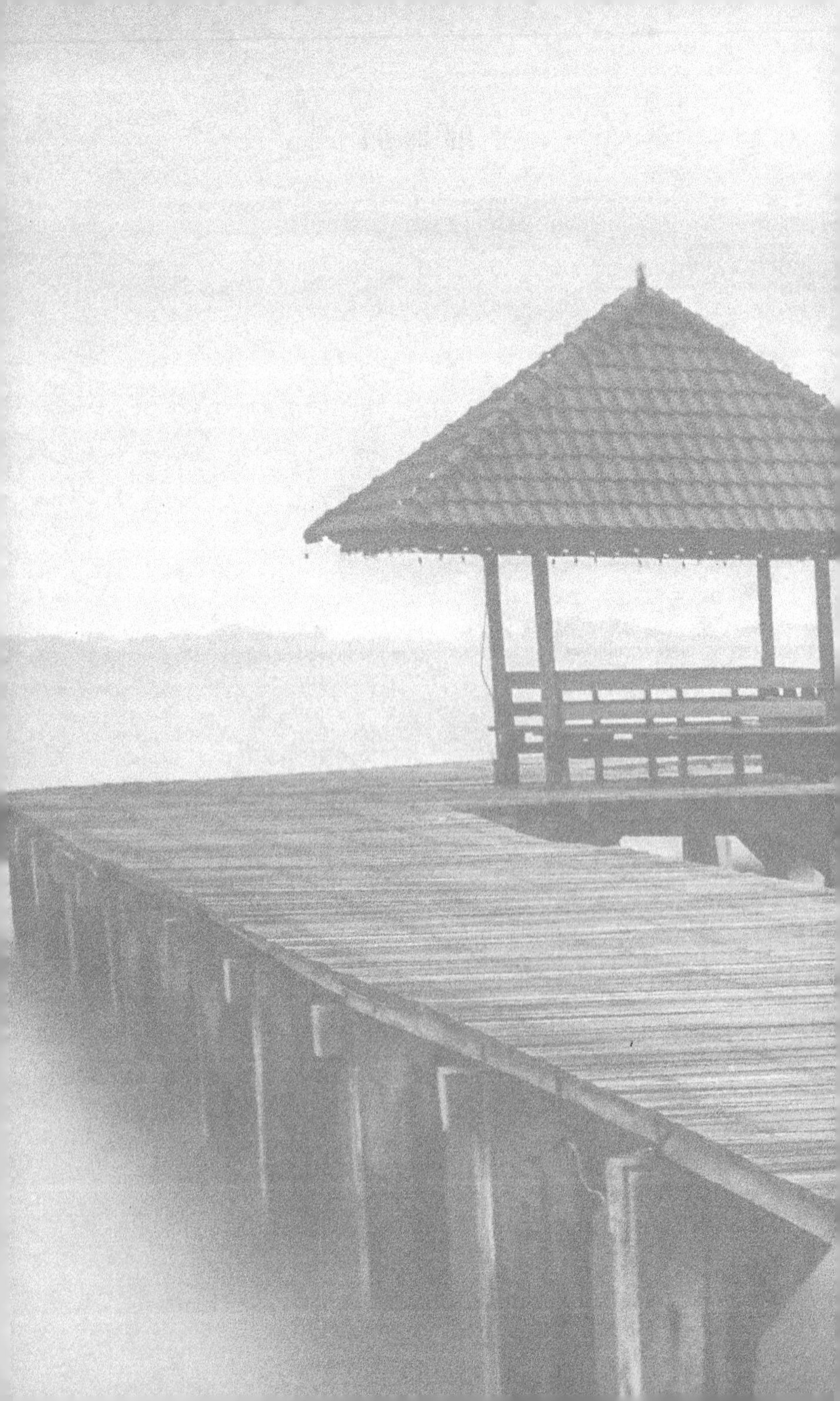

# 9

## REMY

DEAN SMIRKED AT me as I made a plate from all the food he'd prepared for the crew this morning because, of course, I accidentally woke him up when I came to our room last night. Well, I wasn't sure how accidental it was when he set something on the floor, so I'd trip over it and make enough noise to rouse him.

Placing a steamy cup of coffee in front of me, he winked. "Do enjoy. I'm sure you'll need it after last night."

"Oh," Jolene and Kylie both said at the same time. Their eyes were alight with curiosity. "What happened?"

"Personal business," I gave them a polite smile and then turned my head so they couldn't see the side-eye I was giving our Chef.

With the trap he set, Dean had to have known what was

going down last night with Stella and me, but how?

"I hope everything's okay," Kylie frowned as Jolene placed her hand on top of mine.

At least they didn't seem to know about my extracurricular activities. Maybe that meant Ophelia wouldn't know either.

"It's fine," I told them before I took a long drink of my coffee. Dean had put my favorite creamer in it, so I knew instantly with that one taste he'd meant to set up that trap so he could give me shit for the day.

"Outside crew, I want everyone up on deck in ten minutes. Captain Dan informed me our weather conditions are optimal for leaving the dock so let's make their last day aboard the best with all the water toys, including the slide. Before that, let's make sure everything looks like the day they boarded."

Scout and Owen let out a low moan, and I understood because it sucked hard dealing with the slide. I also knew we wanted to give them a day to remember so our tip would be fat.

"We're working for our tip," Owen said as he slipped from his seat. He was probably going to have a cigarette before he had to start working for the day.

"We're going to make it their best day yet. Maybe we can still get in their beach picnic."

"Yes, I'll talk to the Captain and see if he can anchor us near one of the secluded beaches." I looked to the two girls to see what they thought, but they were too busy staring at Dean's ass as he cooked.

## THE BOSUN

"Chef, do you still have provisions for a picnic lunch on the beach?" I hid a grin, knowing he probably already had the menu down for the whole day and hated it when anyone changed it.

Dean looked over his shoulder and glared at me. "*If* that's what we're going to do, I'll chat with the ladies and see what they'd like and go from there."

"That's fine with me. I'll go speak to the Captain now and let everyone know." Taking my plate over to the sink, I rinsed it before I headed upstairs with the hope I'd be lucky to see Stella.

I got my wish, but not the way I wanted it. I was close to the bridge when I heard Ophelia talking. I almost turned and went the other way to avoid her when I caught what she was saying.

"Since we didn't get to finish talking yesterday, I wanted you to know you should stay away from Remy." Stella opened her mouth to speak, but O kept on talking. "I know you only have today, but I thought you should know it's all a game to him. We've been together for the last two years, and nothing you can do will change that."

What the hell was she going on about? I moved so they wouldn't be able to see me, but I'd be able to watch them.

"So," Stella drew out the word, tilting her to the side, "you let your boyfriend cheat on you as part of some game. To me, that sounds like you're the one losing."

She would be if we were actually together, which we never had been.

Stepping forward, I wanted to tell Stella not to believe O, but the inside crew girls started to head in their direction, and I didn't want them to find out.

"Ladies," I called out to them, hoping to break up Stella and O's little rendezvous in the hall, "have a good day."

"You too, Remy. If you need anyone to talk to, you can always come to talk to me." Kylie gave me a sad smile.

Ophelia's head whipped around like she was possessed by Medusa after overhearing Kylie's words.

God only knew what she was thinking or what she'd say to poor Kylie now.

I hated that Kylie likely thought something bad had happened, going by the smile she gave me. In reality, the secret was the time I'd spent with Stella last night, but I couldn't tell her until Stella and her friends were off the boat. I could already imagine the looks on their faces when they realized I'd let them think something horrible was most likely happening at home. If they knew anything about my life, they'd know I hadn't spoken to anyone in my family for over three years.

For the next few hours, I tried to get Stella alone when I was free from work, but it seemed the world had different plans for us. Maybe we were only meant to have one night and few stolen moments on the Seas the Day, but I wanted to at least explain before I never saw her again.

## THE BOSUN

Stella tried her best to not be alone with me, and she must have told her friends what had happened because every time they saw me, they tried to murder me with their eyes.

What had Ophelia said?

The girls huffed in frustration as we all lugged the table, chairs, a makeshift bar, and food. The sun was out in full force today, and the humidity was slowly killing all of us. I wasn't sure if the guests would enjoy it now that we were setting up.

Ophelia looked around to assess the environment. "I think we're going to need to bring a tent for them to sit under, or they're going to melt while they eat."

Nodding in agreement, I looked back at Seas the Day. "If we had power, I'd bring a couple of fans, but a generator would ruin the ambiance."

"We could always fan them ourselves. That should earn us a good tip if you haven't already done that for us, Remy," Ophelia's face twisted up as she spoke.

"He's only doing what was asked of him by the guests. You should be thankful he's taken quite of bit of the load off us," Jolene shot back.

"Really? Is sticking his dick in one of the clients what's best for us? Remy was only thinking with his dick and not thinking about how it would affect us. If he had, we wouldn't be setting up this little excursion for them as a last-minute effort."

All eyes were on me as Ophelia spoke. A giant lump

formed in my throat at what they'd think of me now. We still had half the season left, and I had to work and live with them. My dick had gotten me into trouble.

"Oh please, you're just jealous and wish it was your pants he was getting into," Jolene stepped closer with her shoulders squared off to O. "Everyone, and I mean everyone, including you, could feel something happening between them from day one. I, for one, am happy if there was a love connection."

"Oh my God." O's tone dripped with disgust as she narrowed her eyes at her steward. "Stop living in a fairytale world. No wonder you don't have a boyfriend. Your head is living in La-La land."

"Alright, O, you need to back off the girls. It's me you're really mad at, so don't take it out on them. Kylie and Jolene, please come over here for a second." I wanted Ophelia to know she wasn't included in my little powwow with the others. She huffed and went about unfolding the chairs and setting them up around the table.

"Girls, I don't want to lie to you, and that was never my intention. Something did happen between Stella and me." Their eyes lit up with happiness, and it killed me that I was going to extinguish the light. "I love that you're happy for me or us or whatever, but I don't think it's in the cards for us. Ophelia is trying to kill any chance I have."

Kylie's brows furrowed. "Of course, she is. Well, I, for one, am not going to let her win. I'll get Stella off to the side and

## THE BOSUN

tell her not to listen to O."

These girls were too sweet.

"Don't do that. It will probably make it worse. She's leaving tomorrow, and we're not docked, so our time together is over."

"Yeah, she's leaving tomorrow. Do you want her to think you're a total douchebag for the rest of her life?"

"I wouldn't care if it were true, but she's lying to Stella to keep her away from me." I shook my head. Why was I telling them all this? It would likely only cause problems, and I didn't need more. "I shouldn't be airing all my dirty laundry to you, but I want you to know not to believe everything O says. Especially about me."

"We got the memo loud and clear. Unfortunately, we have to be civil to her because she's our boss and can make our lives a living hell."

"Oh, I understand that all too well. I hooked up with O early on in my first season, and I've regretted it ever since. Trust me, unless she drugs me, it will never happen again."

'Wow,' they mouthed.

I clapped my hands, letting them know our talk was over. I was sure they'd love to drag more information out of me, but I was done. "Alright, let's get back to work and make this the best picnic we've ever had."

After that, we all worked quietly and as fast as possible so we could retrieve our guests and get on with the hot day. For the first time in this charter, I wasn't looking forward to seeing Stella. I let Scout and Owen go back to the boat to pick them up while I helped with the last-minute details of the setup. The atmosphere was charged with hostility coming from O. She was snapping orders at her girls left and right and sending daggers my way. I wasn't sure what she thought was going to happen. Did she really think I was going to let her spout her lies about me and do nothing?

Once done and waiting for the guys to be back with the guests, I pulled O to the side so the other two girls wouldn't overhear.

"What do you want?" She wouldn't look at me as she stood with her hands on her hips.

"You gave me no choice but to tell them the *truth*. I wasn't going to say anything to Jolene and Kylie." I was, but she didn't need to know the timetable.

"I don't know what you're talking about." O turned to me with her narrowed gaze all but drilling into me. "All I've said was the truth from day one."

Closing my eyes, I took a deep breath so I wouldn't yell at her. My fists opened and closed as I tried to rein myself in. "While I don't know everything you've said, I've heard some, and what I've heard has no founding. You blatantly lied."

O got in my face, poking my chest with her fingernail with each word she spoke. "Don't believe all the precious words coming out of her mouth. It's her who's lying to you."

## THE BOSUN

Throwing my head back, I laughed. O had no idea that I had overheard her talking to Stella. "She didn't tell me anything." Her lips parted, probably ready to spew more lies, but I was done. "No one said a word to me. It was my own two ears that caught your lies, and I'm here to tell you that it needs to stop. I don't want my name on your lips ever again, do you hear me? I will make your life a living hell if I even catch wind that you've said my name in any manner that isn't involved directly with work."

An ugly smirk spread across her face. "And I can go to the Captain and get you fired."

"Do it. Unlike you, I have other skill sets besides what lies on that boat. I've got bigger aspirations than being a Bosun for the rest of my life."

Ophelia let out a frustrated noise and stomped off.

On the horizon, I could see Owen and Scout bringing our guests and braced for impact. I wasn't sure if I'd made things worse with O or if she'd keep her big mouth shut. At this point, I couldn't say. It was like she was living in an alternate timeline where we'd been together ever since our one-time hookup.

Turning back to the girls, they quickly went back to work as if they hadn't likely heard every word O and I had spoken. I didn't care. All I had was my pride, and there wasn't much of that since my time in the military, and I wasn't going to let anyone take what I had away.

None of the women looked my way as Scout and Owen

helped them off the boat and onto the shore. As the guests were served drinks, Scout came over to me, his lips set in a fine line.

"What the hell happened while we were away?"

Keeping my eyes on Stella, who was avoiding me at all costs, I gave Scout the shortened version. "I had to set O straight. She'd been telling lies about me to the girls and the guests. I called her out on it and told her under no circumstance did I want to hear my name come out of her mouth to anyone or I'd go to the Captain."

When I was done, I looked to my side where Scout stood. "Is it that far of a stretch that O's gone mental?"

We both laughed at that, causing everyone's eyes to drift over to us and then away as quickly as they came.

"Maybe you should go back, and we'll radio you when we're ready to leave. Write Stella a note explaining the circumstances and leave it in her room. Because if the Captain sees how they're all trying to avoid you, he's going to start asking questions."

Scout was right. It would be bad if the Captain thought I was making the guests uncomfortable. I think in his eyes that would be worse than sleeping with a guest.

"I think I'm going to take you up on that. It's not like I'm needed here. I did what I came to do." I stepped away and started in the direction of the water.

"Remy," Scout called after me. When I turned around, he was right there. His voice was only a whisper on the breeze.

## THE BOSUN

"Are you going to try and make it better?"

Nodding, I backed away. "I'm going to do my best."

As I walked to the boat, I could feel eyes on me, but I didn't turn back. I didn't want to see them look away again. Especially Stella.

Once I was back on Seas the Day, I went to my room, trying to find a piece of paper and pen with no luck. I knew Dean would have something since he was always making lists for food orders and menus.

Dean was cleaning up his kitchen when I stepped inside. He always kept it clean enough you could eat off the floors if you had to.

He must have heard me walk in because he didn't turn around to greet me. "Hey, what are you doing back?"

"First of all, how did you know it was me?"

He shrugged as he kept cleaning. "Who else would it be? Plus, you walk like a ten-ton elephant when you're distracted."

"A ten-ton elephant, huh?" I came to stand on the other side of the counter from him. "Can I borrow your notebook and pen?"

That caused him to halt his movements. "Why?" he asked slowly.

"I need a piece of paper and a pen to write a note, and I knew you'd have some."

Moving out of the kitchen, Dean went into a little storage area and came out with a legal notepad and a pen. "Here," he thrust them at me. "Now leave me be. You know I can't concentrate on anything else until my space is clean."

I did know that. Dean would freak out if I left even a sock on the floor in our room. I would make sure to never room with him again after I found everything of mine rearranged because Dean stated it was all wrong. Why he was looking in the drawer under my bed, I'll never know, but I didn't like people going through my things. Not that anyone did, but we had so little we could bring with us, and he'd gone through all of it. Dean didn't have OCD or anything like that, so I was betting he was trying to find out more information about me and had gone through all my belongings and then didn't know the order I had them. I was a tidy motherfucker after being in the military, so I knew my shit wasn't messy.

"I'll be downstairs in the crew kitchen until I have to go pick them up." I wasn't sure why I told him where I'd be, except in the hope he'd leave me alone to write my note. A note where I had no idea what to say. Who was to say Stella would believe me after she read it?

I stared at the paper in front of me, trying to come up with what to say and knowing that my time was limited. I wasn't trying to be a poet or write a sweet love note. Putting the pen to paper, I started to say my truth.

*Stella,*
*I know you don't want to hear from me, but please don't*

## THE BOSUN

*throw this away until you've read it through.*

*While I don't know everything Ophelia told you about her and me, what I do know is we've never been in a relationship. Not for one single day. I was having a bad day, got drunk, and wasn't thinking straight when I slept with her. It was only that one time. I promise you. Has she offered it again? Yes, many times, and I always turn her down. Nothing could make me have sex with her again.*

*I'm telling you this because I don't want you to leave and think I'm a cheater or a liar. I'm neither, and I couldn't bear to think of you leaving here having that impression of me.*

*Our night together was special. You're the first and only guest I plan to ever have sex with. I only wish we'd had more time, but maybe that's for the better. I already can't imagine not seeing your beautiful face on this boat every day, and I know it would only be harder the closer we got.*

*I wish you all the best once you get back to California and start your new life. You're a wonderful person who deserves the best. Don't let anyone tell you differently.*

*All the best,*
*Remy St. James*

Folding up the note, I went back up to the kitchen to find Dean leaning back against the counter, gulping down a bottle of water. He set it down when he saw me come in.

"Did you get your letter written?"

"I did. Do you by any chance know if we have any envelopes I could put it in?"

His face scrunched up while he tapped the bottom to his chin. "I can't remember seeing one, but I wasn't really looking. Are you mailing something?"

"Something," I answered back.

He had a triumphant look on his face as he replied. "If you can't answer me, then I can't help you."

"Fine." I rested my hands on the counter and leaned forward. "You're so damn annoying. I wrote Stella a letter, and I want to make sure no one else reads it before her."

Cocking his head to the side, Dean asked with a smirk, "Has O been on the warpath?"

"You know damn well she has. She's been telling Stella lies. I don't want her leaving here thinking I was a mistake."

"See what happens when you can't keep your dick in your pants? Nothing but trouble."

"Tell me something I don't know. From now on, he'll stay nicely put away for no one to see."

"You say that now until the next pretty lady comes along and bats her eyelashes at you." He laughed, slapping the countertop when he saw the murderous look in my eyes. "I'm joking, mate. You need to lighten up a little."

"My dick is no laughing matter," I said with a straight face, only to crack a smile.

## THE BOSUN

"No, it's not. You know, if you ever get tired of the ladies, I'm waiting for you."

"As nice of an offer as that is, I don't think it's going to happen. Sorry, dude."

"You can't say I never offered."

That was true. At least once a charter, Dean offered. At first, I thought he was joking, but I quickly learned he was serious. I think the entire crew was shocked to learn he was gay one night when he got drunk and told us all about his ex-boyfriend who stole his credit card and maxed it out while he was away one season.

Dean was rugged with muscles that were always popping out of his shirt and the kindest smile you ever saw. Not one thing about him said he was into men until he opened his mouth and started to talk about dick.

"I don't think you have anything to worry about if you put it in her room. All the guests will probably go to their rooms when they get back, and if not, they will before turndown service. If you're afraid O's going to find it, put the letter in her bag or something."

I could very well see O going in there after I'd been onboard this whole time.

"Thanks, man. I'll do that. It's not like I can get her alone to tell her I left a note. If it was that simple, I would tell her what I had to say. I'm the bad guy now. All the guests look at me like they want me dead, so it's obvious Stella told them what O said, and they all believe her." I stretched my neck out, trying to loosen the tight muscles.

"Sucks to be you." Dean patted me on the back as he walked past me. "I'm going to go rest before I have to start dinner. Good luck."

"Thanks again."

On my way to Stella's room, I decided I'd put the letter I wrote in her bag, that way no one else would find it. I only hoped she'd read it when she saw it.

The only problem was I had no idea which bags or even which side of the room was hers. There were two purses on the dresser: one black and the other a dark purple. From what I knew about Pen and Stella, I was guessing the purple was Pen's and slipped the letter into the black one before I zipped it shut.

Backing out of the room, my radio went off, letting me know it was time to pick them up.

I'd finished my mission just in the nick of time.

# THE BOSUN

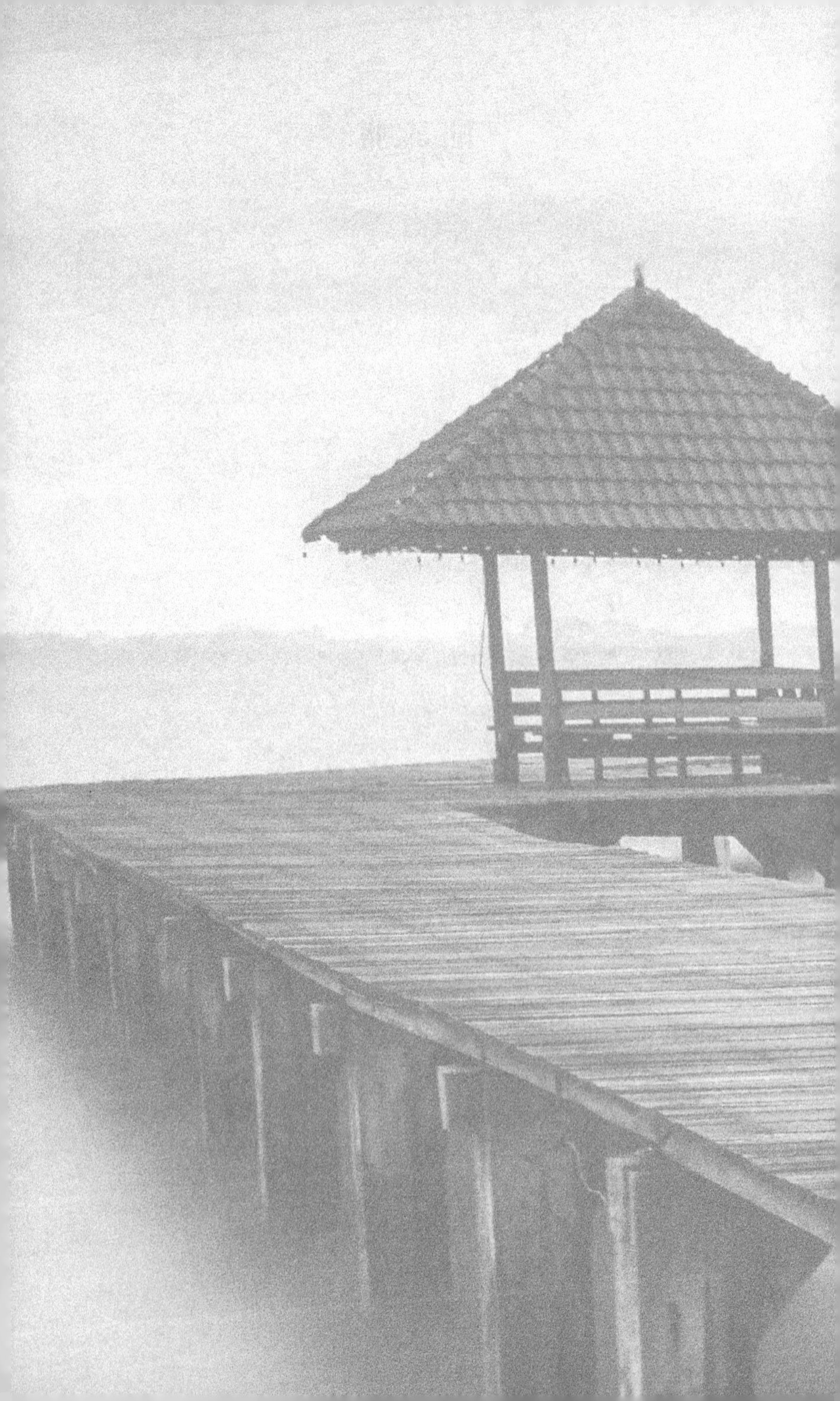

# 10

## STELLA

PEN SQUEALED AS she spun around like a little kid trying to get dizzy and fall down. "I can't believe you're finally here and unpacked," she said as she plopped down beside me on my plush white couch and closed her eyes.

"I certainly didn't think it would take this long to find a place to live." I looked out my wall of windows to the Pacific Ocean that was now my daily backdrop.

"Real estate is a hot commodity in Malibu." Pen rolled her head to look at me. "Plus, you wanted to find your dream house. There's no sense in buying a house you're not in love with."

That was true, but I was desperate to get out of Oasis once we got back from our trip. Since then, it had been four long months of watching Brock's fiancée get bigger and bigger and then giving birth and the town talking about it. I hated seeing the pity on their faces every time I went out that it got to the point I pretty much stayed at home unless I was house hunting.

"Hey," Pen turned toward me and grabbed my hand. "I found something in my purse last night, and I feel so stupid it took me so long to see it."

"Okay," I drew the word out, wondering what the hell she was talking about.

"Listen, I know you've been bummed about Remy, and I get it. You put yourself out there only to find out he was a cheater, but the thing is, I don't think he is an actual cheater."

Now that got my attention.

"What do you mean? Why are you all of a sudden coming to his defense?"

Pen had been the leader of the hate Remy bandwagon, telling us we should ice him out, and it had worked. Remy stayed away as much as he could, and when he had to be around us or me, he kept his head down and went on with his work.

Her mouth thinned out into a grimace. "Because I found a note from him in my purse."

"What?" I jumped back into the cushions and shouted. "Did you read it?"

"Kind of. I didn't know what it was at first, and then…" She pulled a piece of paper out of her hoodie pocket and handed it over. "Read it and see for yourself."

## THE BOSUN

Plucking it out of her hand, I slowly unfolded the piece of paper, unsure if I was ready to read what Remy had to say. And did it really matter when I'd never see him again? Not really, but it would make me feel better that I didn't make the worst choices in men.

Tears filled my eyes as I read it. Not because Remy said he wasn't a cheater, but from his belief in me and that he thought our time together was special. Without the ugliness that ensued, our time together had meant something to me. It signified that I was ready to move on with my life.

As the first tear fell, Pen's arms wrapped around me as she laid her head against mine. "See, he's not a bad guy."

All I could do was nod. I knew if I spoke, I'd turn into a sobbing mess.

"Too bad he didn't leave his number."

Something that sounded like a mix between a laugh and a sob came out as I opened my mouth. "I wouldn't use it if he had."

Pulling me closer, she whispered, "Why not?"

"Because what good would it do? It's not like I'm going to fly to Spain for a booty call. If I had his address, maybe I'd write him a letter saying I forgive him and no hard feelings. Really though, what can I do?"

Pen sighed, making my hair blow in my face. "Nothing, but I thought it might make you feel better about the whole experience."

"Really?" I asked with a raised brow. Remy wasn't the only downside to the trip.

"Well," she pulled back enough so that our eyes locked, "to feel better about letting him bang you. I'm not sure you'll ever get over the way Reagan was toward you."

"Would you get over it?" She shook her head and let me continue. "All my life, I've been told how I'm not white enough or not black enough, and all the stereotypical things that go with being black because then I'm black to them. I know how to swim, goddammit, and I hate fried chicken and watermelon. If they don't like it, they can all stick it up their asses."

"I know you have, and you know I've loved you for who you are since the day I met you. You're beautiful inside and out, and don't let anyone tell you any different."

"Hey," I pushed her shoulder, "did you steal that from my letter?"

"Doesn't mean it's not true, and it proves I'm not the only one who sees it. Fuck Brock and his racist family. If I ever find a guy and his family hates me, I might have to break up with him."

I laughed at that until it sparked a memory that I wanted to talk to her about; why hadn't she been boy crazy lately? I noticed it on the boat, but after we got back, I hadn't thought of it with everything else going on. While Pen had been around to help me house hunt, she'd been working more than usual, even

## THE BOSUN

for her. That, along with not saying she wanted to hook up with just about every guy who crossed her path, was not like her, and now was the perfect time to find out what was going on with my friend.

Positioning myself on the couch, so I was facing her with one leg bent, I leaned back and examined her. "You know," I smiled, knowing she was not going to like what I was about to say, "thinking back to when we were on that trip, I remember I wanted to talk to you about something when we got home, and I never did. It's crazy you didn't remind me."

Pen threw her head back against the couch and moaned. "Because there's nothing to talk about."

"If there's nothing to talk about, why have you been working so much?"

"Because the band I'm working with has amazing potential, but they needed a lot of guidance." She looked away before she could finish her sentence, proving to me there was more.

"Why do I think there's more you're not telling me?" She shrugged, not looking at me. "Come on, Pen. You can tell me anything. You know I won't judge you the same way I know you won't judge me."

"I know, but I didn't want to say anything until I knew if it was anything to even say anything about, you know?"

"No, I don't know because you haven't told me anything." Jumping up, I went to the kitchen and started to make a pitcher of margaritas. "Do we need alcohol for this?"

"You know I can't turn down a good marg, but yeah, make it strong." She bit her bottom lip as I started to pour the tequila into the blender. "While I know you won't judge me, I guess I'm judging myself and haven't wanted to admit it out loud."

"Admit what, Pen?" I asked as I poured one of our frothy drinks in my lapis blue margarita cup.

Taking her drink from me, she took a long sip before she spoke. I was afraid she was going to get brain freeze before I ever got anything out of her. "You know the band I'm working with, Crimson Heat?"

"I know they're a college band from Willow Bay University. What about them?"

"So, the lead singer is the youngest of the four as a junior, and I've kind of been having sex with him for the last six months." Her cheeks pinked up, and then she downed the rest of her drink.

My mouth hung open as I digested her words. My best friend in the whole world had been keeping it a secret that she was having sex.

"Why are you ashamed? Is he bad in bed?"

Pen let out a peal of laughter. "If he was bad, I wouldn't keep having sex with him. In fact, he's the best fuck I've ever had. I'm ashamed because he's barely legal to drink."

"As long as he's legal, who cares?"

"The world?" She laughed humorlessly. "My bosses will definitely care that I'm having sex with one of my clients who

## THE BOSUN

I'm supposed to be looking out for to make sure he and his fellow bandmates don't get into trouble."

I took a sip of my drink and tried to process what she'd told me. "It sounds like you're doing a good job of keeping him out of trouble. If he's in your bed or vice versa—since I don't know your situation because you didn't tell me—he's not out doing drugs and getting all the ladies at his college pregnant."

"Oh fuck off," she swatted at me. "Why did I have to find a guy I'm interested in, and he's practically a kid?"

"Are you really interested in him or just his dick and stamina?" I already knew the answer since she hadn't told me about him. If it was only sex, she would have told me about it when it started.

"He's smart. Smarter than any of the guys I've dated in the past, and he's sweet with this bad boy vibe that I can't resist."

"Obviously. What will happen if Christiano finds out?"

"I'll be fired from Titan Records, simple as that."

"And he's worth your dream job?"

Taking my drink out of my hand, she sucked down the rest. "I think he is."

Smiling at her, I took my glass from her and picked up hers to refill them. "If that's the case, I need to see a picture of him and for you to tell me his name."

"What makes you think I have any pictures?" She giggled like a damn schoolgirl.

"Because I know you and how you like to take pictures. I

bet if I opened your phone's gallery, I'd find all kinds of things you don't want me to see."

"Oh no, that won't be happening. I've got them hidden so only I can enjoy them. I'm not that stupid."

"Of course, you're not. You've had enough clients get in trouble because of pictures. Now," I steepled my fingers under my chin. "If I don't get to see a picture right now, at least tell me his name."

"His name is Walker Pierce." Pen practically swooned at saying his name, and I knew right then she was in trouble and more than likely in love with him even if she didn't know it yet.

"That's a hot fucking name. Now, I need to see if he's as hot as his name, so dig through your phone and find me a picture you can show me."

"Oh my god, you make it sound like there's a bunch of porn on there or something. They're not all bad."

"There's a reason why you're not showing them to me," I pointed out.

Pen held her phone to her chest. "Maybe I don't want you to steal him away," she laughed.

"Ha, as if. You know I'd never do that." Poking her in the side, I demanded she show me a picture. This was so unlike Pen that I was dying to know what this mystery guy looked like.

"Fine," she rolled her eyes but had a smile on her face.

## THE BOSUN

"Give me a minute to find a good picture."

"Damn girl, how many nudes do you have on there?" I was only sort of joking because why else wouldn't she show me? And I knew my friend, she liked to take trophy photos of the men she slept with.

"Not nearly enough." She bit her bottom lip as she looked down at her phone. "Okay, here he is." Slowly she turned her phone my way, but once it was facing me, I grabbed it out of her hand so I could get a good look. "No, what are you doing?" She laughed while she tried to take it back.

"I'm not going to go to any other pictures. I don't want to see your man naked. Well, maybe now that I've got a good look of him." My eyes devoured the image in front of me. Her guy was shirtless with tattoos all over his finely sculpted chest and arms. His eyebrows were a dark slash over broody eyes and long hair that hung almost to his shoulders. I knew the man I was staring at had all the college girls swooning, as well as my best friend, and I didn't blame them.

"What are you thinking?" I heard her say quietly as if she was afraid I wouldn't approve.

"I think I see why you're willing to lose your job over him. He's hot." I was tempted to swipe to the left to see what I'd find, but I handed her back her phone. "I wish you wouldn't have hidden him from me."

Moving to sit right beside me, Pen leaned her head against mine. "It killed me, and I'm sorry. Now that you know, I can finally breathe fully. I swear it's been a weight on my chest that I was dying to get rid of."

"Now, when do I get to meet him," I prodded. Seeing his pictures wasn't enough. I couldn't wait to see them together.

"Once you get your edits turned in or," she drew the word out, and I knew I wouldn't like what she was going to say next, "maybe it should be your reward once your book finally publishes."

My eyes narrowed at her. "You know that's out of my control and totally not fair."

"Well, maybe I should give you a deadline. If you don't get your edits done by a certain date, then you have to wait until your book publishes. That should get your ass in gear."

Since this was my first book, I was having a problem trying to change a few things the publisher wanted once they read through my first draft. There were days I sat in front of my computer and stared at it all day while I tried to figure out a way to incorporate what they wanted.

"You don't play fair, but it might be the push I need to finish." I took a long draw of my drink. I needed it from just thinking about my deadline.

"Wow," Pen stood and ran to the window. "Have you seen your neighbor? He looks like a fucking supermodel."

Oh, I had seen him and drooled over him when I thought no one could see me. He was by far the hottest guy I'd ever seen with the most perfect body and blondish-brown hair. I hadn't

## THE BOSUN

gotten a chance to see what color his eyes were yet. "No, I haven't met him yet, or his wife or girlfriend or whoever she is. I'm not sure which, but she's gorgeous with blue hair and tattoos. They have a blonde little girl that's adorable or who I assume is their daughter. They spend a lot of time in that pool."

"Their house is sick." She let out a dreamy sigh. "I don't doubt he's got a gorgeous woman. Let me know when you meet them because I want all the deets."

I came to stand next to her and shrugged. "Maybe, or maybe I'll tell you in a few months."

Pen glanced at me for only a moment before her attention went back to my new neighbors. "You're never going to let me live it down, are you?"

"It's possible when we're old and gray. I'll think about it, but not likely." I hip-checked her to let her know I was only joking.

"Oh my god, they're getting it on in their pool, and she is gorgeous." Pen squealed with wide eyes.

"I told you they spend a lot of time in their pool."

"But you didn't say you watch them have sex!"

No, I hadn't mentioned what activities they got up to when they were in the pool. It happened day or night. I'd gotten a little show my first night in my new home. It was a wonderful welcome gift, even if they didn't know it.

"We should go back to the couch and finish our drinks and give them their privacy."

"Why? They obviously don't care if they're doing it in broad daylight."

"They probably haven't realized their neighbor has a prime spot to see what they're up to."

It wasn't like you could see much of anything. Maybe a boob, but their lower halves were always underwater. Still, I felt bad about being a Peeping Tom.

"Fine," Pen huffed and slowly turned away from the window. "Maybe you should go over there and ask for a cup of sugar or something."

"And when they find out I'm incompetent in the kitchen, they'll wonder why I asked for sugar when they met me."

"Ugh, why do you have to be so difficult? Surely, we can come up with something. I can go with you in case you need backup." Pen screwed up her face as she looked up to the ceiling. "Oh, I know. Maybe ask for a hammer. You need to hang up that picture over your bed."

Maybe the margaritas had gone to my head, but I didn't think it was a bad idea, and I wouldn't be as nervous meeting them with Pen by my side.

"Okay, but let's give them a couple of hours. I don't want to ruin their post-coital bliss."

"How magnanimous of you, but I agree. You don't want to get on their bad side."

Two hours later, Pen and I were a little past tipsy as we laughed in excitement, walking over to my neighbors' house.

## THE BOSUN

Pen rang the doorbell and hopped in place as we waited. When the door opened, we both stood dumbstruck. Standing before us was the most gorgeous creature known to man, wearing only a pair of light gray sweatpants that hung obscenely low on his hips. I could barely keep my mouth closed as I followed his 'V' into those damn pants. His feet were bare, and even they were beautiful. This man had won the gene lottery when his parents made him.

"Can I help you?" he asked with a dreamy voice.

I cleared my throat, which was full of lust, and had to remember he was with someone and why I was here. "Hi," I thrust out my hand. "I'm your new neighbor, Stella, and this is my best friend, Pen."

His face transformed into a serene smile. I hadn't even realized there was tension in it before. Shaking my hand, he introduced himself. "I'm Ryder. It's nice to meet you. I'm sorry we haven't met sooner. We were out of town for a while and trying to get settled when our daughter Delilah got sick."

"Oh no, I hope she's okay. If this is a bad time, I can always come back later."

"She's feeling better now. In fact, she's staying with her grandma for a couple of days. Do you want to come in?"

"Ryder, who's at the door?" a woman called out from somewhere deep in the house.

"Our new neighbor," Ryder answered while stepping back for us to come in. A moment later, the blue-haired woman I'd seen came around a corner. She was even more beautiful close-up. Her blue hair set off the color of her blue eyes and her flawless skin. My gaze flicked back to Ryder to take in his eye color now that I wasn't struck stupid by his good looks. They were so blue. They reminded me of the water in some tropical location I'd never been to.

"Hey, I'm Lexie." She shook both our hands as we introduced ourselves and smiled sweetly at us. "I guess you've met my husband, Ryder," she said as she wrapped an arm around his waist and leaned into him.

"We did. It's good to meet you."

"I was saying we'd meant to go over to meet our new neighbor, but things have been a little crazy around here."

Lexie moaned as she sagged against her husband. "Yes, it's been exhausting. First, I did an emergency photoshoot, and then our daughter got sick. Excuse me if I look a little haggard. I've had a few sleepless nights, and last night was the first night I've gotten more than a few winks in."

If this is what she looked like with little sleep, life was unfair.

"Don't fret, baby, you look beautiful." Ryder kissed the top of her head. My chest ached for the type of love they had for each other.

Looking over at Pen, who'd remained unusually quiet, I found her staring. I nudged her.

"So, you're a photographer?" she asked with a bit of squeak

# THE BOSUN

to her voice.

"I am, so if you see a lot of people coming and going, it's not because we're drug dealers. Sometimes I do shoots here, but mostly we do them in a warehouse we own on the outskirts of LA."

"What do you do?" She looked at me, but Pen answered before I could open my mouth.

"She's an author and getting ready to publish her first book." Pen's face beamed with pride for me. I didn't know what I'd do without her support.

"That's cool. What's your book about?" Ryder's deep voice asked.

"It's about a wife who starts to suspect her husband of the murders happening in their small town."

"Well, let me know when it comes out, and I'll buy a copy. It sounds right up my alley. I love finding new authors to read, even though I don't have as much time to read now that we have Delilah."

"I will. At least then I'll know I've got one sale," I joked, but I was afraid my book wouldn't do very well, and the publishing company would ask for their advance back because it was such a flop.

"Ignore her. It's going to be a bestseller, I know it. I've been reading her since we met in junior high, and she's amazing."

I shook my head. "She has to say that as part of our friendship agreement."

"No, I don't. Trust me when I say this book is going to be big. You'll be able to say you knew Stella before she was a famous author."

Someone's stomach growled so loud we all laughed at the sound before Lexie spoke up. "Hey, we were just getting ready to grill outside. Would you two like to join us?"

"We'd love to," Pen answered a little too quickly, making us seem desperate.

Lexie linked her arm with her husband and beckons us. "Let's head out back and get started before my stomach eats itself."

We followed the gorgeous couple outside, and even though I had pretty much the same view, I sucked in a breath as I took in their backyard with the pool and ocean. Somehow it seemed so much better than mine.

"Wow," Pen exclaimed. "This is beautiful. If I lived here, I'd spend all my time out here."

"We try as much as possible, but we're pretty busy with our careers and Delilah." Lexie walked over and sat down in a little cabana-type area that had a fireplace, two couches, and chairs off to one side of the pool.

"And what does your husband do?" Pen blurted out. It had probably been killing her to hold in that question as long as she had.

Her eyes landed on her husband, who was lighting the grill.

## THE BOSUN

"He's a model."

Not surprising.

"Have you ever done a photoshoot with him?" Pen was all but eye-fucking Ryder as she took him in.

"That's actually how we met. After that, Ryder's career blew up. We try to work with each other as much as possible. It's a bit of a juggling act with how in demand we both are. If one of us goes out of town, we all go."

"How old is your daughter?" I asked. Even though I'd been married to a pediatrician, I was a horrible judge of age with children. I either guessed way too low or high.

"She's almost three. I wish she was here for you to meet her, but she's with Ryder's mom for the weekend. She wanted to give us some time to rest. We're leaving tomorrow to drive up to where she lives in Washington. We'll be there for a few days." She let out a sultry laugh. "I don't know why I'm telling you all this. You must think I'm crazy."

"Not at all. I do the same thing sometimes when I meet new people that I—"

"Feel a connection with," she interrupted.

"Yes." My eyes widened that she felt the same way, even if I hadn't opened up to anyone since I met Remy.

"Even though I don't know you, I like you. I'm happy to have a neighbor that I like. Have you met your other neighbors?" When I shook my head, she continued. "I'm not a fan. They all seem like a bunch of rich snobs who think they're better than everyone else."

"Alright, ladies. We've got steak or chicken, which would you like?"

"What about hamburgers?" Lexie pouted, looking up at her husband.

"Or hamburgers," he laughed.

"I can tell just from the way she looks, Stella wants a burger."

I did want one, but I wasn't sure how she could tell.

"I'll have one as well," Pen piped in.

"Alright, three burgers and one chicken. Do you want cheese?"

"I always want cheese," I answered. Cheese made everything better.

"Me too," Pen answered in a strange voice. What the hell was wrong with her?

"And I know you want cheese," he leaned down and kissed his wife. When he stood up, Lexie swayed a little.

"I'm sorry, but I can't help but stare at your husband. I don't mean to be rude. I'm sure you're used to women not being able to keep their eyes off him."

Lexie giggled as she eyed her husband. Her lids went half-mast, making me think she was picturing her husband naked or their earlier sex in the pool. "I more than understand. Most of the time, I have the same problem. Wait until you see him with our daughter. Your ovaries will explode."

## THE BOSUN

"Keep me away from that. I am so not ready for children. Hell, I'm not sure if I ever will be."

"You better figure it out before your ovaries shrivel up and turn to dust. Are you sure you don't want any babies with your young buck?"

Pen's eyes turned to slits. "You hush your mouth."

"I love you two already," Lexie clapped. "Where do you live, Pen? I'm guessing not with Stella."

"No, but I'll be here as much as possible to enjoy the beach. It was my idea for her to find a house on the beach when she decided to move up this way."

Lexie's attention swung back to me. "Oh, where did you move from?"

"Oasis, it's a desert city."

Lexie's face scrunched up. "I feel like I've heard of it, but I can't remember why."

"We had a serial killer there a couple of years ago." It was strange how matter-of-factly I said those words now. When it was happening, we were scared to even utter the word in case the next victim was one of us.

"Oh, that's right. Ryder, do you remember that serial killer from a couple of years ago?" she yelled.

Ryder turned around with a deep v between his brows. "Down in the desert?"

"Yeah, that's where Stella's from." She looked back at me. "No wonder you're writing about one. Was it scary living there? Is that why you moved?"

"It was scary at the time, but that's not why I moved. My story is the old husband got his assistant pregnant. Living in a small town, I got tired of being the talk of the town and the looks. The looks killed me the most, especially after the baby was born. Luckily, I'd already found the house next door and was waiting for it to close." I looked around at the beauty surrounding me and felt everything in me relax. "Living here is so much nicer than the desert."

"I agree. I couldn't wait until I could afford a place here. There's nothing better than falling asleep listening to the waves."

"Are you sure about that?" Pen asked, tilting her head toward Ryder.

"You're right. It's second-best to falling asleep in his arms every night."

"She says the sweetest things about me." Ryder looked lovingly over at his wife. "We keep the door open every night so she can hear the waves; that's how much she likes hearing them."

"They're very therapeutic after a stressful day. I hope it's the same for you as well."

"I think it is. My life is already less stressful unless you count the editing hell I'm in. Maybe I'll try sleeping with my door open."

"That doesn't sound very safe. What if someone wants to

## THE BOSUN

break in? You're giving them an easy way in." Pen shook her head at me.

"That's what alarms are for, and if they really want to break in, they will. Open window or door, or not," Lexie answered her.

I hadn't thought about someone breaking in. Maybe I'd sit outside and enjoy listening to the waves crash during the day as much as possible; that way, I'd be safe at night. I didn't have someone like Ryder to come to my rescue if anything bad happened.

"Alright, ladies," Ryder's drawl was deep as he set down a platter with our burgers and a piece of chicken for him, "lunch is ready."

"Thank you for inviting us. If I knew how to cook, I'd invite you over for dinner, but I'd hate to poison you, so I'll take you to dinner soon."

"We're down for that. Sometimes I feel bad for eating whatever I want while this guy here," Lexie pointed at Ryder, "is always eating healthy so he can keep his physique. I won't feel so bad if I have a partner in crime."

"I really don't mind. It's so ingrained in me now that I'm not sure I could eat junk food if I tried."

Lexie rolled her lips, but it still didn't hide the grin that was trying to escape. "Do you see the drool at the corner of his mouth as he eyed our burgers? Don't let him fool you. He wants it, but he sticks to his regimen unless he's got a chunk of time off."

"I admire your diet. I like to eat whatever I want whenever I want." That was always why I had curves, and my stomach was not as flat as I wanted it.

"That's why we're going to be the best of friends. Before you leave, make sure I have your phone number. I'll call you when we get back from Washington."

"See, you're already making friends. Now I won't feel bad when I go out on the road next week."

I turned wide-eyed to her. "You didn't tell me you were leaving so soon."

Pen's face softened. "I'll be back. It's only for a couple of months."

"Where are you going?"

"Small venues all around the US." Pen went on to tell them how she worked Titan Records and the band she managed.

Lexie ate the last of her burger and moaned. "You make a mean burger, Dimples. If modeling doesn't work out, you could be a chef."

I couldn't help myself from saying, "You two are so sweet together."

"Hell, yeah, we are." Ryder eyed his wife hungrily.

I yearned to have a man look at me like that someday.

Pen knocked me with her elbow. "I think it's time we leave so the happy couple can be alone."

I had a feeling Pen was right.

# THE BOSUN

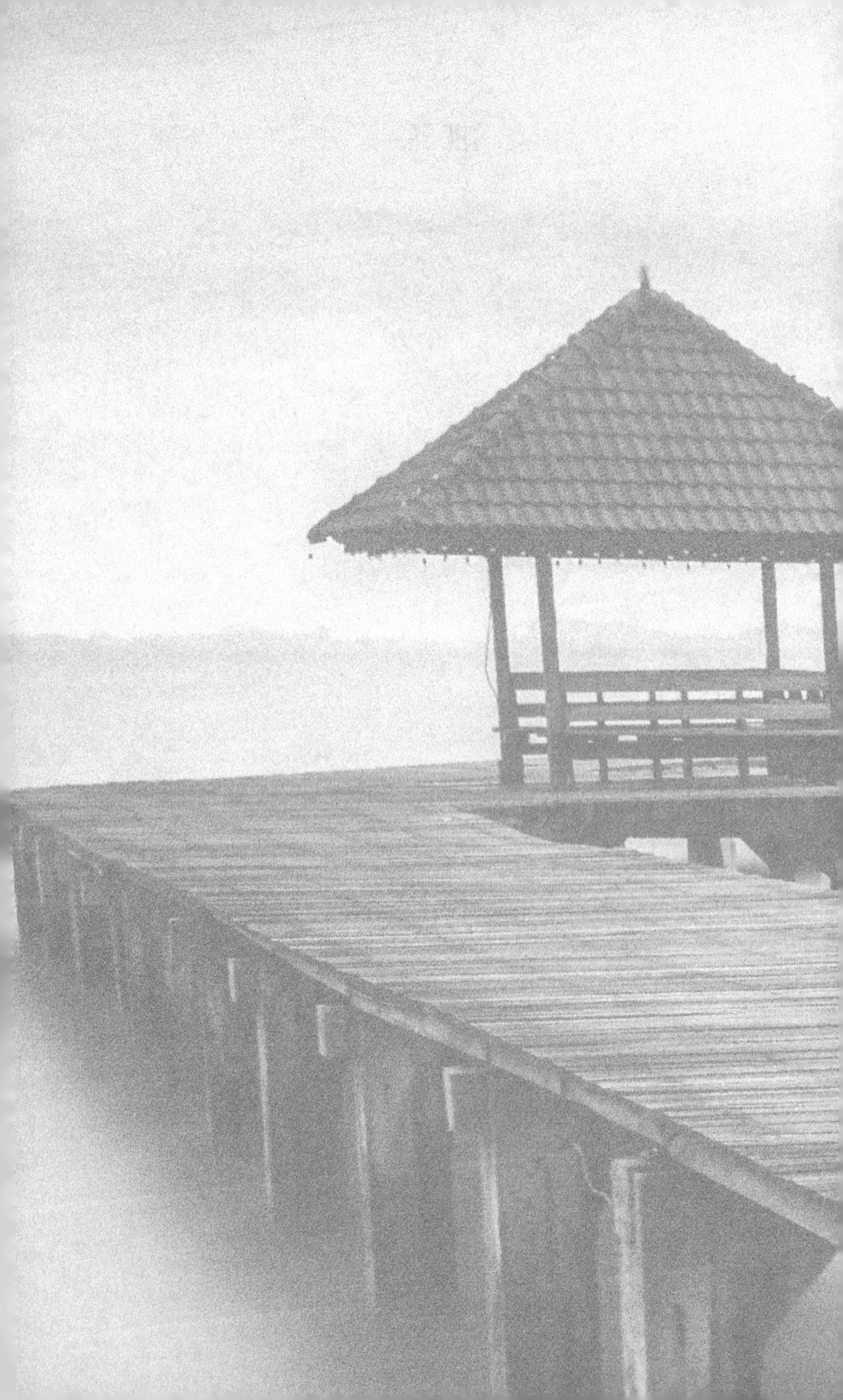

# 11

## REMY

BEFORE ANYONE WAS up, I spent the first thirty minutes of my day looking at all the pictures on Stella's Instagram account. I'd been doing it since she left Seas the Day. I thought it might be difficult to find her, but it wasn't. Zelda and Reagan had posted pictures constantly of their stay and tagged Stella in a few of them.

On her feed, I saw her writing space as she finished writing her book and her celebratory glass of Champagne. There hadn't been much of her life in Oasis. Now all her pictures were of sunsets and the beach letting me know she was living the life she deserved.

There weren't many pictures of her except on moving day with Penelope helping. Both of them looked exhausted but happy. The other was of both of them with a couple.

The woman had blue hair that looked incredibly natural on her, at a restaurant smiling widely for the camera.

I wasn't sure if Stella had read my letter, threw it away, or maybe she didn't believe me. All I knew was she barely spared me a glance the day they departed.

Did she think of me like I did of her? There was something about her that I knew deep down in my bones I'd never find in another woman for as long as I lived. The feeling was unsettling but something I'd come to live with.

After going through all of her pictures and finding nothing new, I went to see how my buddy Tyler was doing. Even though I didn't post on social media much—more like never—I had it to keep in touch as much as I was able to with the guys from my old unit.

Most of them were still enlisted except for the ones who hadn't made it that fateful day. And me. I had gotten out at the first opportunity, unable to handle the guilt of living when my best friend in the entire world died in my arms, and I could do nothing about it. It didn't matter that I knew somewhere deep inside my guilt that Damon's injuries were fatal, and there was nothing I could have done. The fact that I could only hold him and assure him everything was going to be okay when I knew it wasn't still ate at me.

Knowing that Damon left behind a woman who loved him more than anything, and she was pregnant with a child he'd never meet.

## THE BOSUN

It should have been me. I had no one but my dad and Damon's family, who all but adopted me as I grew up. I hadn't seen any of them because I couldn't face them, knowing they'd wonder why I hadn't done more to save my best friend. Knowing they'd never understand the situation we'd been in or what it was like over there.

Instead, I locked it all away, and once every month or two, I'd check Tyler's Instagram to see what he'd posted. Tyler had been there for me after Damon died. If it wasn't for him checking on me constantly and making sure I ate, I wasn't sure if I'd be where I was right now—or dead.

My vision glazed over at the flag on the latest post. It was a memorial postdated three weeks ago. It didn't go into specifics, but it stated Tyler died while in Afghanistan and was laid to rest in his hometown of Macon, Georgia.

Guilt gnawed at my insides and climbed into the deep recesses of my mind conjuring images I'd tried hard to forget these last two years. Closing my eyes, I tried to shut out the sounds and images that haunted me. The sounds of explosions all around me, bullets whizzing by my head, and the smell of dirt embedded in my nose as I ducked for cover. I could hear my men yelling in the background, but I was rooted to the spot, unable to move or speak.

When a hand landed on my shoulder, I nearly decked the person who was touching me. It took several seconds for me to realize I was on a boat in the Balearic Sea and not in the Middle East.

"Fuck, dude, you need to lay off the coffee," Scout quipped as he ducked away from my fist.

"Yeah." I gave a shaky laugh, trying to play it off. "I've had one too many cups this morning." I tried to smile over at him while he poured his own cup of coffee and knew I failed when the corners of his mouth tipped down.

He took a step toward me but stopped when I held my hand up. "Don't lie, man. Are you okay?"

Hanging my head, I picked at the skin around my fingernail as I spoke. "As good as I can be after finding out a friend of mine died."

"Damn, is there anything I can do? Do you need—"

"I just need time." I stopped him. "Once you and Owen have everything clean, your day is yours. I'm going to...go clear my head. I'll let you know if I don't plan on coming back tonight."

"If you want company or to talk—"

"I won't," I interrupted again. The only person I wanted to talk to was Tyler, and that wasn't going to happen ever again. "I appreciate the offer, but trust me when I say I need to be alone."

Scout leaned over the table and laid a hand on my shoulder. "If that ever changes, I'm here for you."

"I know, and I appreciate it. It's not my first loss…" A lump formed in my throat, and it took a few seconds to swallow it

## THE BOSUN

down. "I doubt it will be my last."

"Fuck, man, that's got to be tough. Leave your radio here so no one will bother you."

"Thanks. I'll let the Captain know I won't be around, and I'm leaving you in charge."

Not wanting to see the worry etched on his face, I grabbed my cup of coffee and poured it out in the sink. Grabbing my wallet in my room, I got off the boat before I ran into anyone else. I clearly wasn't doing a very good job at hiding my emotions and wasn't sure I could keep my composure if I was questioned anymore on whether I was okay.

Not knowing where I was going, I walked through the city without seeing its usual beauty. Instead, all I saw was sand, mud houses, and buildings that had seen better days. The salty air was replaced with smoke and death.

My conscience screamed at me that if I had stayed, maybe Tyler would be alive today, joking while lying on his cot in a tent in the Register Desert instead of six feet under in Georgia.

It didn't matter that I knew my mental health would have deteriorated with each passing minute. All that mattered at that moment was Tyler.

I wasn't sure how much time had passed, but it had to have been hours when I found myself at a beach I'd never been to. Shucking off my shoes and socks, I placed them on the ground before I waded into the water. The cool water was refreshing after walking for hours. I stood there looking at miles and miles of water and concentrated on the light sound of the waves lapping at the shore. Reminding myself I was far away from the desert and war. It was both a relief and terrifying at the same time.

What was I doing with my life?

I'd been running from my problems for the last two years and knew I couldn't keep doing it. I needed to face my family and Damon's wife and tell them I was responsible for his death. I knew if I didn't, I'd never be able to climb out of the hole I'd dug myself into.

While there was nothing I could do about Stephanie until the season was over, I could reach out to my dad. But damn, was I scared to make that particular phone call.

Since I didn't have an international calling plan, I came up with a plan of action. I'd find a hotel with free Wi-Fi close to port, book a room, let Scout know where I was, and then call my dad.

Not surprisingly, my footsteps were slow as I walked back the way I came. Now that I was more aware of my surroundings, I was shocked I'd walked so far in a daze. Something so unlike me since I'd been trained to observe my surroundings.

I almost went to get a few things but decided against it. I'd be fine with what I had on me. All I needed was my wallet and phone. Once close to the water, I found a small hotel, Brismar,

## THE BOSUN

and booked a room. It wasn't anything special, but it had everything I needed for the night.

Sitting out on the balcony and looking out at the sea, I messaged Scout.

**Remy: I'm going to stay at a hotel tonight. It's close to port, so I'll be onboard bright and early to help with anything that needs to be done before guests arrive.**

**Scout: Everything is done. Seas the Day is sparkling more now than the day she hit the water.**

**Remy: Good to hear. Thanks for picking up my slack today.**

**Scout: You slack? Your slacking is us on our best days.**

**Scout: If you decide you don't want to be alone, we could do dinner.**

**Remy: Thanks for offering, but I don't think I'd be very good company tonight.**

**Scout: It's not the point. If you want me to sit across from you and not talk, I'd be happy to do it.**

Damn, he was a good friend. Better than I'd ever been to him.

**Remy: If I change my mind, I'll let you know.**

Strangely, after contacting Scout, I felt better about attempting to call my dad. I wasn't even sure if he'd accept my collect call since that was the only way I could get in touch with him. It didn't matter. There were only two more months left of the season, and after it was over, I was headed back to the States where I'd stay. It was time for me to move on with my life. If I couldn't get a hold of my dad tonight, he'd be my first pit stop when I got back home.

Hell, I didn't know how to make a collect call anymore, especially internationally. I'd become dependent like everyone else on their cellphones. After a few trials and errors, the phone started to ring. It was softer than what I was used to, and I wasn't sure if it was from the phone I was using in my room or if it was because of the distance I was calling.

I held my breath as I waited to see if anyone would pick up. What if he'd changed his number, and I was calling some stranger?

"Hello," my dad's voice answered. It sounded tired, and I wanted to slap myself for not thinking about the time difference.

My vision blurred as thick emotion lined my throat. I had to clear it a couple of times before I could speak.

"Dad?" My voice cracked.

"Remy?" he asked in disbelief. "Is that you, Son? Are you okay?"

I shook my head because I wasn't okay—not even close to it after hearing the sound of his voice. It was music to my ears after not hearing it for so long.

"I'm sorry," I muttered. "I'm so sorry it's been so long." Tears ran down my face as I let it hang in shame.

"That's okay, my boy. You're calling me now, and that's all

## THE BOSUN

that matters. Are you safe?"

"I'm safe," I choked out. It amazed me he'd be worried about my safety when I hadn't spoken to him in so long. Why hadn't he given up on me like I'd given up on myself?

"Good. Where are you?" he asked quietly and then sniffed.

"I'm in Spain."

"I always wanted to visit that way. What the hell are you doing there, though?"

His simple question opened the floodgates. Lying down on the bed, I cried for the first time in years. How had I been so wrong about my dad?

"I work as a bosun on a yacht people charter," I tried to explain.

"Never heard of one." He cleared his throat, and I knew the tough questions were coming next. As a child, I always hated it when my dad cleared his throat. I knew he'd squared his shoulders as he prepared to ask the question. "What happened, Son? Why'd you disappear?"

"Because I'm stupid. I thought...Damon died."

"I know he did, Son. It was...is a terrible thing, but it still doesn't explain why you disappeared. It was like I lost two sons at once."

I'd never thought of it that way, but he might not feel the same once he found out what happened.

"I should have saved him, Dad. I should have—"

"And how would you have done that?"

"I...I could have been more diligent in searching my surroundings, kept my ears open to sounds, to—"

"Unless you pushed him in the way of the bullet or shot him yourself, I don't see any way you could have known what was going to happen, let alone saved him and the other men." His voice was no-nonsense as he gave me his truth.

"You weren't there. You can't know," I croaked. The guilt was almost as all-consuming as the day was front and center.

"I know you loved Damon like he was your brother, and you'd never let anything happen to him if you had the choice. Remy, you've got to stop blaming yourself. Guilt will eat away at you until there's nothing left but a hole so deep, you'll never be able to fill it."

He was right. I'd have done anything for Damon. Giving up my life for Damon to have his wasn't too big of a price to pay.

"He died in my arms, and all I could say was that it would be okay. I knew it wouldn't. Help wasn't coming in time. There was so much blood. No matter how hard I pressed, it continued to ooze around my fingers. How could I have let that happen?"

"You didn't let it happen, and it was most definitely not your fault, Remy. Have you talked to the other guys in your unit?"

I shook my head, unable to answer even though I knew he couldn't see.

He let out a deep breath, and I closed my eyes. I would have given anything to be with my dad in that moment.

## THE BOSUN

"Maybe you need to talk to someone. A counselor."

I knew he was right. I did need to talk to someone, but I wasn't sure if I'd ever stop feeling guilty.

"You don't hate me?"

"Remy," he sobbed out. A short minute later, he spoke in a rough voice. "Boy, I could never hate you. Is that why you've stayed away? Why I haven't heard from you?"

"I couldn't face you."

"Can you now?"

"I think so. I still have a couple of months to work, but once this season is over, I'm coming back if you'll have me." I was done running and hiding from my past.

"Of course, I'll have you. Hell, I'll throw you a ticker-tape parade." There was a long pause before he said, "I wish you had called a long time ago. It would have eliminated the agony of the last two years."

The pain I felt from losing Damon would always be there, but maybe if I had been around the people who loved him and went through the grieving process with them, it wouldn't have felt so profound.

"I've missed you, boy. Thought about you every day and wondered where you were."

"I'm sorry. I didn't mean to do that to you." I never wanted to cause my dad more pain.

"I know you didn't, but it's been hard not knowing where you were or how you were doing. After talking to you, I don't think you were doing too good. I wish I'd been there to help you."

"Me too, Dad. Me, too. My head's been so lost in grief, I wasn't thinking straight." I closed my eyes and felt the tears run down my cheeks and into my ears. "I've made a lot of mistakes. Ones I'll never be able to make up for."

"You have nothing to make up for. I'm just happy you're alive and safe. That's all I could ask for. Never did I think you'd come back unscathed. Men never come back from war the same as when they left. All I want from you is for you to let go of your guilt and realize what I know."

"What's that?"

"That you did everything you possibly could to save Damon. I know you did. Just as I know, you'd do it for anyone around you. You've always had a heart of gold, wanting to help everyone around you, but the other side of that is you feel too much. Your heart feels so deeply. You have to know your own limitations because your life is just as important as everyone else."

Hearing my dad say those words was hard to hear.

"You deserve to be happy, Son."

He sniffed, and it broke my heart. How much suffering had he gone through because of me? I knew he worried about me when I was in the service, but I'd never thought about it once I was out. I'd been so selfish.

"I don't think I'll ever be able to apologize enough for what

## THE BOSUN

I've put you through. I'm sorry, Dad. I really am."

"I know you are, Son. Don't worry about your old man. I'm resilient, but I worry about you. If you haven't dealt with what happened..."

I hadn't, and up until today, I hadn't realized how much it had festered inside of me. I was thankful we didn't have a charter full of guests because I wasn't sure I'd have been able to handle today and my duties.

"I'm going to. I promise, but for now, I've got to keep my head on straight otherwise, my crew and the passengers could get hurt."

"That's what I'm talking about. You're caring for others before yourself."

"If someone were to get hurt or worse on my watch, it would only make my guilt escalate. There's no helping that."

It probably sounded like a copout to my dad, but it wasn't. I already had so much death weighing on my shoulders, I couldn't handle more without tipping over the edge and drowning.

"I can accept that. So, you're coming home in two months?"

The hope in his voice would have brought me to my knees if I'd been standing.

"I am, and it can't come soon enough. I'm sorry about the time. I hadn't realized the time when I called."

"Remy...I want you to know if you ever need to talk to me,

you can always call me. I'll accept the charges day or night."

"Thanks, Dad. I don't have an international plan, so I can't make phone calls."

"Where are you now then?"

"I got a hotel room for the night. I needed a break from the crew and to have my thoughts as my own for the day."

"It's good to see you're putting yourself first, at least for today."

"I'm going to try to do more of that when I can. That's not as often as I need, but I'll make do. Hearing your voice has done wonders. Knowing you…" I couldn't finish.

"I would never think that of you. It kills me you thought that. I love you, Remy. More than anything. Even though you're a man now, you're still the most important person in the world to me."

"I love you too, Dad. I should have…"

"But you reached out now, and that's all that matters."

How he knew what I was going to say, I had no idea. I wish I could blink my eyes and be standing in his yard in Florida.

He yawned loudly. Looking at the clock, I realized we'd been on the phone for almost two hours talking and catching up on everything. It was some of the hardest and best hours of my life.

"I should let you get some sleep."

"I don't mind. I'd lose as much sleep as needed to know you're okay."

## THE BOSUN

"I am, or I will be, and I promise to keep in touch. After the next charter, I should have another day off. In the meantime, we can email if you want."

"Of course, I do. I finally have my son back."

Damn, he was killing me.

"Grab a paper and pen, and I'll give you my email. I looked when I got here, and this damn hotel room doesn't have a pad of paper, or I'd write yours down. Once you email me, I'll have yours. We do have Wi-Fi on the boat, so there's that."

After a few more minutes of me telling my dad I'd call him on my next break, which would probably be in a week, we got off the phone. Getting up, I walked back out to the balcony and sat in one of the chairs as I watched the sunset.

My heart was lighter after I hung up. I knew it would still be hard to face Tyler's parents and Damon's wife and child, but it wouldn't be as hard as it was to reach out to my dad. I also knew they might not be as forgiving as my dad, but I'd take that chance. I knew I needed to face my demons head-on from here on out. And maybe, just maybe, I'd open up a little bit to Scout while I was still here.

Taking my dad's advice, I was going to start taking care of myself the way I needed to. Next, I'd live the life I deserved just like I'd told Stella to do.

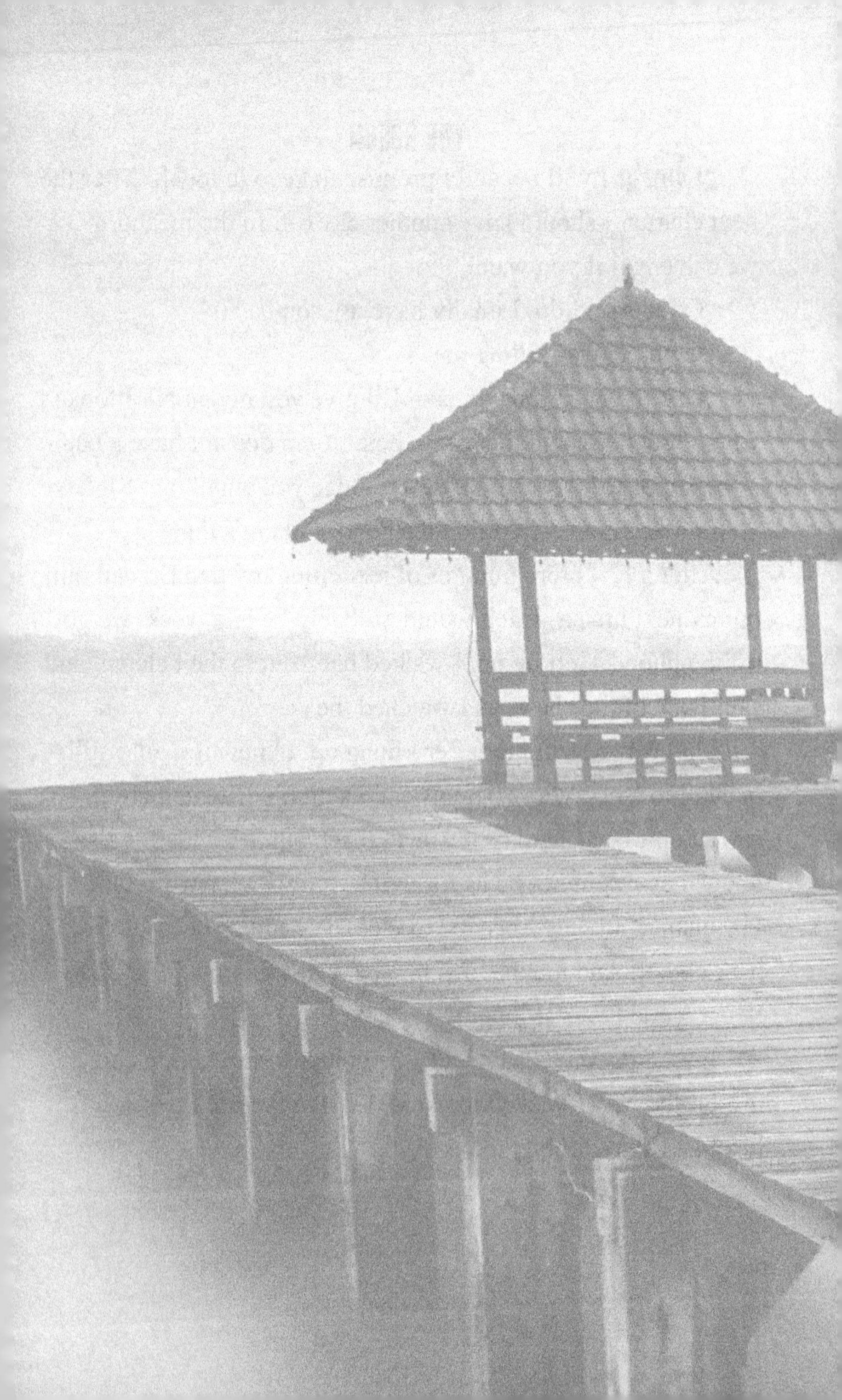

# 12

### STELLA
### 6 MONTHS LATER

"WERE YOU CHECKING out my husband?" Lexie asked as I dried away the small amount of drool that had formed in the corner of my mouth.

I felt bad because Ryder was such a sweetheart, but I couldn't help myself from ogling him. "It's hard not to when first he pops out those dimples of his, and then he took off his shirt." I held my hands up, hoping it didn't offend her. "I'm only doing what any warm-blooded woman would do."

"Trust me, I get it. Those dimples get me every time. But I think it's time we get you a man of your own or at least someone to keep your bed warm."

"And how is that supposed to happen when I'm gone all the damn time or writing?" I asked as I took the lounger next to hers.

Lexie shrugged. "At least get laid. How long has it been since that guy you told me about?"

"Remy? Almost a year now. Ten months is too long to go without sex, but I know he ruined me for all other guys."

"Unless you find a man out there who's better than him," she smirked. "Keep thinking positive, and maybe one will drop out of the sky."

"Or appear out of thin air. Please, tell me how I'm supposed to find a man who's good in bed. Do I get references from his previous bed partners after he tells me what he excels at?"

Throwing her head back, Lexie cackled. "Oh my God, can you imagine?"

"Most definitely not. If that's what it takes, I'm out of the game." I laughed along with her.

Once our laughter died down, Lexie sat up on her lounger and swung her legs around until she was facing me. "How have you been, with the exception of not getting any dick?"

"You know it's not fair that out of you, me, and Penelope, I'm the only one not getting any." Lexie bit her bottom lip to keep from smiling. "Other than that, my life is great. I can't believe people are reading my book and loving it. It's been surreal. I'm ready for a break, but my publisher wants me to get started on another book that I have no concept on yet."

"Sounds to me like you need to find a young stud to please you, unblock your pipes, and then your life will be perfect."

## THE BOSUN

"Is sex the answer to all my problems?"

"It certainly won't hurt, but if you want, I can brainstorm with you." She sat up straighter and got serious. "Are you wanting to continue to write with the same characters like a series or something new?"

"I don't know," I moaned out as I threw my arm over my eyes. "I mean, how much can happen in that little town?"

"It wouldn't be a place I'd want to live if people kept dying, but it doesn't have to be murders. Does it have to be a mystery? Maybe you can have someone kidnapped or sold into the sex trade industry."

"Wow," I blinked. "I'm not sure I'm ready for people to be sex slaves yet in my books or ever, but maybe a kidnapping. A kidnapping would be fun. Although I think that's too much for one small town. Can you imagine? I would move. Hell, I did move, but not because of the serial killer who was causing havoc on my town."

"You're right. I think it should be a new place with new characters unless it's in a big city. The best part is you can travel to those places for research."

"I don't want to go anywhere but my bed for the foreseeable future. I don't know how you do it?"

"It's not easy. Especially with Delila, but we've got a system that works well for us." She turned and looked to the gym, where we could see Ryder working out. I kept my eyes away. "When I first met Ryder, he was traveling nonstop. He didn't even have a place to live since he was never home. I warned him he was going to get burned out even when we weren't together, and luckily, he listened. He scheduled some much-needed time off, and after that, he started to look at the jobs he was offered. Who the photographer was, how much money he'd be paid, and who the shoot was for. If it wasn't worth the time away, he didn't take the job."

"I never thought about all that. He seems so put together."

"Now he is, and he was doing it for a good reason back then. He wanted to make money to help with his mother's hospital bills. I warned him that if he didn't slow down and got sick, it could fuck with his career. You're only as good as your reputation in the modeling industry."

"I'm sure he's grateful he had you in his corner to give him good advice."

Lexie nodded. "I do give good advice, and my advice to you is to enjoy what's happening to you. You only get your first time being a New York Times best-selling author."

"You're right, and I am for the most part. It's been an amazing experience, but with each passing day, my inbox fills up more and more with no time to look at them. It's too much for me to handle."

"Maybe you should look into getting an assistant. You don't even need to have one come to your house. They can live hundreds if not thousands of miles away, but it might be worth it to have someone helping you, and then you wouldn't be so

# THE BOSUN

overwhelmed."

"Damn, you're good. I should have talked to you about this a couple of months ago when I started drowning." If I didn't have to worry about all the emails coming in and a few other things, I wouldn't feel like I was doing a never-ending task, and then I could plot out my next book.

"The hard part is finding the perfect one. Trust me, I'd been through quite a few before Raine came into my life. Now, I don't know what I'd do without her. She wasn't perfect at first, but we just clicked, and I knew eventually she'd get it. If she ever tries to quit, I'll have to tie her up and never let her go."

"Ugh, I didn't think about the process of finding one. I'm not looking forward to that."

"On with brighter news. Since you're now a big shot author, I was thinking we should do a photoshoot. Get you some headshots and maybe take some other pictures if you want."

My face flushed. I certainly didn't feel like a big author. "I would be an idiot to turn you down." I looked down at my lap and picked at the hem of my sweatshirt. "I have to be honest; when I first met you, I had no idea who you or Ryder were. I think after the second time I met you, I looked you up because of something that was said and realized that you're kind of a big deal. Both of you are, and to know how down to earth and sweet you both are made me love you all the more."

"Aw, you're going to make me crazy." Lexie smiled big, making her blue eyes sparkle in the sunlight. "I don't expect people to know who I am. It's not like a lot of people follow photographers. Now that I'm with Ryder and he posts pictures of us, more people recognize who I am, and it's weird. Before, the only people who knew who I was were in the industry, and now they know me because of who I'm with. I'm sure you'll get familiar with it soon enough. Because obviously when you were on your book tour, those people knew who you were, but don't be surprised if you get stopped now and then at the grocery store."

"Really? That's got to be weird and something I'm not sure I'll be ready for when the time comes."

"Oh, it will be here before you know it." Lexie shivered. "What do you say we go inside? This wind keeps picking up, and I'm getting cold."

I wasn't sure how she'd been able to stand it as long as she had on a light t-shirt and shorts. I had on leggings and a sweatshirt and was cold after only about thirty minutes.

I followed Lexie into her kitchen, one that would make a chef jealous.

"When it gets this windy, I get nervous. Do you want a cup?" she asked, holding up a coffee cup. It was too late for me to drink coffee and be able to sleep tonight, so I turned her down.

"Why do you get nervous?" I asked as I sat down on a stool at their kitchen island.

"Fires, plain and simple. It's so easy when everything is so

## THE BOSUN

dry, and then it gets windy like this."

"The one thing that worried me about moving here was all the fires. Have you ever been in one?"

"No, but we haven't lived here very long. The only thing I can say is I hope you got fire insurance."

"Can you even live here and not have fire and earthquake insurance?" It wouldn't be smart not to have it.

"You can, but you'd have to be stupid or insanely rich," she answered over the rim of her piping hot coffee.

"Where's Delilah?" I was surprised I hadn't seen her running around.

"Oh, she's napping a little later than usual. Her energy was boundless today, and she kept going until she couldn't go anymore. Ryder thinks we should get a dog to wear her out, but I'd hate to have to leave a dog at a kennel every time we go out of town. Our next option is swimming lessons, so she'll wear herself out in the pool."

"I'd say I'd watch the dog, but I can't always promise to be home. Although a puppy sounds like what I need in my life. Maybe we should co-parent a dog."

Lexie shook her head at me. "You don't need any other distractions in your life. If we get a dog, and that's a big if, I'll let you see it as much as you want. You can even have sleepovers."

It was sad when I was excited at the prospect of having the company of a dog. Pen had done a tour around the States a few months ago, and it was such a success they were now doing a world tour, so I wasn't sure when I'd see her unless I flew to some random country they were playing in. Thinking about it, it did sound like a good idea because I'd yet to meet Walker.

The mystery of who he really was made me want to meet him all the more.

Lexie leaned over the counter with a mischievous smile. "What's that look for?"

I felt the smile grow on my face as I spoke. "I'm thinking about surprising Pen while she's touring with Crimson Heat since I've yet to meet her beau."

"Oh, yes! That sounds like a wonderful idea and so much fun."

"What sounds like fun?" Ryder asked as he sauntered into the kitchen, a sweaty mess. Sweat had never looked so good on a man before. He pulled out a water bottle from the refrigerator and chugged half of it. I couldn't take my eyes off him as his throat worked. It wasn't fair for a man's throat to be sexy. I really did need to have sex.

"Surprising Pen while she's on tour and finally meeting the guy she's…" Lexie scrunched up her nose and looked at me. "What are they doing?"

"According to Pen, they're just having fun, but I think it's more than that. I think she really likes him, but she's worried if anyone finds out, she'll lose her job."

Thinking of Pen and Walker made me think of Remy and

## THE BOSUN

our brief time together. I wished I could see him again and let him know I'd read his letter, and I didn't blame him. Maybe Pen had a pit stop in Spain, and I could find out where Seas the Day was and surprise Remy as well.

Ryder came up behind Lexie and wrapped his arms around her waist. She melted back into him as they swayed where they stood. "I think you girls should surprise her. I don't have anything planned, so I can stay here with Delilah."

Lexie clapped, excitement lighting her eyes. "Let's find out where we're going."

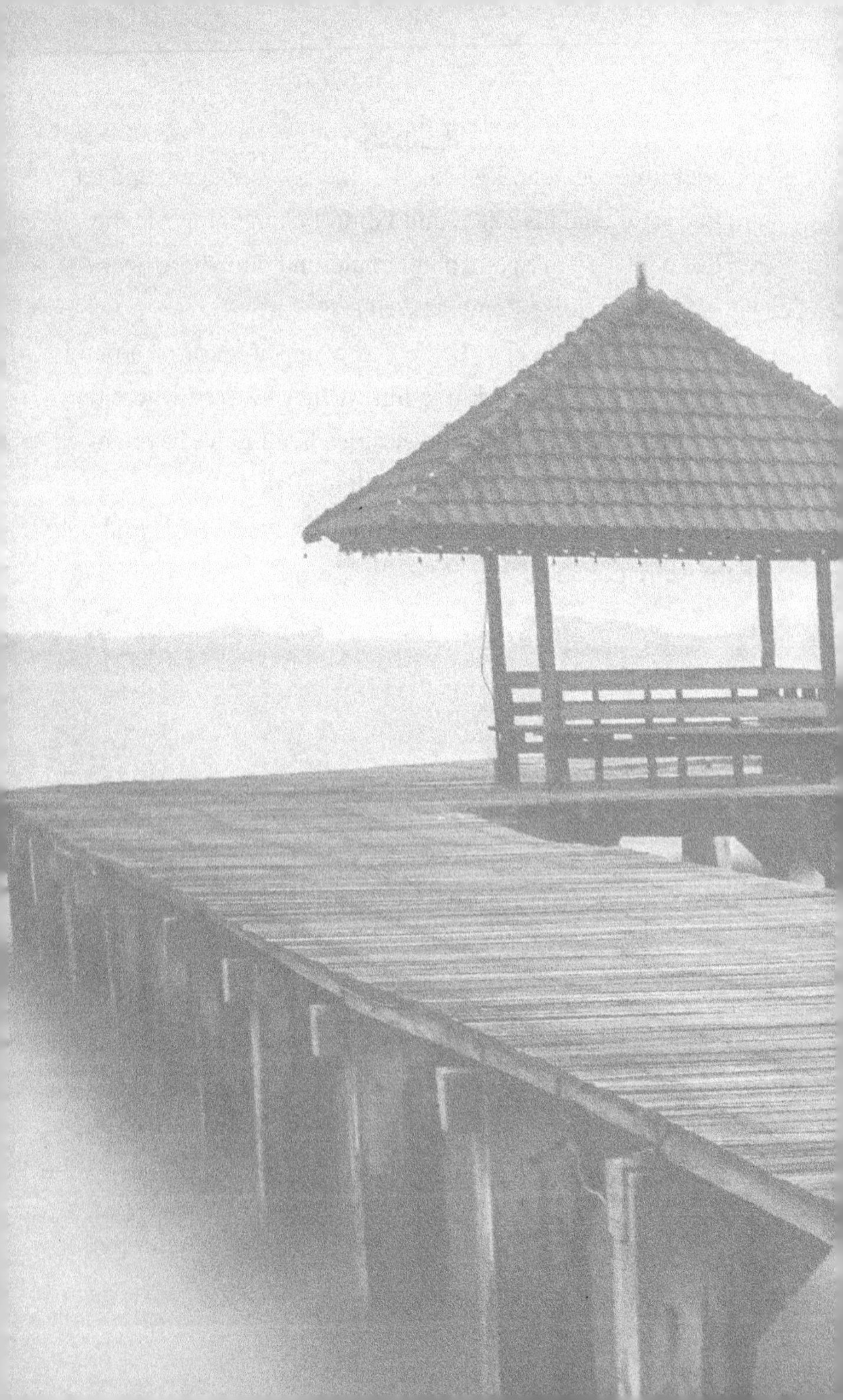

# 13

## REMY

"DO YOU THINK YOU'RE ready for this?" my dad asked from the doorway of my childhood room.

Stopping what I was doing, I turned to him. "I think so, and so does my firehouse captain, but as you know, fire is unpredictable."

"I just got you back and don't want anything to happen to you," he said as he sat down on the edge of my bed. "I'm more scared of losing you to fire than I ever was of you going off to war. Or worse yet, what if something happens to one of the people you're working with and you…"

I watched as my dad's Adam's apple bobbed before he looked at me with glassy eyes.

"I can promise you I won't go MIA on you again. My time with my therapist has shown me there was nothing I could have done to save Damon. All of that therapy doesn't mean I won't miss him for the rest of my life. I can still be sad about it, but I know how to better handle what I'm feeling."

"I just worry about you. Why couldn't you be an accountant or something where you're not putting yourself on the line every day?"

I moved to sit down beside him. I hated seeing the fear in my dad's eyes, but it was in my blood to help people. I wouldn't feel right if I was doing anything else. That's how I knew I couldn't be a bosun for another season. I needed to do what fed my soul, and that meant making another life change.

"Because you taught me that I should always help people in need, and my country needs me. Whether that be overseas fighting for our freedom or saving people and their homes from fire."

Placing his tanned hand on my knee, my dad gave me a shaky smile. "I guess I did something right raising you on my own."

Wrapping my arm around his shoulders, I rested my head on his. "You did, and I wouldn't change one thing about my childhood."

"When are you leaving?"

"In a couple of hours. One of the guys is going to pick me up and take me to the airport in Fort Lauderdale along with another guy from a different station."

"Why do these fires keep happening?"

## THE BOSUN

"California has all the right components to make a fire start, and with the winds they've been having, they're hard to contain."

"And that woman you told me about, she lives out there where the fire's headed?"

"I think so. I don't know exactly where she lives, but it's consuming a large portion of where I think she was supposed to live."

He nodded as if it all made sense to him. I didn't think I'd magically find Stella or come in and sweep her off her feet, away from the fire. That wasn't why I was going to help. I wanted to help, and California just happened to be where there was a fire raging out of control.

Standing, my dad looked down at me. "All I ask is that you be safe and come back to me."

"I promise I'll always be as safe as I can and that I'll come back to you. You can't get rid of me that easily. Although I might get my own apartment when I get back."

"You know you can stay here for as long as you want, but I understand you might want your privacy as well." He waggled his brows at me.

Bringing home a girl was the last thing on my mind. But I wanted something more than four walls that surrounded me. I wanted my own space for once in my life and not just a small room and bathroom that I had to share with someone.

Clapping me on the shoulder, my dad only nodded for a

moment. Maybe he finally understood why I had to go to California. "I'll let you finish packing."

"It shouldn't take me too much longer."

I had very few possessions—something I had done purposely over the years. First being in the military and then living in a room the size of a bathroom while on different boats, it was sad almost everything I owned could fit inside one duffle. Slowly, I'd started to accumulate more things over the last few months, but not much. I'd been too busy with my training, seeing a therapist that was recommended to me from one of the guys in my unit who'd been home for the last year, and spending some much-needed quality time with my dad.

I'd been more engaged in life and happier since I arrived in my hometown than I had been in the last two years, even as I worked through my crippling guilt.

Seeing my dad for the first time had been bittersweet. My parents weren't young when they had me. My mom was thirty-five, and my dad forty. He'd aged a lot since I'd last seen him almost four years ago, making him look older than his sixty-seven years, and I knew a great deal of it was because of me. He'd been worried sick about me when I didn't come home for Damon's funeral and then when I didn't try to contact him. I'd been the worst son in the world, and I'd been trying to make it up to him any way I could. I knew it would kill him if something happened to me and I didn't come back to him. It nearly killed him when my mom left and never came back while I was

## THE BOSUN

at school. As far as I know, he'd never heard from her after her initial phone call saying she wasn't ever coming home.

Once packed, I took my gear and my bag and set them by the front door before I went to join my dad in the living room. He was watching a baseball game with a bottle of beer in his hand. I wished I could have had a beer with him before I left, but that wouldn't have been smart with the anti-anxiety medicine I was taking.

Sitting down in the recliner next to his, I reclined and tried to watch the game, but my mind was racing with everything I'd learned in the last few months. It helped I'd had training while overseas. I wasn't a newbie, but it would still be my first time being in front of a fire of this magnitude.

"You know I'm proud of you, right?" My dad continued to stare at the TV as he spoke. "Even if I don't fully understand why you do it, it's honorable. Something I never had the courage to do."

It meant much more than he'd ever know to hear those words from my dad. Growing up, we'd always been close. That is until I vanished out of his life, but now we were closer than ever.

My eyes teared up. I wasn't as courageous as he thought. It was hard to leave him again. Life was uncertain, but I'd do everything in my power not to hurt him again. "I know, Dad," I choked out.

My phone pinged with an incoming text.

**Jason: Picked up Eric and should be there in twenty.**

**Remy: See you then.**

Dad glanced at me as I slid my phone back into my pocket. "Is that your buddy?"

"Yeah, he'll be here soon. He was leaving from picking up the other guy."

He eyed my bags by the door. "Are you sure you got everything you need?"

"I think so. I know I'll have to do laundry while I'm there, but if I need anything else, I can buy it. Don't worry about me. I'll call you once I get settled into where they're housing us, and I'll either call or text you every day."

"It's hard not to worry about you. There was a boy no older than you, who died two days ago."

He hadn't been a firefighter. He had tried to fend off the fire headed straight toward his house with only a hose hooked to the spigot at the front of his house. I understood he didn't want to lose his house or worldly possessions, but it shouldn't have been at the cost of his life. There were too many people who hadn't evacuated from the area from what I'd last heard. They needed more manpower to try to get the residents to see the best thing for them was to evacuate until the fire wasn't endangering their lives.

"I probably won't even be put in the front lines, but I've got to go. It's hard to be here when so many are in need in South-

# THE BOSUN

ern California."

My dad stood, holding out his hand for me to take. The moment I stood, he wrapped me up in a bear hug. I hugged him back just as hard when I heard his deep inhalation of breath.

"I love you, dad."

"I know. I love you too," he said gruffly.

My phone buzzed in my pocket, letting me know Jason was here and it was time to go.

Squeezing me one last time, Dad patted me on the back before he pulled away, his eyes glassy. "Call me when you get there to let me know you landed safely."

"I will," I promised. I was never going to leave my dad in doubt again.

Striding over to the door, I picked up my things before I headed out on my next mission.

⚓

Eight hours later, Eric and I were stuffed into the back of a van to be taken to the firehouse that would be housing us while we were in California.

"Alright, boys, we're not going to throw you out into the thick of it first thing," Donnie, our stocky liaison, said as he drove. "More than anything right now, we need men to go door to door seeing who's home and who isn't. If they're home, it's your job to try and convince them to leave."

From beside me, Eric's entire face furrowed. "But when

can we fight the beast?"

Donnie shook his head and let out an annoyed sigh. "I can't say. You'll have to take it up with the chief, but don't hold your breath. While we need help, we don't need some guy we don't know putting himself and others in danger."

Crossing his arms over his chest, Eric sat back and fumed. Not knowing his background, I couldn't say if he was justified in being irritated by the possibility of not being up close and personal with the fire. All I knew was I was here to help in any way possible, and it looked as if they needed it. The closer we got to our destination, the brighter orange the sky became. I couldn't imagine what it would be like closer since it looked like this, and we were fifty miles away. How people thought it was safe to stay in their homes was beyond me when nature was giving them a big warning in the sky.

The other guys who were in the van talked quietly to each other, but I kept my eyes on the sky. Eric wasn't up for talking anyway as he tapped his fingers on his knee, huffed every few minutes, and glared up at the front. After being stuck in traffic for almost two hours, Donnie swung the van into a spot at the firehouse.

As we all piled out, Donnie stood off to the side, his gaze directed at Eric. "Are we going to have a problem?"

"No, sir," Eric replied stiffly.

"Good, now I'll show you where you can store your things. It's not much, but we've got more guys here than usual with all

## THE BOSUN

the volunteers." He held open the door for us as we all walked in. "There should be dinner, so grab a bite to eat, and we'll have a meeting to brief you on the status of the fire along with where you'll be going tomorrow morning. I suggest you get some good sleep because it might be the last time you get a full night."

Taking a look around, it wasn't much different from the station I'd been training at, but it felt different. The energy was electrified. Creating a buzz through my body, making me feel like, for the first time in years, I was right where I was supposed to be.

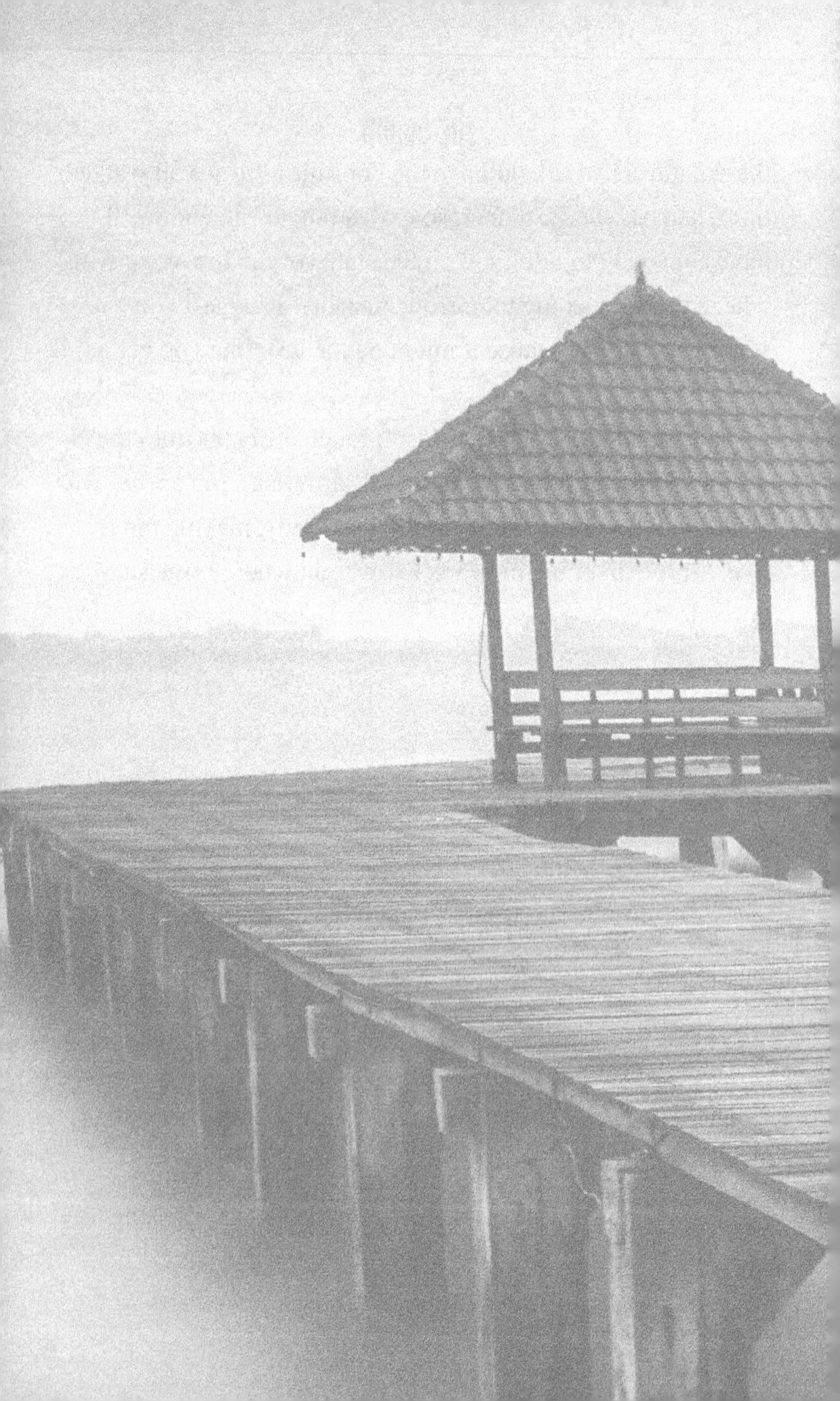

# 14

## STELLA

UNFORTUNATELY FOR ME, Pen and Crimson Heat had already made their pass-through Spain a couple of months ago, so I wouldn't be able to see if Remy was working on Seas the Day. Even if he was, it would have been awkward as hell for me to call and then show up out of the blue. If he was there, he'd probably be working, and it was possible he'd forgotten about me.

Since we weren't going to hijack a yacht in Spain, I didn't care where we went. The sooner, the better was what worked for Lexie. She had a big photoshoot in a week she needed to be back for, and then Ryder had one someplace I'd never heard of.

It wasn't easy trying to get Pen's boss, Christiano, to give me the information on what hotel they were staying at, but I assured him I wouldn't do anything that would make Pen deviate away from her job. I knew he didn't know me, but what did he think I'd do. Pen had never given him a reason to think she wouldn't be one thousand percent professional. That was unless he thought she was doing the lead singer of the band. Still, Pen seeing me was no cause for concern, and after about thirty minutes, Christiano gave me the address of the hotel they'd be staying at tonight. He even threw in tickets with backstage passes.

"I can't believe we're going to Amsterdam," I said a little too loudly, going by the looks I got from the rest of the people on the plane. "Have you ever been?"

Lexie's brows furrowed as she thought about it. I wished I had the problem of not remembering all the places I'd gone. I'd never traveled since Brock's going to medical school took precedence over everything else.

"Actually, I don't think I have. I've been to quite a few countries around the Netherlands, but never there." She leaned her seat back and closed her eyes. "If it's okay with you, I'm going to try and get a little shut-eye before we land. Ryder and I haven't been apart for more than a day in three years, and he kept me up way past my bedtime." One eye opened as she smirked at me and then promptly closed.

"I understand." If I had a man, I'd have done the same thing. "I was up too late trying to plot out my next book but didn't get much accomplished. I was too excited to surprise

## THE BOSUN

Pen."

The corner of Lexie's mouth kicked up. "She's going to be so surprised."

Hopefully, in a good way because I wasn't going to wait any longer to meet this Walker guy who was taking all of my best friend's time.

"She is. We're lucky we're to show up tonight since they won't be heading to the next venue until tomorrow afternoon."

Curling up onto my side, I closed my eyes in an attempt to fall asleep. I wasn't sure if I'd be successful with how excited I was, but one minute I was thinking about the look that would surely be on Pen's face when she saw us, and the next, I was woken up by the captain of the plane saying we'd be landing in forty minutes.

Lexie stretched beside me and let out a long yawn. "I can't believe I slept the whole time. I'm sorry if you were bored. I thought it would only be for a couple of hours."

"Seems like your husband wore you out more than you knew." We both laughed like schoolgirls. "I slept the entire time as well, but even if I hadn't, I could have been plotting or reading. I'm rarely bored. More often than not, I feel anti-social. I'm happy staying at home, ordering and having everything delivered to me, and catching up on reading books or TV when I'm not writing. It's when I finally do something else that I realize what I'm missing out on not doing more with my days. That's why I started to do that yoga class down on the beach. I thought it might help clear my mind and get me to socialize more. At least I'm doing more than sitting in front of my computer all day. Does that make any sense?"

"Perfectly. Ryder, Delilah, and I live in our own little world for the most part. We don't do much that's not work-related, but that's fine with us since work takes us all over the world. We're happy being at home enjoying our house, the pool, and the beach. We worked hard to get to where we are now. What's the point in life if you can't enjoy what you've attained?"

"There's isn't. You should enjoy what you have because your family and house are both beautiful."

"Thank you," she laid her hand on my arm and looked at me softly. "You'll meet someone one day who will make you his world. Just don't make the same mistake I did?"

Mistake? I had no idea what she was talking about. "What's that?"

"When I first met Ryder, well, not the first time, but after some time apart and we saw each other again, I lied to myself about what he meant to me. Raine tried to make me see reason, but I was having none of it. I didn't think I could hold Ryder's attention for long with him constantly traveling and being around beautiful women. Trust me when I say it doesn't matter the age or distance; if a man makes you happy and wants to be with you, you try to make it work. It's better than being miserable and alone."

"I had no idea. You're so beautiful and confident, and the

## THE BOSUN

way Ryder looks at you."

"That's the thing, though. Doubt can make you blind to what's right in front of you. Raine told me over, and over again, she could see how much Ryder was into me, but I didn't see it, and once I did..." She let out a sad sigh. "I thought he was with someone else. To make matters worse, it was with a person he knew I didn't like. It felt like such a betrayal, but if I'd been thinking with a clear head, I would have known Ryder would never do that."

"So, you're saying that I need to be more confident in myself and to listen to those around me? Easier said than done."

"I know it is. I was damaged from having multiple men cheat on me, and that made it hard for me to trust even though Ryder never once did anything to make me think he'd betray me. I know you've been burned by your ex, but don't make the next man pay for your ex's mistakes."

Again, easier said than done, but it was good advice. I shouldn't put all the baggage I had onto someone else because of what Brock had done.

"Well, if I ever met a guy I'm interested in, I'll do that or at least try."

"What would you do if the guy from the boat showed up on your doorstep tomorrow? Would you be with him?"

I sputtered, making Lexie's sultry laugh fill the compartment. Everyone was looking at us, but we didn't care.

"That's a leap. I'd probably wonder how in the hell he

found me, but I wouldn't be opposed to...I barely know the guy."

Lexie turned to look at me. "We can never know a person unless we give them a chance. Think about when we met. We didn't know each other, but there was an instant connection. We built on that connection, and now it's like we've known each other forever."

She was right. How was I ever going to meet a man if I never gave him a chance? If by some miracle, Remy did walk into my life, I needed to give him a chance. I already knew there was an insane physical attraction between us. Plus, I liked talking to him the little I had when I was in Spain. There was something about him that made it easy for me to open up to him, and that had to mean something. I didn't go about telling everyone I met my life story.

A thought came to me, and I felt the blood drain from my face. "Please don't tell me you somehow tracked him down, and he's going to surprise me in Amsterdam. I'm not sure I'll be able to take it."

"Oh my God, you should see your face. At least now I know you do not like surprises. Good to know." Her face cracked into a large grin.

"I like doing the surprising, not the one being surprised, so please, no matter how much Pen tries to tell you I love them, trust me when I tell you I really don't."

"Okay." The word hung in the air, and I could tell she want-

## THE BOSUN

ed more from me.

"Let's just say I've never had a good experience where surprises were involved. In fact, they've all ended up being complete disasters."

"Then I promise not to surprise you. If it makes you feel better, I haven't tried to track down the man you met on the boat. If I wanted to, I'm sure I could pull a few strings to find out his contact information, but I won't unless you tell me you want me to."

I did, but I was afraid of what I'd find out. It had been almost a year since our time together. Who was to say Remy hadn't met a woman and fallen in love with her?

"Stop thinking about it for now and enjoy our little impromptu vacation. You deserve one after that hectic book tour."

I had been busy. It showed me what Pen did when she was on tour with a band; only hers was ramped up times a thousand.

"I kind of feel bad that I'm keeping you away from your family, especially now that I know you haven't been apart. They could have come."

"They could have, but that's too much flying back-to-back with Delilah. If we could have stayed longer, I would have brought them with us. They'll be fine, and I'll be fine. Dillie loves her dad, and I'm sure she'll love all of his attention solely on her for a change."

"When you look at him with your daughter, do your ovaries ache for him to impregnate you?"

"Something like that." She leaned closer as if she was going to tell me a secret. "We've been talking about having another baby, and I stopped taking my birth control." She shrugged. "So, we'll see. It'll happen when it happens."

I had a feeling it would happen very soon.

"I'm not sure I'm equipped to handle seeing your husband holding a baby. If you're planning to get pregnant, then I need to get a boyfriend stat."

One eyebrow rose in question. "One that you want to have a baby with?"

"Maybe," I shrugged one shoulder. "I don't even know if I can get pregnant. I tried for years with Brock, and no matter what we tried, I never got pregnant. Maybe it was a sign I'm not meant to be a mother."

"Or maybe it was a sign that you weren't supposed to get tied down to an asshole who'd cheat on you."

I couldn't imagine how complicated everything would have been if I'd been pregnant or if we'd had a child. I wasn't going to plague myself with what ifs though. I knew one thing. "I'd like to be a mother one day. If I can't have a child of my own, I'd happily adopt. There are so many kids out there that need a home."

"Maybe you should look into it when we get back. See what it would take for you to adopt. You don't have to wait for a man to be in your life."

Logically I knew that. I wanted a man and a child, but just

## THE BOSUN

because I wanted them didn't mean I had to do them in order.

"Why are you so damn smart?"

"I just am." She giggled. "But seriously, if you want a family, you don't have to wait for a man."

"I'm going to give myself until the end of the year because I can't imagine writing a book while going through the process. I want to be able to devote all of my headspace to it."

"Now that we slept almost the entire flight and won't need a nap, what should we do until tonight?"

"Why don't we walk around and check out the architecture, maybe do a little shopping, and then head to the Red Light District?"

"I knew there was a reason we were friends," Lexie laughed.

⚓

Several hours later, Lexie and I were crammed into the front section of the venue, jumping around as Crimson Heat belted out their encore. They were good. Better than good, and I knew after this tour, they were going to blow up the world with their music.

As the song started to slow, Lexie grabbed my hand. "We should try to make our way backstage now before things get too crazy," she yelled over the music.

I nodded in agreement and let her lead the way since I had no idea where I was going. Neither did she, but she certainly acted like it. We were stopped by a big burly man who was half as wide as the hall. Lexie flashed her badge and smile and then picked up mine to show. The guy didn't speak. He only nodded and moved enough to let us slip by.

Lexie and I moved quickly down the hall. Our excitement built off the others as we spotted Pen standing off to the side with big headphones on. She hadn't seen us yet. We moved to the other side of the hall and slinked down it slowly, hoping she wouldn't turn around and catch us until we were directly behind her. Lexie clapped a hand over her mouth as her body shook, trying to hold in her laughter.

Sneaking up behind Pen, I placed my hand on her shoulder. She turned around with a pinched face until she took us in standing before her. Mouth hanging open, Pen pulled me into her arms and hugged me until I couldn't breathe. Next, she gave Lexie a hug before taking a step back and looking us over as if she couldn't believe we were standing before her.

Jumping up and down in place, Pen yelled. "What are you guys doing here?"

"We thought we'd come and surprise you since it's been forever since we saw you."

"And to meet your man," Lexie supplied.

"Shh," Pen hushed her. "Don't let anyone hear you say that. We're keeping it on the down-low. The only ones who know are you two and Walker's bandmates because they found us in a compromising situation."

## THE BOSUN

"Sounds exciting." I winked at her.

"Try embarrassing. Oh my God, I can't believe you're here. Did you see the concert?" Lexie and I both nodded. "Aren't they great? Everyone overseas loves them, and Titan keeps putting more dates on the tour. I'm just..." She looked back in the direction she'd been looking when we surprised her.

"It's your baby. You're proud of them," I finished for her.

"I really am. They're about ready to come off stage. Please don't say anything. I'll introduce you to them once we're back in the green room. And then...how long are you here for?"

"We fly back tomorrow, so you only have us for tonight," I pouted. "Are you happy to see us?"

Pen rolled her eyes as she pulled me to her side. "Of course, I'm happy to see you. Never in my wildest dreams did I think you'd fly to see me."

"Well, I missed you. Plus, I wanted to procrastinate on this book, and visiting you is the perfect excuse."

"Ha, ha. I told the band I now know a famous author, so don't make me a liar."

"Thanks for the pressure." As if there wasn't enough after my first book did so well.

"Did your husband come?" Pen asked, looking around.

"No, I thought it was best if this guy you're seeing or whatever you are," Lexie amended after Pen gave her a sour look. "No guy wants to see his woman drooling over another man."

"You two are full of jokes tonight, aren't you?" The loud

sound of the crowd erupting had us all go quiet. Pen smiled and then motioned for us to follow her. "Stay here, or you'll likely get run over. They are full of energy when the show is over."

One by one, we watched as the band walked by us. They each gave Pen a greeting before they proceeded down the hall. Walker moved by only muttering Pen's name, giving nothing away.

Once he was a few feet past us, Pen turned to us. "Are you ready to meet Crimson Heat?"

"Oh, I've been ready for quite some time," I told her as we started walking.

Stopping in front of a closed door, Pen turned to us. Her hands were clasped together as she spoke. "Please don't embarrass me. I have to be on the road with these guys, and they'll use any ammunition you give them against me."

"I guess there goes our plan," Lexie said as she went for the doorknob. She was about to open the door when Pen slammed her hand on the door to stop her.

"What do you mean plan?" She looked back and forth between the two of us.

"There is no plan. The only one we had was to surprise you. Now quit stalling before we have to do something to embarrass you in front of them."

"Fine," she hissed as she opened the door. We were accosted by the sound of four guys wrestling each other on the

## THE BOSUN

ground. They stopped and jumped up the moment we walked in.

"Hey, P, who's your friends?" one of the guys said with a wide and infectious smile. He had blond hair in a crew cut and colorful tattoos up and down his arms.

"These are my friends they came to surprise me, Stella and Lexie. This is Cross," she indicated the one who'd asked who we were. "This tall beast of a man is Kenton," Pen pointed to a guy who looked like he was almost seven feet tall. His height could have made him scary, but he had the kindest brown puppy dog eyes I'd ever seen. "This is Greer," she hooked her thumb his way and moved to stand in front of Walker. From what little she'd told me about the band, Pen and Greer didn't get along. He stood with his lips curled up in a half snarl and silvery-gray eyes taking us in.

"Last but not least, this is Walker." He tipped his chin up at us but didn't say a word. Even with his hair a sweaty mess and sticking to his head, he was still hot. Looking at them all now, he looked like the oldest of the bunch instead of the youngest.

"If any of you want to go to dinner with us, I suggest you get cleaned up because I don't want to smell any of you while I'm trying to eat." Cross opened his mouth, but Pen cut him off. "And neither do my friends."

Walker started to walk away until Pen stopped him with a hand to his chest. They talked in whispers as Greer plopped down on a couch and made himself comfortable. The other two guys argued about if they should stay to pick up some girls here or later while they were out. After a few minutes, they parted ways, and Cross stepped up to Pen. "I think we're going to skip dinner. That way, you can spend time with your friends."

Pen closed her eyes and inhaled deeply. When she reopened her eyes, they narrowed on the man who stood before her. "Don't do anything stupid just because I'm not there. Remember, if I get fired, the person who replaces me won't be as lenient as I am."

"I know, Momma P. This isn't our first rodeo. We won't do anything you wouldn't do." His face transformed into a devilish smile for only a moment before he schooled his features.

"Please don't call me that," Pen moaned.

"Tell Bob to let the people back so we can get this over with," Walker muttered from the other side of the room.

Pen pulled a walkie-talkie I hadn't noticed before from behind her back and spoke into it. "They're ready. Let them through." Turning to us, she said. "If it gets to be too much, you can always go out into the hall. Sometimes the women can be a bit much." She leaned in to whisper. "You'd think with the way some of the women act, these guys were world-famous. When the squealing gets too much, I hide out in the hallway until they leave."

I had a feeling it was also to not see the women pawing at Walker. Women had been screaming his name, flashing their boobs, and throwing their underwear at him all throughout the

## THE BOSUN

concert. If Walker was my man, I wouldn't want women throwing themselves all over him.

After only a few girls nearly blew out our ears with their high-pitched squeals from meeting the band, Lexie and I went to wait out in the hall. She walked further down the corridor but was where I could see her so she could check in with Ryder.

It was only thirty minutes later when Pen and Walker walked out and left the rest of the band with about twenty women.

"Walker's going to take a quick shower on the bus, and then we'll be ready to leave. Would you like a tour of the bus while we wait?"

"Why not? When am I going to get another opportunity?"

Lexie and I walked behind Walker and Pen, and I could tell from Pen's body language it was killing her not to be able to touch him. The moment we stepped inside the bus, Pen's hand went to Walker's lower back as she trailed behind him in the cramped space.

"I'll be right back. Make yourselves comfortable," he murmured before walking off into the back.

"So, this is it," Pen laughed. "Their bus isn't as nice as some big-name people, but it's still pretty nice. There's a bedroom in the very back, and here," she walked a few steps. "This is the bunk area. The back bedroom is on rotation so whoever isn't sleeping back there is in one of these."

"Do you have sex in this tiny area?" Lexie asked as she crouched down to get a better look.

"Only once. It was...difficult would be the word. Normally we wait until one of us has the back bedroom or is staying in a hotel like tonight."

Scrunching up my nose, I backed away from the bunk beds. "It smells like Doritos and feet."

"Yeah," she sighed. "Coming from being an only child to sharing a small space with four males has been trying."

"I'm sure Walker makes handling the situation a whole lot easier."

Pen looked over her shoulder and then ushered us closer to the front of the bus. Speaking in a hushed tone, she said. "Most of the time, but he can be moody after a show. I don't know why and from what I gathered, neither do the other guys. Like tonight, he's being unusually quiet. I don't know if he had a bad night because from what I saw and heard, they were amazing, or if it's because you guys are here and he's giving me my time with you."

Hopefully, it was the latter, and he just needed to get to know us.

Walker stepped out of the bathroom shirtless with his long hair dripping and his shirt balled up in one hand. Pen let out a noise that was a cross between a sigh and a whimper. She had it bad. I only hoped Walker felt the same about her.

Shaking out his shirt, Walker slid it over his head before he

## THE BOSUN

looked to us. "I'm ready whenever you are."

"So, I did a little research on places to eat here, and there's a place close to the hotel we're staying at. We could get an Uber there and then walk. Shit, where are you guys staying?"

"Funny you should ask that. I thought I was going to have to give my first-born child to Christiano to get any information out of him. He pretty much told me not to get you into trouble while we're here. What have you told him about me?"

"Nothing at all. I wouldn't tell that man anything voluntarily about my life." She let out an annoyed huff. "He's so fucking annoying. I can't believe he said that to you. Did he at least tell you where we're staying?"

"He did after a lot of begging and promising that I really knew you. We were lucky to get a room. The hotel said they only had a couple that weren't booked."

"At least we're all staying at the same hotel. We can eat dinner and then chill out at the bar downstairs or something."

"Perfect, now let's get ourselves a ride because I'm starved, and you don't want to see me when I get hangry."

⚓

Covering my mouth and speaking low, so Walker didn't hear from his spot next to Pen, I asked. "How do you sit by and let those women, and I use the word women loosely, hang all over him?"

Pen leans back, not caring if anyone hears her. "I don't really have a choice. If I acted all possessive over him, that would only stir up rumors. What about you? How do you handle it?"

"There's not much to handle. Everyone we're around knows Ryder and I are together. I can't do a thing about all the women who eye-fuck him." She tipped her head in each of our directions. "You two included."

It was fun to watch as Walker, who'd be acting uninterested in our conversation, stiffened.

"When we were first together, Ryder took care of it for us when we were around new people. He'd claim me on the spot with a kiss that would leave me breathless and a whole lot more if you know what I mean."

Oh, we knew exactly what she meant. Ryder would kiss her, and she'd want to jump his bones.

A sigh escaped her, and I knew Lexie was missing her husband and child. It meant a lot to me that she came on this trip with me. I needed to do something to repay her. Maybe I'd watch Delilah while they went out on a date or something.

"We were going to wait if you hadn't stopped in Spain so we could make a little pit stop, but it wasn't meant to be."

Pen's eyes went wide. "Were you going to look him up?"

"I mean, I was thinking about it."

"This is new." She wrapped her hand around Walker's bicep and shook it with excitement. "Do you want to talk to him or just have great sex again because I bet Zelda would try to get his number if you really wanted it."

## THE BOSUN

"Well, in a perfect world, I'd like both and for him to be at least be on the same continent or sharing the same body of water. That's not too much to ask for, is it?"

"I don't see how you're going to get laid if you're not even on the same continent as the guy," Walker muttered.

"See," I slapped my hand down on the table. "He gets it."

"Maybe you should stop focusing on that guy and find one more…" his eyes lifted to mine, "attainable."

Ouch.

"Don't listen to him." Pen glared at Walker. "He doesn't know what he's talking about or what you've been through. But," she drew out the word, "maybe you should think about starting to date. Maybe download a couple of apps."

"She should not do that." Walker leaned forward with his elbows on the table and gave me the hard facts. "Listen, you don't want to meet a guy off an app. They are there for one thing only, and that is to get laid. You're a beautiful woman, and if you put yourself out there, any guy in the vicinity would want to date you."

Throwing up my hands, I smiled over at the two of them. "Well, he won my vote. I say you keep him. Anyone who can simultaneously tell me something I don't want to hear and compliment me at the same time is good in my book."

"Is that really all it takes?" Pen silently shook with laughter from her side of the table.

"Well, I mean, you seem to like him since you've kept him

around for a few months, which isn't typical for you."

Pen's eyes narrowed as she shot daggers at me. "How about you don't spill all of my secrets, so I can maybe keep him around for a bit longer?"

Walker looked to Lexie. "It's like I'm not even here. Do they do this often?"

Lexie tilted her head to the side and smirked. "I've spent a lot more time with Stella than I have Pen, but I can't say that they do."

Turning to Walker, I apologized, trying to explain. "Sorry, we know you're here. I wanted her to know you've got my seal of approval. I was worried that after I found out about you, I might not like you. That there might have been an ulterior motive as to why Pen kept your existence all to herself."

Walker sat back and put his arm around Pen's shoulders. "She felt bad about it if that helps."

I would hope she felt bad about lying to me for months. As far as I knew, it was the only secret she'd kept from me.

"It helps some," I murmured.

Our waitress brought out our food, and we all sat in silence for a few minutes as we ate. Lexie and I were starved since we hadn't eaten since early in the morning, which seemed like ages ago. Pen had found a quaint little café that had a little bit of everything.

"You did good picking this place," I said before I took another bite of my mini pancakes.

## THE BOSUN

"Yeah, it's good, or it could be because it's been hours since we ate," Lexie pointed out.

"You did good, babe," Walker nodded. "How did you two like the show?"

"It was a damn good show. I wouldn't normally go see a band play if I didn't know their music, but your music sucked me in, and I was dancing along like I knew every word."

"That's a good thing." He bobbed his head with an uptick of his lips.

"I'll definitely be buying your music once I get home. I know my husband will love it too, so you've got three new fans. I know that's not much—"

"No, it's everything. It means a lot to me that you both liked our music. The whole band is astounded by the way everyone has embraced our music, and we have Pen here to thank for that. If it wasn't for her giving us a chance, we'd still be playing at college parties and at the one bar that would let us play."

I loved seeing the passion he had for his music and how humble he was.

"That gives me all the feels. I'll have my husband download it and do something on his Instagram story, TikTok, or something like that showing that he's listening to it. You'll have a lot of new fans or at least sales if he does that."

"Get their IG handle as well so he can tag them. They'll get a lot of new followers," Pen instructed, going into manager mode.

Walker sat up straighter. "How many followers does he have?"

Lexie scrunched up her face in thought. "I don't know. Let me look." She pulled out her phone and smiled down at her phone. Her home screen was a picture of the happy couple in an exotic location with Delilah on her dad's shoulders. It was a gorgeous shot of them. The moment she clicked on Instagram, it lit up with notifications as she went to Ryder's profile. "He has a little over a million."

"How does he not have more?" Pen questioned while her boyfriend blinked rapidly.

"While I don't have nearly as many followers as Lexie or Ryder, like not even close, I could get a picture with you and post it on mine. Every little bit helps, right?"

"Your friends are too nice." Walker's Adam's apple bobbed as he looked over at us. "I don't have words for how grateful I'd be."

"That's enough for me," Lexie said before she finished off the last of her pancakes.

"Me too," I said around a bite of mine. The Dutch knew how to make some mean pancakes.

"I told you they're the best." Pen laid her head on his shoulder. She looked so serene as she snuggled up to him. It was a sight I hadn't seen from her in all the years I'd known her. It looked good on her.

## THE BOSUN

"You kind of have to say that about your friends." He chuckled all low and rumbly.

"Clearly, you haven't heard her talk about our friends Zelda and Reagan. Especially Reagan." I couldn't even say Reagan's name without my lips curling up in a snarl.

"I can't say that I have."

"Yeah, I don't always have the nicest things to say about the two of them. Mostly Reagan, but I'm not sure I'd count her as a friend anymore."

"She's certainly not mine," I added.

Pen raised her hand in the air as our waitress went by and made a checkmark in the air, signaling for our check. "Do you want to go back to the hotel after this, or do you want to see the nightlife of Amsterdam?"

"I wouldn't mind walking off some of these pancakes." I patted my full belly. "Seeing a little more would be nice and then heading back. We did as much touristy stuff as we could after we checked in since both of us slept for most of our flight."

"We even hit up the Red Light District. Although, I'm sure it's much more entertaining at night than it was during the day."

"Oh, we should go there." Walker's eyes lit up.

Pen rolled her eyes. "Of course, you want to go where the prostitutes are."

"Are you jealous?" He pulled her close and lightly kissed

the corner of her mouth. "It's not like I'm going to do anything. They went, and you didn't assume they paid for any services."

The man made a point.

"Who knows if I'll ever be back here? While I'm here, I want to see what the big deal is. Don't you?"

She shrugged as if she didn't want to, but I knew she wanted to go. Who wouldn't?

Walker pulled Pen even closer and spoke against her ear. Pen looked down as her cheeks pinked up at whatever he said. I was pretty sure it was something dirty.

"You're right." She nodded. "You only live once, and who better to share this experience with than you three."

Lexie slapped the table as she stood. "Now you're talking. Let's go. The only thing I ask is that we don't do anything that will get us arrested."

"What?" I nearly shrieked, turning on her.

Pen rolled her lips. "Did you see the look on her face? I thought she was going to pee herself." Unable to hold back her laughter any longer, Pen leaned against the booth as she laughed.

"Relax, no one is getting arrested."

Walker wrapped an arm around Pen's waist and started to guide us out of the café. "You can't be too sure. The guys might decide to do something stupid without you there."

"Do you know something you aren't telling me?" He shook his head, but that didn't stop Pen from continuing to ask ques-

## THE BOSUN

tions. "Are you trying to make me feel bad for doing something with my friends? Should we find them?"

"No, I'm fucking with you. No one is getting arrested. Tonight, tomorrow, or any other night if I have any say on the matter." He looked over his shoulder to Lexie and me. "She takes her job way too seriously sometimes."

"Because I like my job and don't want to get fired, and I want Crimson Heat to be the best. That's not going to happen if you guys are out partying every night, doing drugs, or getting arrested."

"I know, babe. Tonight, we're going to have a little fun, but not too much fun. Okay?"

I liked that even though Walker was young, he seemed to have a level head and knew how to calm Pen down when she needed it. Seeing them together made me feel better.

"Let's go have some fun, girls!"

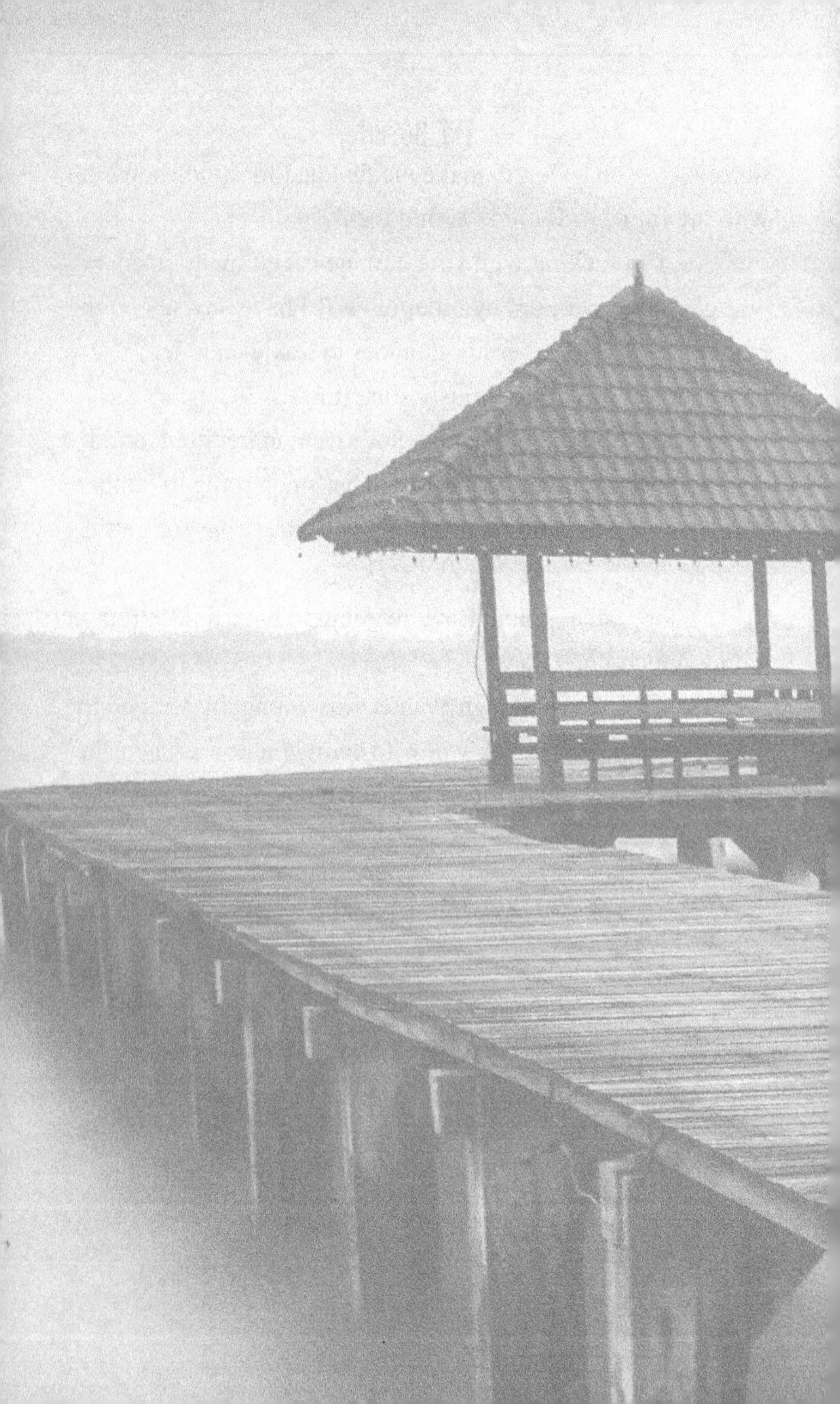

# 15

## STELLA

LEXIE AND I stood outside by her pool, looking at the angry sky. We'd only been home from Amsterdam for two days, and there was a fire threatening to burn down our homes. If the wind shifted even the tiniest amount, it could very well send the flames to our little town. While I'd said I wanted to live in Malibu because everyone knew of it, I lived a little further south between the Pacific Palisades and Santa Monica. Up until now, the location hadn't mattered as much.

"I can't believe this. Do you think we'll have to evacuate?" Lexie held her camera to her chest after taking about a hundred pictures of the sky.

"Maybe. I really don't know. They think it's possible it might reach us if they don't get the fire contained."

"Will you keep us updated?" She glanced over at me and then back to the sky. Lexie and Ryder would be gone for the next two weeks on jobs, and I knew it was hard for them to leave with the uncertainty of what would happen.

"Of course, I will. If you want to pack a bag or bags of things you'd like for me to take if I have to leave, do it. After you leave, I'm going to pack a bag to be ready just in case."

She nodded. "You know you could come with us if you want to. I hate leaving you here alone."

I wasn't too thrilled about it either, but I couldn't run from all my problems. "I know, and thanks. You don't need to worry about me. If I need to, I can always go stay at Pen's house until it's over."

"Baby, it's time to go," Ryder called from the door with Delilah on his hip. "Stella," he called to me, "be safe."

"I will." I'd won the lottery having those two as my neighbors. They could have been stuck-up assholes like the rest of my neighbors, but instead, they'd become some of my closest friends.

"I'll see you in two weeks," Lexie said as she leaned over and hugged me. "I expect you to have the first five chapters of your book written when I get back."

Pulling back, I laughed. "Now you," I accused her. Pen was always on my case about how I procrastinated. I didn't need Lexie to start in on me as well.

Walking backward to her house, she only grinned at me

## THE BOSUN

until she reached the door. "What can I say? You need someone to hold you accountable."

I did need the accountability, but it was hard to write when you thought your house might burn down with you in it.

Heading back over to my house, I grabbed my computer, not wanting to think about the fact that I was now alone. All my friends were off living their lives while I sat in my office, stuck somewhere between my past and the present.

Pulling out a stack of index cards, I wrote down all the pivotal points that would occur in my story and tacked them up on the wall. Before I'd moved in, I'd had a person come out and make one wall in my office a tack wall so I could pin all my notecards to it.

Some days, I'd stare at it for hours as I tried to conjure up the twist that would keep my readers reading.

After covering a fourth of my wall with my notecards, I was wiped out. Now that I had my key components done, I'd start writing in the morning.

It felt like my head had barely hit the pillow when I was woken up by my doorbell ringing. Cracking open my eyes, I looked over at my clock to see it was a little after ten in the morning. The blackout curtains I had installed were doing their job at keeping out the bright morning sun. I liked to wake up when my body told me it was time to wake up. It usually resulted in a better writing session than when I woke up with an alarm.

As I trudged downstairs, I already knew today wasn't going to be a good writing day. My head felt fuzzy from not enough sleep.

My doorbell went off again. Whoever it was was impatient. "I'm coming," I yelled as I hit the first floor. Swinging open the door, it occurred to me I should have looked at my phone to see who was at the door. It could have been some annoying salesperson or one of my neighbors. All people I wouldn't answer my door for.

"Good morning, ma'am, I—" He stopped talking the moment our eyes landed on each other.

Standing before me was Remy. Remy from Seas the Day in a...firefighter uniform. Was I dreaming?

"Stella?" he asked in disbelief.

"This has to be a dream," I muttered as I turned to look around. The sky outside my living room windows was a darker orange than it was yesterday.

"It's not a dream, Stella. This is real. You need to leave."

"Leave? Why? What happened?" My brain was trying to catch up to what was going on around me and how Remy was now standing just inside my front door.

"The fire shifted and is headed this way. I'm part of the team trying to get residents to vacate from the area."

"But I didn't pack a bag yet. I didn't…"

He moved quickly. One second, he was a few feet away, and the next, Remy was toe to boot with me cupping my

## THE BOSUN

cheeks in his warm, calloused hands. "Hey, it's going to be okay. You have time to pack a few things if you need to, but then you have to leave. Do you have any place to go?"

"Um...Pen has a place in LA where I can stay. I don't mean to be rude, but what are you doing here? I thought you were on a yacht in Spain."

Smiling down at me, he shook his head. "Not for about six months now. I needed a change." He shook his head, and a big smile grew across his face. "Damn, it's good to see you. I never thought I'd see you again."

"Same." I giggled. "I thought about trying to get your number somehow after I read your letter, but—"

"You read it?"

"Four months later, Pen found it in her purse. After I read it, I had no way of contacting you. I even thought about flying to Spain to find you."

"Well, I'm glad you didn't." Knowing my feelings were only one-sided, my face dropped, and pain shot through my chest. "Hey, look at me and let me finish." Slowly tipping my chin up with his index finger, Remy didn't speak until our eyes locked. "I'm glad you didn't try to find me because I was in Florida. I would have hated for you to spend all that money for nothing."

"Oh," was my simple response.

"Yeah, oh. I've thought a lot about you. Make no mistake thinking otherwise. Now, why don't you go pack a bag?"

"Can you stay? While I pack," I amended. He obviously had more important things to do than sit around with me.

"Yeah, sure, but you need to make it quick. Do you know if your neighbor is home?" he asked as we climbed the stairs. "I tried the house, and no one answered."

"They're out of town, but I'll let them know what's happening. What is happening?" I turned around at the entrance to my bedroom.

"We're trying to get as many people out as we can in case the fire reaches here. I only got here yesterday, so I don't know much, and I haven't been on the front line to know much more."

Shakily I went to my closet, changed my clothes, and pulled out a suitcase. "Do you think my house is going to burn down?"

"I can't say, but I hope not." He looked around the room as I threw anything I thought of into my suitcase. I wasn't sure how long I'd be gone or if anything would be here when I came back. "So, this is your house."

"It is. I haven't even been here a year, and now this," I laughed without humor. It would be just my luck that I'd finally move on with my life only to have my house burn down.

"Is there anything else you need?"

Looking up from my bag, I answered. "My laptop and all the cards on the wall in my office."

"I'll be right back." He turned on his heel and was out of

## THE BOSUN

the room quicker than I could blink.

I was packing my toothbrush when he came into the bathroom. "We really should be going. I have a long list of houses to go to. Um...I..." I stopped what I was packing and looked up at him. It was strange seeing him in his firefighter garb, but I liked it. "I don't want this to be the last time I see you. I mean, I know where you live now, but this is coming out wrong. I still can't believe I'm standing in your house. In your bathroom. Can I get your phone number? Maybe I can call you tonight when I get back to the firehouse."

Warmth filled my belly and up through my chest and arms. "I'd like that. Maybe if you're not too tired, I can take you to dinner or something like that."

"Sounds good. I don't know when I'll be free, but I promise to call." He held out his phone, and I promptly snagged it and put in my number.

"Oh, I need my phone and charger. It should be by the bed. Can you grab it?"

"Of course, and then we need to leave."

I couldn't believe I was leaving my house. At least I was lucky enough that I had a place to stay. Once I was on the road, I'd have to leave a message for Pen to let her know that I was at her place, and I'd need to leave an update with Lexie.

"Do you need this?" Remy asked as he held up my vibrator while he tried to keep a straight face.

Tilting my head to the side, I asked. "I don't know, will I?"

Throwing it over his shoulder, Remy moved into my space. His large hands came to my waist as he bent down until his lips were only a breath away. "Not if I have anything to say about it."

"Good, then leave it here." Stepping out of his grip, I grabbed my bathroom bag and took a look around my room. It was mostly dark with only the lamp on for light. My bed was unmade, and Remy stood in the middle of my room with a heated look in his dark eyes.

As I went to pick up my suitcase, Remy did it for me. He didn't say anything as I slowly walked down my stairs and through the lower half of my house, silently saying goodbye just in case.

As the garage door opened, I turned to Remy and placed my hand on his cheek. "I really thought you were a dream when I first saw you."

"Do you dream of me often?"

"That's for me to know." Pushing up on my toes, I grazed my lips over his. "Stay safe."

Opening the driver's door for me, he waited until I had my seatbelt on. "I will. You do the same."

As I backed out of my driveway, I watched Remy go to the house next door and ring their doorbell.

*Who knew all it would take was a state of emergency to bring us together again?*

# THE BOSUN

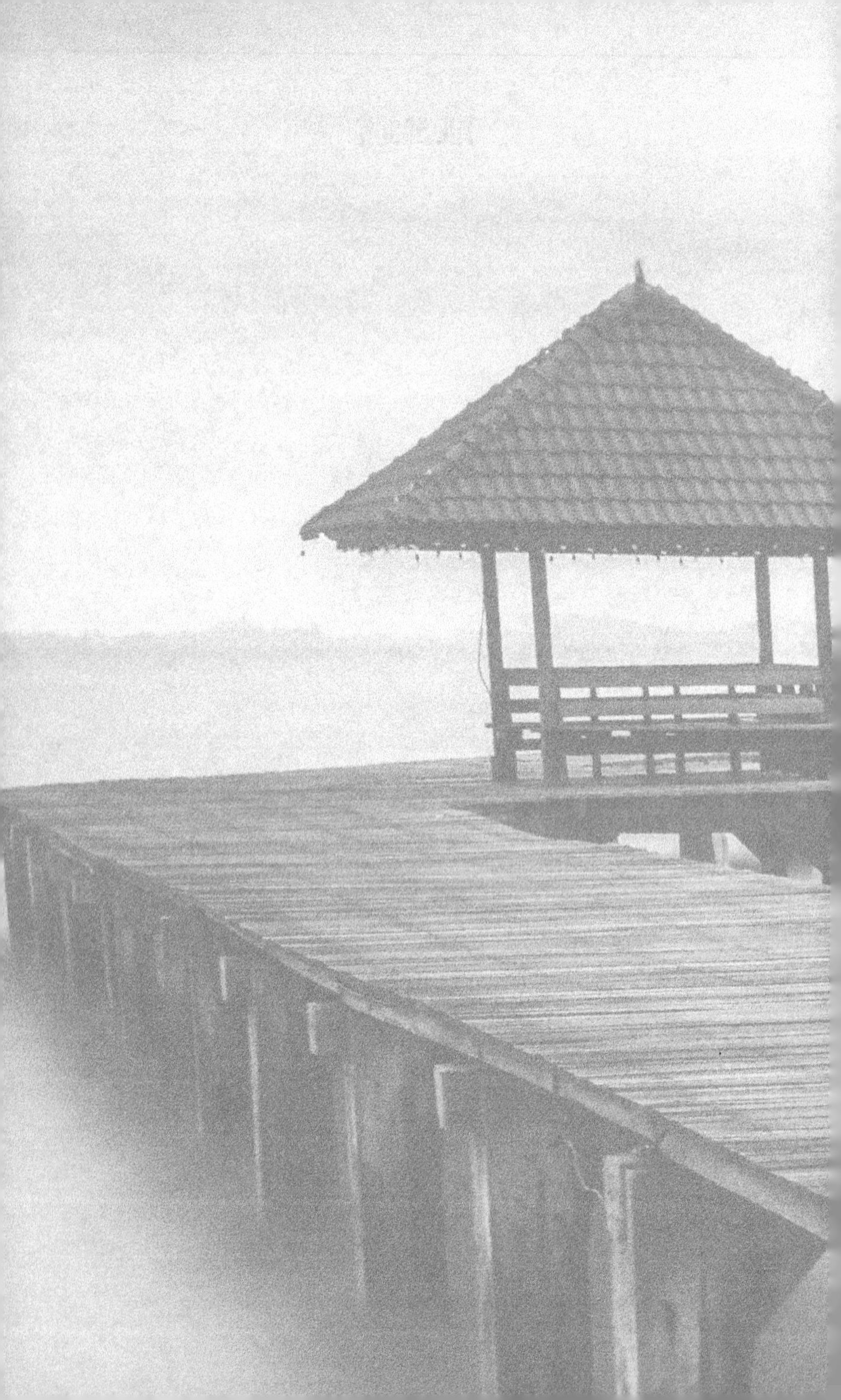

# 16

## REMY

FRESH OUT OF the shower, I went in search of Donnie. Even though he wasn't the Captain, he'd been put in charge of all the volunteers since Captain Rodrigo was overseeing Station Nineteen's firefighters.

I knocked on his door and waited until I heard him call out. Donnie looked up from behind the desk he sat at as I walked in. "What do you need...sorry, I can't remember your name?"

"Remy St. James, sir."

"No need to call me sir. We're pretty laid back around here. Is there something you need?"

"Yeah, I was wondering if it would be okay if I went to dinner with a friend."

He stopped typing and leaned back in his chair. "Are

you expecting me to drive you to meet this *friend*?"

"No, I just wasn't sure what the protocol was and didn't want to do something that would piss anyone off."

"I appreciate you asking. You can do whatever you want in your free time, which there won't be much of, I can assure you. Just be back before we roll out in the morning. Did you only come out here to spend time with this friend?"

"No, sir. It was a coincidence I even ran into her. She was one of the houses I was sent to evacuate. Before that, it had been almost a year since I'd seen her."

"No need to explain all of that." Donnie gave a tight smile. "I only ask because we've had a couple of guys who only came for a free plane ticket. Like I said, you can do what you want in your free time. No one is going to come looking for you if you're not here in the morning."

"I'll be here," I promised.

"Today, we went easy on you. Tomorrow night there will be a skills test so we can see what you're capable of."

"I'm ready to prove myself."

"Good, now go see your lady friend." He chuckled.

"Have a good evening," I said before I closed his office door. Pulling out my phone, I pulled up Stella's name and hit the phone icon to call her. It rang twice before she answered.

"Hello?"

"Are we still on for that dinner you promised me earlier?" I answered in reply.

## THE BOSUN

"Um...yeah, of course." She giggled, and I felt it in my bones. "It got late, and I thought maybe you changed your mind."

"That would never happen. I'm a man of my word. If I say I'm going to do something, I will do my damnedest to do it. Do you by any chance know where Station Nineteen is?"

"I don't, but I don't know where most stuff is here. I have to use my GPS wherever I go. Let me see." Her voice was muffled as she continued to speak. "It says it should only be about thirty minutes from where I am, but I'm not sure if it's taking traffic into account."

"If it would be easier, I can get an Uber and meet you someplace to eat?"

"Are you sure?"

"Positive."

"Okay, do you like Mexican?"

"Love it. Send me the address, and I'll meet you there."

A moment later, a text came in with the address. Looking forward to seeing Stella, I went into the bathroom and slicked my hair back, and sprayed myself with a touch of cologne as I waited for my Uber to arrive.

⚓

Stella walked into the restaurant wearing the same clothes I'd seen her in earlier today. She made a simple pair of cutoff shorts and a t-shirt look downright exotic with the way she filled them out.

The moment she saw me, a bright smile lit up her face, and her steps quickened until she stopped right beside me. Leaning down, she kissed my cheek before moving to sit across from me. "I hope you haven't been waiting too long."

"Not long," I held up my drink that I'd only taken a few sips of.

Clasping her hands together under her chin, her assessing gaze took me in. I was in a pair of cargo shorts and a gray t-shirt. Nothing much, but I hadn't planned on going out while I was here. "I still can't believe you're here. The whole day has seemed surreal. I think I've checked my security cameras at least a hundred times, trying to see if I can see any fire."

"And?" The one thing that killed me was I wasn't given any updates on the fire. I should have asked Donnie before I left, but my only thought had been meeting up with the woman who sat across from me.

"Nothing so far." She sighed and looked sad. "I don't want my house to burn down. Not that anyone does, but it felt so monumental getting there and to have it taken away from me after a few months would be a difficult pill to swallow."

"At least you had somewhere to go." Although I couldn't imagine knowing there might be a chance my house would be gone when I went back to it. "You're at Penelope's house, right?"

"I am. She has a condo that she's never at since she's

## THE BOSUN

always on the road. I'm lucky I have someplace to go because I know there are lots of people who are displaced right now." Her eyes became glassy as she spoke. "On top of all the stress, and then not having any place to go. I feel for them." A tear escaped and slid down her cheek before she brushed it away. "I could use a drink."

I spotted our waiter and signaled to him. After dropping off an order, he came over, devouring Stella with his eyes. "What can I get you, hermosa dama?"

"I'll have a margarita and…" she looked to me, "are you ready to order?"

"Go ahead, and I'll figure it out while you order."

Stella murmured something about a burrito, and our waiter went on to tell her all about his favorite dishes at the restaurant. With each word he spoke, I became angrier. What gave him the assumption she wasn't with me?

Most likely feeling my eyes burning into him, he turned his attention to me. "And what would you like?"

"Well, first, I'd like you to stop eye-fucking my girl here, and second I'll have three of the tacos de fuego."

"I...I meant no…" he stuttered.

"I think you did, so how about you place our orders, and you keep your eyes to yourself for the rest of the night," I gritted out.

"Of course, señor." He walked backward a few steps before turning on his heel and scurrying away.

I wasn't sure how Stella would take the way I reacted to our server. When I looked over at her, I was shocked to see she was biting her lower lip.

"So I'm your girl, huh?" she asked with a raised brow.

"I hope so because I plan to sink into that sweet pussy of yours tonight, and I'd hate for you to be anyone else's when I do that."

"I'm not." Her cheeks pinked up, and I wondered why until she quietly added. "I haven't been with anyone else since Spain."

"I haven't either."

One of her brows quirked up. "Really? I find that hard to believe."

"Do you find it difficult to believe that not a day has gone by since you walked away that I haven't thought of you?"

"How is it we both felt something so strong and yet didn't get each other's numbers?"

"Because Ophelia was being a bitch and lied to you."

"There was her interference."

"But I do think things happened the way they were supposed to in the end. Otherwise, I might not be here right now. If circumstances were different, I might have still been working on charter yachts."

"And I might still be in Oasis living a very unhappy life." The waiter brought Stella her drink and promptly left us. Holding up her drink, Stella clinked it against my glass. "Here's to

## THE BOSUN

fate bringing you to my doorstep."

"To fate," I cheered and took a long pull of my beer.

"How long are you here for?"

"I can't say since no one knows how long it will take to get this fire contained. It could be a week or a month. What I do know is I'd like to spend more time with you while I am here." There were a lot of things I wanted to do to her, and I couldn't wait to get her someplace alone.

"I'd like that, too."

I felt a 'but' in there, but she never spoke it. Instead, she sipped on her margarita until our food came.

"I think he's scared to even look at me now," she whispered after our waiter left.

"Good, he shouldn't have been trying to flirt with you in front of me, to begin with."

"If Brock had done that, it would have pissed me off, but with you, I found it to be quite the opposite."

"Oh, yeah, how's that?" Although I had a pretty good idea going by the way she licked her lips and looked at me with hooded eyes.

"It was hot. I wanted to crawl over the table and jump you." She clapped her hand over her mouth and laughed. "I can't believe I said that. They put a lot of tequila in this." She shook her almost empty glass.

"I like your honesty." Picking up her hand, I kissed her knuckles. "I wouldn't mind you sitting on my lap and going for a ride."

Watching her bite down on her bottom lip, my dick got impossibly hard.

"No one has ever looked at me the way you do." Her words came out in a breathy caress. "Do you think you have time to make a detour to Pen's condo?"

Was she kidding? My dick had been hard since the moment she answered her door. No matter what I'd thought about through the day, I'd had a semi.

"Nothing could keep me away."

"Check," she called. She pulled out a few bills and threw them on the table before she stood up and took my hand in hers. "Ready?"

Her impatience made me laugh as I let her lead me to her car. Her hand left mine the moment the lights flashed, indicating the doors had unlocked.

Sliding inside the plush leather seat, I couldn't help but look around. Back in Florida, I had an old beat-up truck. Seeing her house earlier and being inside her car showed me how different our lives were. It still astounded me that Stella wanted me. She could literally have anyone she wanted. How she was still single after all these months confused me.

"I live like a hermit. The only people I see are my neighbors and Pen when she's around."

"I hadn't realized I'd said that out loud." Hopefully, she didn't hear the rest of what I was thinking.

## THE BOSUN

Her hand came to rest on my arm. "It's okay. I could say the same thing about you. Why are you single?"

"Because I wanted to be." It was true I could have had a relationship with someone or had sex numerous times since I'd last seen Stella, but no one interested me like she had. Maybe if she hadn't been a constant thought, it would have been different, but as I sat in her car, I was happy with the way it worked out.

"Same for me. It has sucked because my neighbor and friend, Lexie, is so in love with her husband it sometimes hurts to think of how alone I am. Pen has a guy. She even had him when we were in Spain. It still didn't force me to go out and date. I think I was waiting for you to magically appear." Even with only the light of the dashboard, I could see her cheeks pink up.

"And here I am. You should get prepared for all the wicked things I'm going to do to you now that we don't have a boat full of people to hear. I want to hear you scream my name over and over again."

"Yes, please." She wiggled her ass in her seat, and I knew she was turned on.

"Drive faster," I demanded. I wasn't sure how much longer I could hold myself back from touching her.

Doing exactly as I asked, Stella sped up, and with each passing building, I swore I could smell her sweet pussy. Fuck, she was so ready for me.

Pulling up to a tall building, she put her car into park. One second, she was behind the wheel, and the next, she was straddling my lap. Her hands went to my hair as she tilted my head back and consumed my mouth in a desperate kiss.

She tasted of tequila, lime, and something that was only Stella. She was intoxicating.

Her hips swiveled, grinding down on my erection and making us both moan. Breaking from the kiss, she panted as she looked down at me. "I wish I had a skirt on. I'd push my panties aside and fuck you right here."

Oh, how I wished the same.

"I think we can manage until we get upstairs, don't you?" Opening my door, I placed my hands on her hips and helped her outside before I slid out myself.

With our fingers laced together, I followed behind Stella in case we came into contact with anyone they wouldn't see my tented shorts. I barely registered my surroundings as she guided us through the lobby and onto the elevator. The moment the doors closed, we were on each other. My hand went up to grab her breast as her leg wrapped around my hip. Our mouths fused together as we all but fucked each other with our clothes on. When the elevator doors dinged open, it was all I could do to break apart from her. I'd forgotten how amazing her body felt.

She ran down the hallway with me following after her. My body pressed to hers as she unlocked the door. My hands roamed over her lush curves, and I couldn't wait to touch every

## THE BOSUN

inch of her skin.

When the door opened, we stumbled inside, laughing until I heard the click of the door lock. Once I heard that sound, I was like an animal stalking after its prey. Pressing her body into the door, I wasted no time removing her clothes. With each piece of clothing removed, I got harder until I thought I was going to explode. My need for her was visceral and all-consuming.

Her hands frantically went to the button of my shorts, undoing it first and then my zipper. She tugged my shorts and boxer briefs down. Stepping out of them, I picked her up and brought her over to the couch, where I laid her down to feast on her.

It was dark except for the moonlight shining in through the sliding glass door, but even with only the small amount of light, I could see the hunger in her eyes.

I stood, removing my remaining clothes, wanting to feel every inch of her skin on mine. Getting down on my knees, I started kissing the arch of one foot while I ran my other hand up the inside of her thigh. Spreading her legs wide, I kissed and nibbled until I reached her soaked center. I could see it glistening in the moonlight, and damn if that didn't turn me on even more.

Dipping my head down, I licked her from her opening up to her clit where I flicked it with my tongue. Stella's back arched as she moaned, her body already writhing under my touch.

"How did I forget how good you taste? I could feast on you for days."

"Please," she begged. I wasn't sure if she was asking me to let her be my meal for the next few days or if she wanted more.

Running my hand between her breasts and over her mound, I used two fingers to hold open her hood as my thumb made slow circles over her clit. I fucked her pussy with my tongue, devouring her as her honey spilled across my lips and tongue, and didn't stop until her entire body was shaking and she was chanting my name like I was her religion.

Placing a kiss on the inside of her thigh, I moved up her body until I was seated fully between her legs.

Throwing her head back, a low moan came from her lips as I slide inside. Her pussy contracted around me, making it hard not to come. Taking a deep breath, I grabbed one of her legs and placed her foot on my shoulder. It was then I started to move. I couldn't hold back any longer. It was a dream come true to have Stella under me, listening to her come undone.

Taking one breast into my mouth, I flicked her nipple as I pistoned inside of her slick heat.

"Oh, Remy," she moaned. "I think I'm going to come again."

Her words were my undoing. Slamming into her, my balls slapped against her ass with each thrust. When my spine began to tingle, I took her leg off my shoulder and placed it on the ground, letting me sink deeper into her.

"Remy," she shouted as her pussy started to squeeze my dick in waves of pleasure. Her nails found purchase in my back

## THE BOSUN

as I drove into her one last time and unloaded inside of her.

My head fell to her shoulder as I caught my breath. Placing a kiss on her neck, I moved to lie on my side, taking Stella with me until I took her spot and Stella was draped on top of me.

Her heavy breaths puffed out, making her hair tickle my chest with each exhale. "I don't think I'll be able to move for the foreseeable future. That was ten times better than on the boat."

"As much as what we experienced back in Spain was good, great even, you're right. What just occurred between us was phenomenal, and it makes me think sex with us will only continue to get better."

Stella hummed. "I like that challenge. I've never felt so blissed out in my life." Her fingers skimmed up my ribcage and along my shoulder, until she was tracing the tattoo I got with my unit when we were on leave. Some days I wished I hadn't gotten it so I wouldn't have the reminder etched into my skin forever, but then there were days like today when it was easy to think of all the good times and the amazing men I served with.

"I'm glad I could be of service." My hands skimmed along her silky skin, making my already semi-erect cock harden further. Leaving her and going back to the station was going to be difficult. After everything, I hoped Stella wouldn't think it was a wham bam, thank you ma'am type thing. If it was up to me, I'd stay here like this with her until she kicked me out.

We lay like that until her breathing slowed, and at one point, I thought she'd fallen asleep until she spoke. "I know you're going to have to leave soon. This has been nice, though." She snuggled further into me, wrapping one leg with mine.

"It has, but just because I have to leave tonight doesn't mean we won't see each other again. I know where you live and have your phone number, and you've got mine. There's no excuse for us this time."

She tilted her head up to look at me with strands of hair all over her face. "I know you're going to be busy, so whenever you can give me your time, I'll take it."

Brushing her hair out of her face, I leaned down and sucked on her lower lip. "You can count on it. I'm not going to let you disappear out of my life again. Now, what do you say we see if I can make it impossible for you to walk until tomorrow?" I swiveled my hips, sliding the tip of my cock through the wetness between her thighs.

Grinning like a cat that ate the canary, she straddled me. "You read my mind."

# THE BOSUN

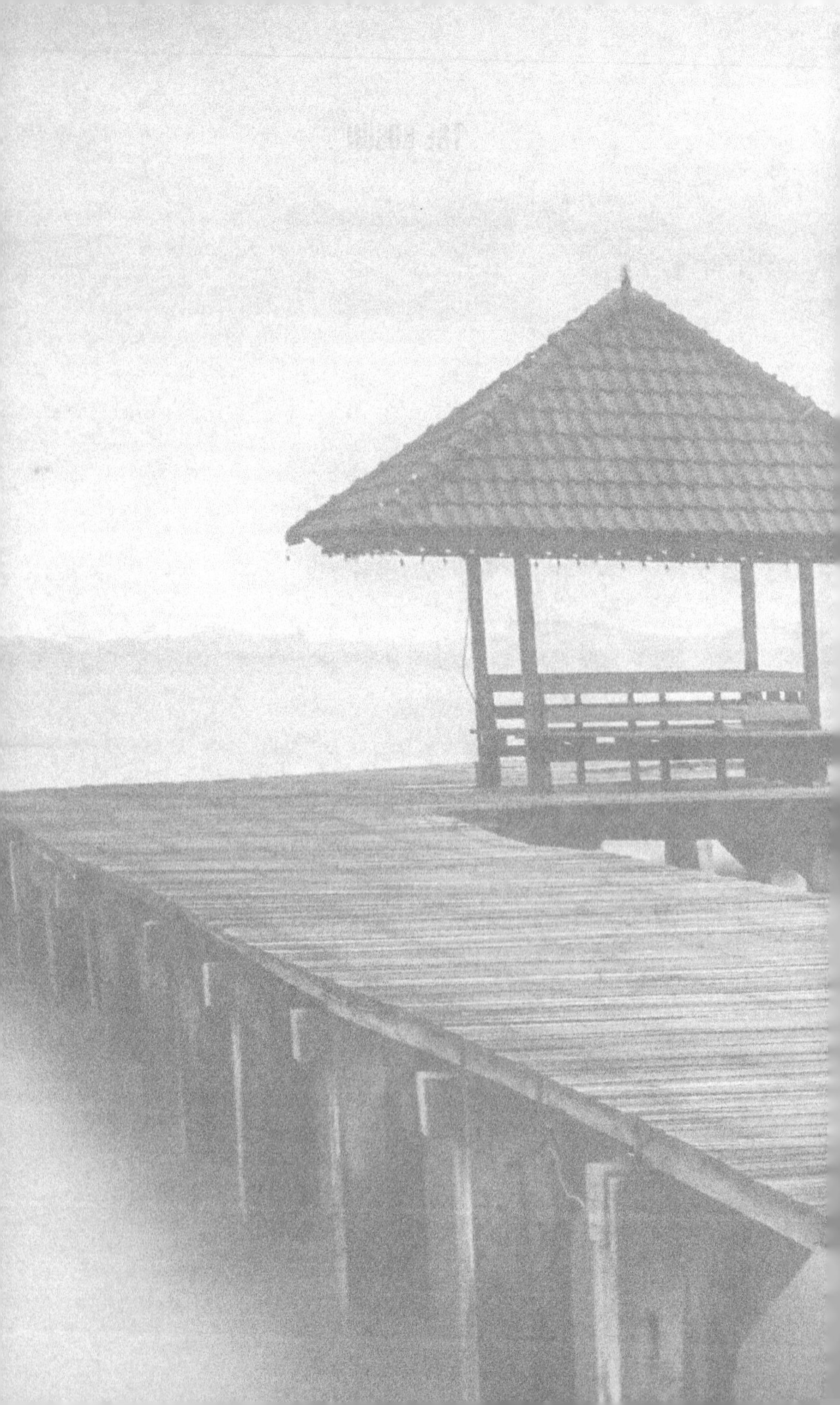

# 17

## STELLA

SPENDING MY NIGHTS with Remy was wonderful. The Earth-shattering sex will make it hard to forget him, but in the back of my head, I was always wondering what was going to happen when he left and went back to Florida. He'd told me all about his dad, and the few times I'd heard him talking to his father, it was sweet the way he'd reassure him he was fine and hadn't been put in any danger that day.

I also didn't know *when* Remy's time here would be up. The fire seemed to be better contained, but I wasn't back in my house yet. I didn't want to risk having to leave again, and Pen's place was much closer to Remy. I didn't want to waste our time driving back and forth when we could be doing other things.

"I can feel you thinking." His voice rumbled through

his chest where I had my head resting.

"I'm always thinking about what I'm going to write next." It wasn't a lie. Usually, I was thinking about what I'd write about the next day, but not when I was with Remy.

"Is there something else on your mind?" The hand that had been sifting through my hair paused at the nape of my neck.

Damn, I guess I wasn't as good at hiding what I was thinking or feeling as I thought. "How did you know?"

He let out a long exhale. "I've been feeling it since we ate at the Mexican restaurant. I let it go then, but I thought eventually you'd tell me what's on your mind."

Rolling onto my front, I crossed my arms over his chest and rested my chin on my arm as I looked up at him. Remy's hair was flopped down over his forehead and sexily tousled from my fingers pulling on it earlier.

"It seems too soon to say anything." My gaze shifted, unable to look at him. Instead, I let my eyes roam over the tattoos on his arm. "I didn't want to run you off before anything got started between us."

"Something started between us back in Spain. It might not have been what we expected, but that something lingered inside both of us during the months we were apart, even though we never thought we'd see the other again. Correct me if I'm wrong."

Lifting my lashes, I found Remy's eyes locked on me. "You're not wrong."

## THE BOSUN

His hand slid from my hair and around to cup the side of my head. "Then it's not too soon for you to tell me whatever it is that's been on your mind for the last week."

"If you say so, but if you run, I'm going to hunt you down and smother you." I cracked a grin to let him know I was only kidding. Kind of, anyway. "I've been wondering what we're doing here. Is this going to end when you go back to Florida? Every night I wonder if it will be our last."

"Oh, my Stella Bella." Remy rolled us until I was on my side, tucked against his warm, toned body, and we were nose to nose. "I can't say how long I'm going to be working here, but I can tell you one thing, I'm not going to be on a plane back to Florida the next day if you're not with me."

I blinked several times as I tried to comprehend what he was saying. "You want me to go to Florida with you?"

"Why not? You can meet my dad and see where I grew up." He said it as if it all made sense to him. "It doesn't have to be difficult. I like you and everything I've learned about you this last week. I hope you feel the same. Since we don't know when I'll be done here, I think we should continue getting to know each other and see how we feel when the time comes."

I already knew I didn't want him to leave, but I couldn't ask Remy to leave his dad behind. I knew how important his dad was to him.

Snuggling closer into his body, I asked. "What do you want to do once you leave California?"

"I want to be a full-time firefighter, but first, I have to take and pass my test. I'm not worried about that part of it, though. What I don't know is where I want to work."

"Do you get to put in a request for which station you want to work at?" I really had no idea how becoming a firefighter worked, but I guess I always thought he'd work at the station he'd trained at.

"Nothing like that. I guess I should have been clearer when I spoke. I don't know if I want to be a firefighter in Florida or in California. I like the guys here, and the station house has an energy about it that speaks to me." His hand moved to start tracing circles on my lower back as he spoke. "While I've known for some time that being a fireman was what I wanted to do, the station I trained at in Florida never felt like home. Not that I don't like the guys there, but I guess I never felt like I fit in, but I've felt the exact opposite since the moment I stepped foot into station nineteen."

"So, you're thinking of staying here?" I tried to tamp down my excitement in case I'd heard him wrong.

"If they'll have me. And maybe a certain special woman I know will also want me to stay."

Pressing my lips to his, I smiled and licked along the seam of his mouth before I spoke. "I do want you to stay. I just wasn't sure we were at the stage where I could ask that of you."

"You're not asking. I want to be here if you and the station will have me." I couldn't contain my smile. "Our relation-

## THE BOSUN

ship isn't normal. We didn't start out normal, and that's okay. Normal is overrated. Our relationship will go at our own pace. I may be younger, but I've been through things you can't imagine. Through all of that, I've learned a lot about myself and to trust my gut. My gut is telling me I'm right where I'm supposed to be." Leaning in, he pressed a kiss to the tip of my nose. "What is yours telling you?"

It was amazing how by opening up to him, Remy was able to push all of my fears to the side. In the short time we'd spent together, I knew I was already falling for him. "That I need to not be afraid of my journey with you, and I can open up to you, and you won't go running for the hills."

"Nothing could make me run from you." His hand started to rub up and down my back while the other played with the loose strands of my hair. It was soothing. Remy St. James was the perfect mix of the tattooed bad boy who was a beast in bed and then a gentle lover afterward.

"That feels good," I murmured sleepily. With each pass of his hand, I could feel my eyes droop a little more until I couldn't hold them open. Each night Remy had to go back to the station, and I never got to sleep in his arms. I only wanted to experience it for a moment, I told myself as I let myself fall asleep.

Startled awake, I blinked as Remy thrashed beside me, moaning in his sleep, sounding hurt and afraid. Placing my hand on his chest, I tried to gently wake him up with no success. I had no idea what to do in this situation. Was I supposed to let him wake up on his own or save him from his dream?

Sitting up on my knees, I shook him harder and was about to throw a glass of water in his face when Remy stopped moving. The sound of his ragged breathing filled the otherwise silent and dark room.

I started to rub my hand up and down his arm, trying to soothe him when Remy jumped out of bed. He seemed lost as he walked around the room a few times before he disappeared into the bathroom. I started to get up to see if he was okay or needed any help, but the click of the door lock had me getting back into bed. Turning on the bedside light, I moved to rest against the headboard and rubbed at my tired eyes while I waited for Remy to come out.

It was hard to calm down, wondering what happened as I worried about him and adrenaline pumped through my veins. More than once, I wanted to get up and knock on the bathroom door, but I held myself back.

Ten minutes later, Remy came out of the bathroom with dark circles under his eyes that looked haunted. "I called an Uber to take me back to the station. It should be here in a few minutes."

Of course, an Uber would get here fast when I didn't want Remy to leave. At least not without first talking to me about what happened.

"I could have driven you back." I sat up straighter against

## THE BOSUN

the headboard, clutching the sheet to my chest. "I still can if you want to talk."

Not looking at me, Remy dressed without saying a word. I didn't understand what was going on. Why was he shutting me out, and what was that dream about? Had he seen something horrific from the fire and didn't want to mention it? Whatever it was had taken its toll on him, going by the way his shoulders were hunched over and the desolate look in his eyes.

"Remy," I called out to him, my voice shaky, "please talk to me. I don't want you to leave like this."

"It's...I can't. Not tonight." He looked at me only for a moment before he looked away again. "Anyway, I need to get back to the station, and we both need to get some sleep."

"I wish you could stay and sleep here." And talk to me.

"You know that's not possible. I need to go." He moved around to my side of the bed and kissed the top of my head. Never once did his eyes meet mine as he spoke. "I'll try to call you tomorrow night, but I might be wiped, so if you don't hear from me, don't be alarmed."

How could he say that? Tomorrow Remy would be placed closer to the line of fire. Of course, I was going to worry about him. Now even more so.

"Remy," I grabbed his hand, not wanting to let him go. With tired eyes, he met my gaze. "Please be careful tomorrow, and if you don't have the energy to call me, then send me a text letting me know you're okay."

His eyes fell to my lips and lingered there before he spoke. "I'll try. Now I really need to go. My ride is waiting for me downstairs." Every word that came out of him sounded like it was coming from a robot. There wasn't a hint of the man I'd come to know there.

I kept my grip on him even as he started to pull away. After being woken up the way I had, I was desperate to touch him in any way I could, wanting to go back to those minutes before I woke up. When my fingers slipped from his, Remy turned on his heel and walked away.

"Be safe," I called out as a tear ran down my cheek.

Without looking back, he replied in the same robotic tone as before, "Always."

# THE BOSUN

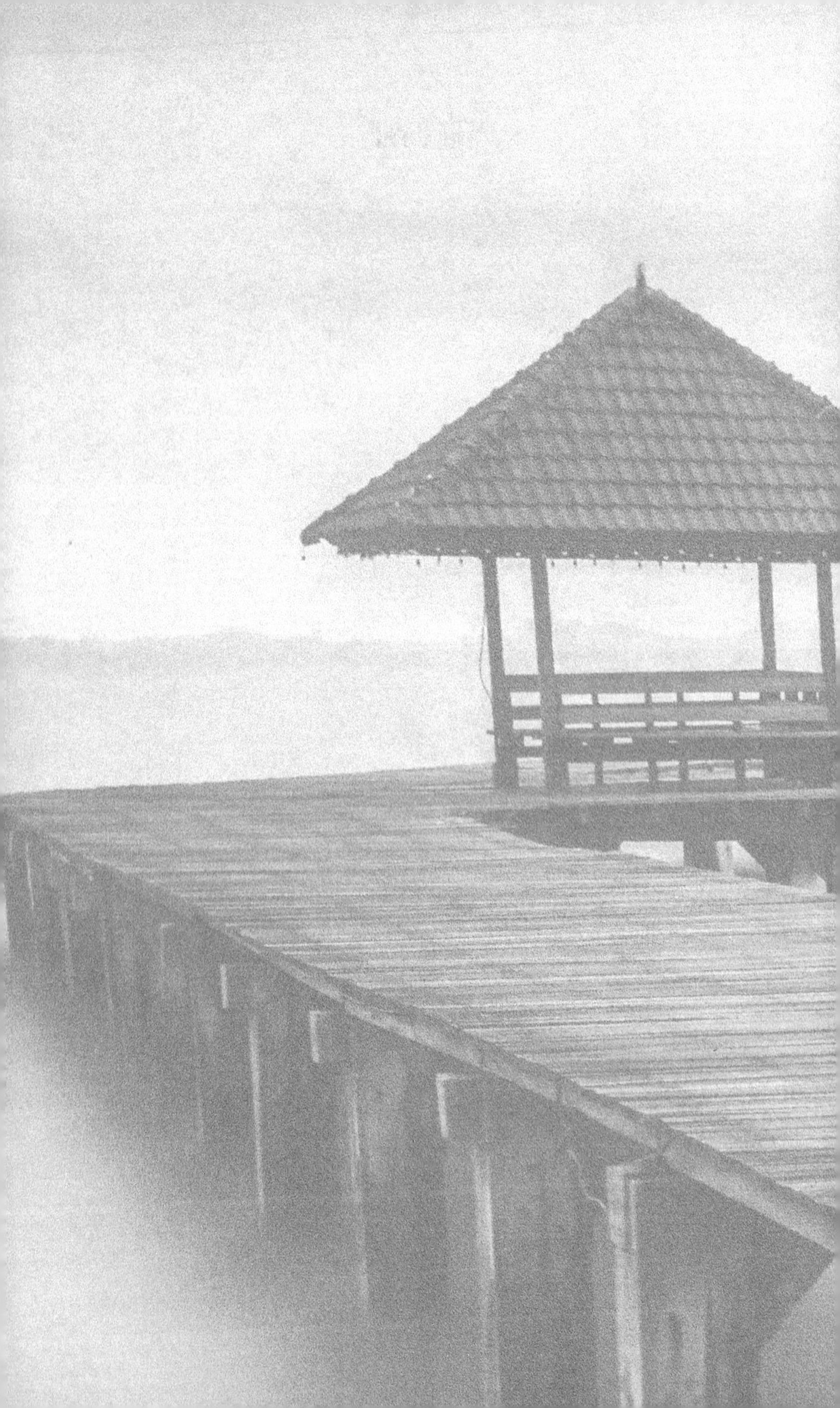

# 18

## REMY

LYING ON MY COT, I knew I should text Stella to let her know I was okay, but the truth was I wasn't okay. I was fine from today, but my dream from last night kept haunting me. Also, I couldn't get the way Stella looked at me when I told her I was leaving out of my head. She'd opened up to me earlier in the night and then I did what I said I wouldn't do, I ran.

Blowing out a breath, I thought back to my call with my therapist. He knew what I'd been through, and I'd hoped he could shed some light on what was going on with me. I'd talked to my dad earlier, and he told me I needed to give Stella my past, but I didn't want to fill her with my darkness.

Dr. Rivera said the same after I explained to him how I

was feeling about Stella, but I couldn't do that to her. He also suggested maybe I wasn't ready for the situation I'd put myself in with volunteering in a life or death situation. We went over some of the exercises that had helped me in the past, and he said to call him day or night if I needed to talk.

I wasn't ready to face the reality that doing the one job I wanted to do might set me back. I was no longer able to suppress what happened when Damon died.

Knowing I needed to open up to Stella about my past and worrying she might not want the damaged man inside kept me from calling her. I couldn't be another man in her life that let her down. First, her father for not accepting the way she looked, and then Brock for using her to make his way through medical school only to cheat on her when she didn't become pregnant with his child. What kind of man did that? And how could I be another man she let into her heart only to break it with the shattered pieces of me I hid from her?

I knew what I needed to do, but I had to wait until I was face to face with her. This wasn't something I could say through a text or over the phone. Tomorrow, I would tell her. For now, I'd send her a message letting her know I was safe and I'd see her the next day.

**Remy: It was a tough day but I'm at the station house and safe.**

**Remy: I'll see you tomorrow.**

**Stella: Thank you for letting me know.**

## THE BOSUN

**I can't wait to see you.**
**Stella: Good night, Remy.**

**Remy: Good night.**

⚓

    Closing my eyes, I willed myself to come up with another alternative to deal with the pain that was trapped inside me. All night and day, all I could think about was how I'd thought I was better and not as damaged as I'd been since the moment Damon died. Even now, knowing it wasn't my fault that he died. The pain of losing him and Tyler all came rushing back after my dream. The only time it went away was when I was working and out risking my life to save others.

    Not wanting to be around others when I saw Stella, I took a taxi to Penelope's condo. My leg bounced the entire way there with nerves about what I was getting ready to do.

    The moment Stella opened the door, and she took me in, her eyes filled with tears. "Come in," she said on a shaky breath as she moved to the side to let me in.

    Following her to the couch where we reunited, I sat down and left a couple of feet separating us. I knew if I felt the heat of her body, I would cave and not do what needed to be done.

    "You look like shit."

    I knew I did. I'd barely slept the night before, and it been a long and difficult day.

    "I guess I look like I feel."

"What's going on with you?" She started to move closer but stopped when I held my hand up.

"Please, I need to say this, and I won't be able to if I can feel your heat or smell your coconut scent."

"Oh." She curled up on her end of the couch with her arms wrapped around her knees. "What is it you want to tell me?"

"After the other night, I realized I'm not who I thought I was. There's so much darkness and pain inside of me just waiting to get out, and I can't let it infect you the way it has me."

Her glassy eyes locked on mine. "What are you talking about? You're not making any sense."

"I thought we could be together. That we'd...but we can't. I'm sorry, Stella, but I won't be another person in your life who tries to ruin the beautiful soul I see shining back at me. I wish your light could cut through my darkness, but no, I'm too damaged." I swallowed the emotion that formed in my throat. The devastation written on her face as she continued to look at me nearly had me changing my mind, but I knew I'd only ruin her, and I wouldn't do that to her.

Standing, I moved until I was in front of her and cupped her face in my hands. "Forget about me and find a man who isn't damaged beyond repair." Leaning down, I closed my eyes and kissed her soft pouty lips one last time.

"Are you breaking up with me?" Her chin trembled a little more with each word she spoke.

Running my hand along her jaw, I soaked in the way she

## THE BOSUN

felt under my touch. "I'm setting you free from the darkness."

She opened her mouth. Surely a protest on her tongue, but I hushed her with a finger.

"Goodbye, Stella. I wish I could have been what you needed." Before she could speak or try to talk me out of what I'd done, I left.

The taxi was waiting for me. I didn't want to go back to the station, but I had nowhere to go. I was alone again. As soon as my time in California was up, I'd go back to my father, who I knew once again would be disappointed in my choice to cut Stella out of my life.

Instead of going inside, I sat out on a bench by the volleyball court and looked up at the stars. It had been months since I'd done that when before it was a nightly occurrence.

I missed the tranquility of it.

As the moon started to head for the horizon, I picked myself up and went inside. What was done was done, and I had to live with it. Even if Stella was the best thing to ever happen to me.

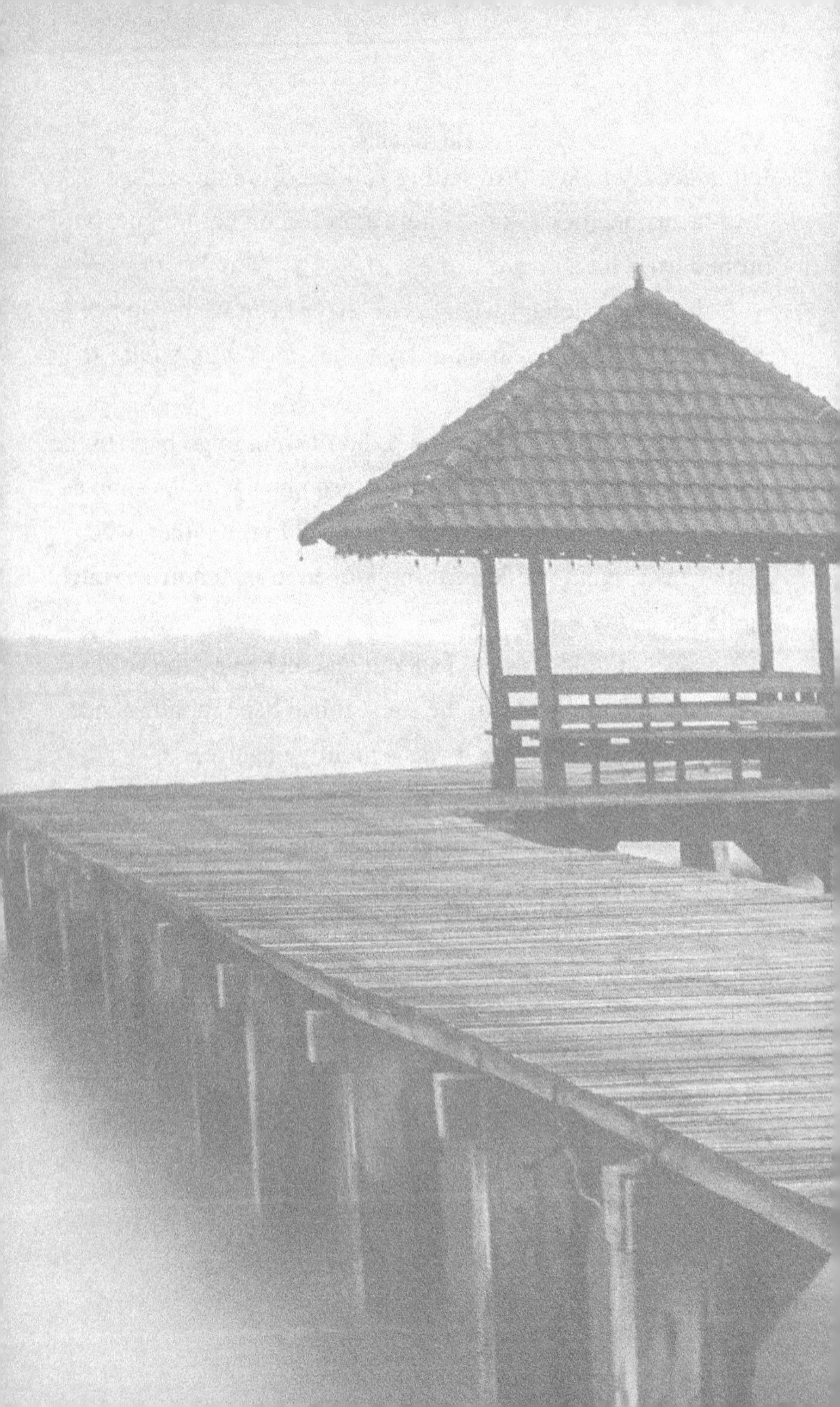

# 19

## STELLA

"WHAT DO YOU MEAN, he broke up with you? I wasn't gone long enough for him to come into your life and walk right back out. I didn't even get to meet the jackass," Lexie growled out as she brushed my matted hair away from my face, reminding me of the time when Remy had done the exact same thing. A new round of tears started.

"Just what I told you," I cried. "He had a nightmare one night, and after that, he wasn't the same. The next time I saw him, he ended it. Something about darkness and light." I hung my head. "I don't know. It doesn't make any sense to me."

I'd run over everything in my head at least a million times since he walked out the door that night over a week ago. I'd tried to text him, but he never responded. Eventually, the messages never even said delivered. I wasn't sure if he turned off his phone or changed his number to avoid me. Either way, I knew then it was over, and there was nothing I could do about it.

"I'm sorry, sweetie. If you had told me how bad it was, I would have come back sooner."

Wrapping my arms around my middle, I tried to hold in the aching pain that was permanently etched into my heart. "I couldn't ask you to skip out on a job because I got my feelings hurt."

"They're more than a little hurt, Stella. You're a wreck." She scooted closer to me on the couch and wrapped an arm around me. "You could have a least called me. I swear you've lost ten pounds while I've been gone, and you look like you haven't slept." Probably because both were true. Food was unappealing, and sleep rarely found me. When I did sleep, I dreamt of Remy walking out on me over and over again. Reliving it every time my eyes closed had me consuming copious amounts of coffee each day.

"Have you talked to Pen yet?" she asked quietly.

"No," my chin wobbled, and I knew I was close to losing it again. When I woke up the next day after crying myself to sleep, I knew I couldn't stay at Pen's place any longer, so I packed everything back in my car and drove home. The worst of the danger was over, and all I wanted to do was be somewhere I wouldn't see Remy everywhere I looked. Once I got home, I fell onto my couch and had been there ever since. It

## THE BOSUN

felt like I hadn't stopped crying since.

"What are you waiting for?"

"I don't want her to leave the tour so she can come and pick up the pieces of my life once again. Pen deserves to be happy, and she's finally found it."

Resting her head to mine, Lexie spoke softly. "She is happy, but she'd still want to know. She's your best friend. How would you feel if Pen and Walker broke up and she didn't tell you?"

"I'd be pissed, but this is different. Remy and I were barely together." My eyes filled with tears, and I tried to rein in my emotions. "It shouldn't hurt this much."

"I know, honey, but it will be okay. Maybe Remy was only put in your life to help you move on, and there's someone else out there who you're meant to be with."

I knew her words were only meant to help, but they didn't. They stung worse than any other thoughts I'd had since the breakup. I wasn't sure if I could put myself out there again for another man to trample on my heart.

"Why don't I draw you up a hot bath and maybe make you some tea? I think that'll make you feel better."

She was probably right. A nice shower or bath always made things better. Even if it was only a small amount, it would be better than nothing.

"That would be nice. Thank you for coming over here to check in on me. I know I can't mope around and cry forever."

She stood and helped me up before guiding me to my bathroom. "It's okay to be sad. You saw something in him that spoke to your heart."

"What if I never find someone? Am I destined to be alone for the rest of my life? Maybe I should get a cat and start hoarding them now."

Lexie turned on the water and tested it before adding some oils to it and looked to me. "I can't say when you'll find your someone, but he's out there. I know he is. He has to be because you deserve to be loved."

I wanted to believe her, but it was hard when I couldn't understand why Remy had ended things.

Stepping to me, Lexie took me in her arms and gave me a big hug. "Get in the water, and I'll bring you your tea when it's ready, okay?"

All I could do was nod and hug her back. Once I was alone in the bathroom, I stood in front of the mirror and took in my disheveled state. I was a mess with my hair all tangled, looking like a bird had started a nest in it. My eyes were red-rimmed with dark circles underneath them, and my skin was pale.

Doing as ordered, I removed my clothes and threw them in the trash, not wanting to see them again.

Slowly, I lowered myself into the steaming water. With each inch submerged, I felt my body relax a little more until only a small amount of my shoulders and head were above water. The smell of lavender filled the room, further relaxing me

## THE BOSUN

until all thoughts seized. I was only in the here and now.

A few minutes later, Lexie came in and crouched beside the tub. She spoke quietly, as if she was afraid she might break the peaceful bubble I found myself in. "Do you want me to stay?"

Keeping my eyes closed, I spoke just as quietly. "You can go. Thank you for everything you've done. I already feel better. Once I get out of here, I'm going to sleep, but I'll call you whenever I wake up."

"If you're sure," she said lightly.

"I am." I nodded and felt little waves of water lap at my neck.

"Okay, I'll lock your door and talk to you tomorrow. If you need anything at all, Ryder and I are here for you."

Cracking one eye open, I raised my hand and patted the hand she had perched on the side of the tub. "I know you are. Thank you again. I really needed this."

She patted my hand with her other one before she stood and left. Sitting up a little more, I took a sip of the tea Lexie had made for me. It warmed my insides just as the water was doing to the rest of my body, making me relax even further. Sinking deeper into the water until only my face wasn't submerged, I closed my eyes again and took in the smell of lavender. All of it combined was enough to have me fall asleep in the water.

Not wanting to drown from heartache, I decided to get out. After drying myself off, I wrapped my fluffy towel around me, took my tea, and got into bed. Taking another sip of tea, I lay down and pulled my comforter up to my chin, letting the warmth from my bath, tea, and blanket lull me to sleep.

Waking up to darkness, I had no idea how long I'd slept. My phone wasn't on my bedside table, and the curtains were drawn tight so as to not let in any light. What I did know was I felt better. Did I still feel sad over Remy? Yes, I wasn't sure when or if that ache would ever go away, but I'd live. I knew I had to get back to living my life the best way I knew how and that involved calling my best friend to let her know my heart had been broken but I was okay, get back to writing my book, and finding some food because I was starving.

Getting out of bed, I got ready and pulled my still messy hair into a bun, so I didn't scare any of the patrons at our local coffee shop. I walked along the beach from my house with my laptop in hand as I traveled down to The Dream Bean. It was only about a ten-minute walk, but feeling the sun on my face for only a few minutes along with the sleep had done me wonders.

I bought their biggest coffee and a blueberry muffin to devour and took them outside on their back patio to watch a group of guys play volleyball. Once I finished my coffee, I went inside to get another. Getting comfortable, I opened my laptop and read the last bit of what I'd previously written since it had been so long. After catching myself up, I placed my fingers on the keys and started to type. I wrote without a break; it was long enough for my coffee to go cold and the sun

## THE BOSUN

to dramatically shift in the sky. I couldn't remember the last time I'd written three chapters in one sitting. I would have kept going if my laptop hadn't flashed a notification to let me know its battery was almost dead.

With each minute of the day that passed since I woke up, I felt more and more like myself. How could I let a man almost ruin me? Again? Picking up my laptop and cold coffee, I vowed to myself I'd never let a man wreck me or break my heart again.

As I got close to my house, I saw Lexie, Ryder, and their daughter out on the beach splashing in the water. I could hear Delilah's squeals each time the water went over her feet, making me smile. I wasn't sure why seeing them out there together now over all the other times I'd seen them made me want a family more than any other, but it did.

I waved to them, not wanting to interrupt their family time as I went up the walk to my place. Once again, I was hungry with no food in my house. The muffin I'd had earlier wasn't cutting it after so many days without food. Pulling out my phone, I pulled up my favorite Chinese restaurant, deciding I'd treat myself to a feast. My finger hovered over the order button when I heard a knock on my sliding glass door. Lexie rarely came to the front door. It was kind of how we knew it wasn't a salesman. I didn't bother getting up, knowing she'd let herself in.

"You look better."

Looking over at her, I smiled. "I feel better. I was getting ready to make a big order at Yin Chang. I didn't want to bother you guys, but I should have asked if you all wanted to join me. Do you want anything?"

"We already ate, but thanks for asking. I just wanted to come over and check on you. I saw you had your laptop with you, so…" She paused, waiting to see if I would finish the thought.

"I went to get coffee and breakfast down at The Dream Bean when I realized I had no food. I have no idea how long I was there. Not once did I look at the time, but I wrote three chapters." I leaned back into the cushion of my couch with a happy smile on my face. "I can't remember the last time it was that easy to get down my words. When I woke up today...I felt like a new woman. Something inside of me changed. I'm not saying I'm not still sad because I am, but I know I'm going to get through this. I'm going to write this book, and then I'm going to look into starting a family of my own. When I close my eyes, I can see myself holding a little baby in my arms."

Rushing over to me, Lexie plopped down beside me and hugged me to her sides. "This is good news." She shook me a little, making me laugh as I hugged her back. "I have to say I was worried about you. I even thought about calling Pen."

"I'll call her after I eat." Starving, I woke up my phone. "If you're sure you don't want any Chinese, I'm going to get my order going."

## THE BOSUN

"I'm positive. Ryder made Delilah and me some amazing chicken Alfredo, and I'm stuffed. That's why we were out on the beach. I was trying to work off some of it."

"And what did your poor husband eat?" I felt bad for him when he'd watch us all eat whatever our hearts desired while he stuck to a regimen of almost all chicken and vegetables.

"He actually had a tiny portion of the noodles and sauce, and then he had a chicken breast and broccoli." She let out a dreamy sigh. "I don't know how he does it, but I admire his dedication to his body. I worship it nightly."

I bet she did.

"Soon, you'll be pregnant with baby number two if you're not already."

"I don't know. You can never tell how long it will take once you stop taking birth control, but it doesn't matter to me because I'll have fun trying to get pregnant all the same." Getting up from the couch, Lexie looked outside. Probably to where her family was still out playing on the beach. "Now that I know you're doing okay, I'm going to get back to them. Even though the air isn't too bad, I still don't want Delilah out in it too much."

I understood that. Who knew what it might do to her little lungs?

"But if you need anything, and I mean anything, you know where to find me. Day or night, you know I got you."

Even more than when we met, I knew I was one lucky bitch

to get Lexie and her family as my neighbors. She was the best.

Standing from my perch on the couch, I gave her a big hug. "I feel like I'm always saying this on repeat with you, but thank you. Don't bother to hesitate to call me if you need anything. In fact, if you and Ryder want to go out or have a night alone, I'd love to watch Delilah for you."

"We'll definitely take you up on babysitting." Opening the sliding glass door, she looked over her shoulder. "Enjoy your Chinese. Next time you plan to order the entire menu, let me know, and I'll join you."

"Deal," I laughed. "At least I have a good excuse. I need the leftovers since I have no food in my house."

"You never need to have an excuse for ordering from there. If I could, I'd eat it every day, but then my husband would probably kill me. It's one of his only food weaknesses."

I tapped my temple. "I'll remember that."

"Enjoy the rest of your night, and congrats on your chapters. If you keep that up, you'll have your book finished in no time," she said before she closed the door and walked back to her family.

My fingers were already itching to get back to hitting the keys on my keyboard. Maybe if I was lucky, I could write another chapter before my food got here.

Taking one final look at my neighbors as Ryder ran through the water with Delilah on his shoulders, I let out a sigh.

Soon.

## THE BOSUN
Soon I'd have something like that—minus the dad.

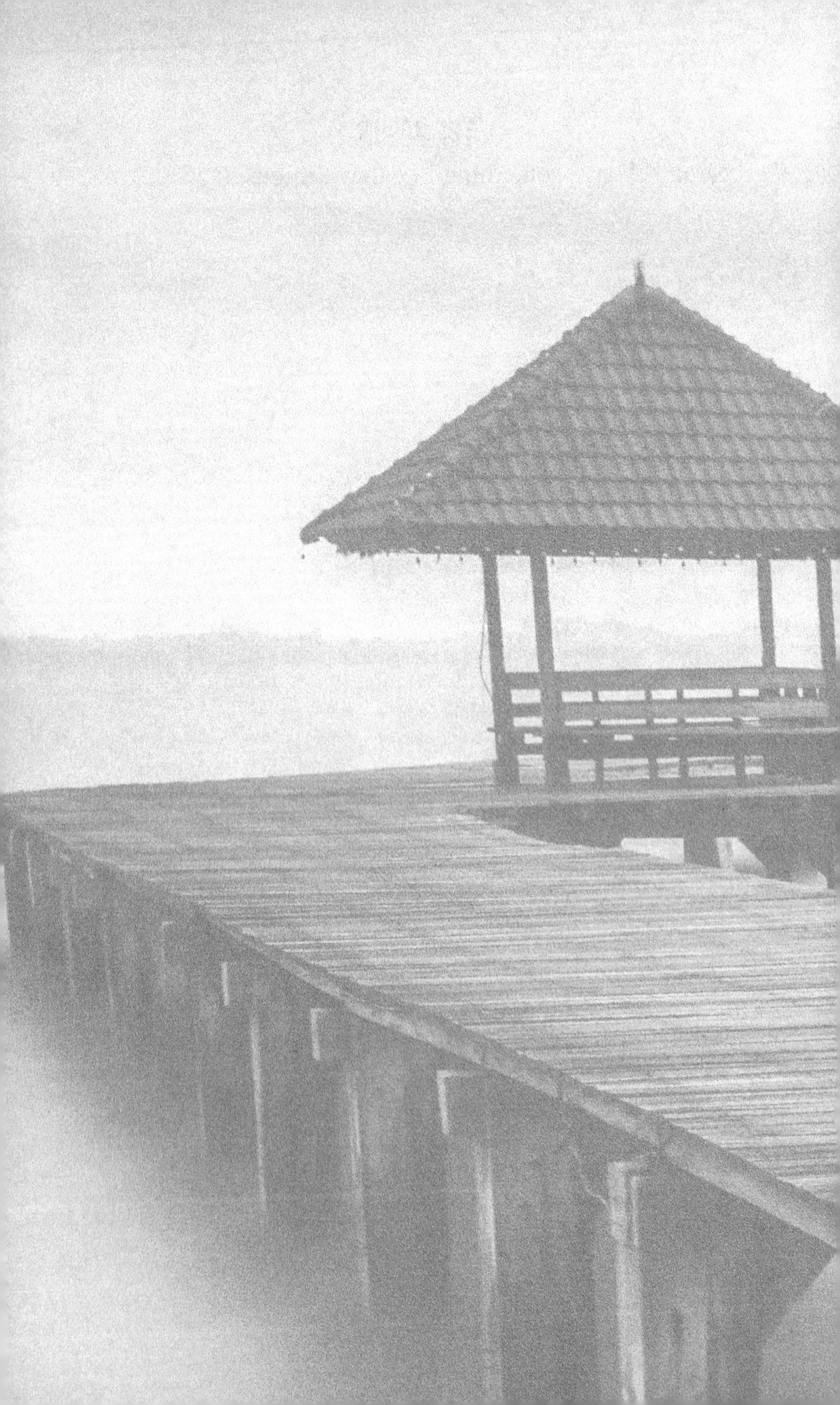

# 20

## REMY

"YOU DON'T LOOK like a guy who passed his test," Eric said as he sat on the stool beside me.

I shrugged and finished off my drink.

"How long are you going to mope about this girl? You've been back a month, and every time I see you, you look like someone kicked your puppy."

"I guess when I stop thinking about her every second that I'm not working or studying. Now that I don't have to study, I guess I'll have more time on my hands to try and get over her."

Eric let out a frustrated huff before he lifted two fingers in the air and then motioned down to my beer. A few moments later, the bartender set a beer down in front of each of us.

"From what you told me, which isn't much I might

add, you're the one that broke up with her. There had to be a reason." He took a sip of his beer and then placed both elbows on the sticky bar, not seeming to care what he was sticking to. "Why did you cut things off with this woman if you're so hung up on her, huh? Did she cheat on you?"

Narrowing my eyes at him, I growled. "Stella did absolutely nothing wrong. It was all me. I was the stupid motherfucker."

Turning on his stool, Eric squared his shoulders as he took me in. "Why the fuck did you cheat on her if you like her so damn much?"

"I didn't cheat on her asshole. That's not who I am." Never in a thousand years would I cheat on Stella, not after what she told me her ex-husband had done.

"Then what did you do to fuck up so royally?"

Closing my eyes, I tried to center myself even though I knew it wouldn't do much good. "I'm not good enough for her, plain and simple."

"Why do you say that? Women seem to gravitate toward you wherever you go. You've got to have something they like."

His words made me chuckle. It was obvious Eric didn't usually have these types of conversations, so it was something he was trying with me.

"I have no problem getting women. That's not the problem. I saw some things when I was deployed no person should ever have to see" Looking straight ahead, I told Eric the whole story.

## THE BOSUN

Eric clapped a hand on my shoulder and gave me a tight smile. "You don't have to keep talking if you don't want to, man. I've heard nightmare stories from buddies who've been over there."

I nodded that I heard him, but I kept going. "If it wasn't for another guy in my unit, I probably wouldn't be here right now. He saved me one day when my mind wasn't on the mission. After not resisting, I decided to make some easy cash by working on yachts."

Eric's brows rose. "Yachts, really? What are you doing here then?"

"My life doesn't feel right unless I'm helping people, and as much as working on boats helped me not think about my past, it wasn't fulfilling. Anyway, one morning when I was alone, I was on Instagram checking to see if Stella had posted anything new and decided to see how Tyler, the guy who saved me, was doing. He posted as often as possible, and it helped keep me connected with the guys still over there. When I went to his account, I found out he'd died over there." Picking up my beer, I slammed the whole thing and still wanted more. I signaled for the bartender to bring me another while I stared down at my empty beer bottle, running my fingertip around the edge of the lip. "The guilt of not being there for him the way he was for me was tough. I knew then my time on the boats was over after that season. I'd wanted to be a fireman before, but something was holding me back. After that day, I knew

I couldn't wait any longer. I needed to be out there helping people instead of hiding out in Spain."

"Fuck, that's tough, man. I had no idea." His mouth turned down as he picked at the label on his bottle of beer. "So, what happened?"

"I had a nightmare while in bed with her and kind of freaked out. I knew I wasn't as put together as I thought I was. Stella deserves so much more than me, so I broke it off before I ended up damaging her."

"Don't you think you should have given her the choice?" His face turned serious, and I wasn't sure if I was going to like what he said or not. "I'm not saying I believe it, but maybe she's the one to heal you."

Eric was probably right. They all were. If I'd told Stella about my dream and what occurred while I was deployed, she probably would have understood why I needed some time to myself, but there was a constant nagging in the back of my head saying I might never be over the trauma of Damon's death.

"What if I'm the one to fuck her up beyond all recognition?" I choked out, barely more than a whisper.

"Because that's how you see yourself?" I gave him a one-shoulder shrug. "I didn't know you before, but I do know you now, and you're a great guy when you're not moping around. You're never going to be the man you were before you left. Everyone changes, but you changed even more so while

## THE BOSUN

you were gone. That's okay. She didn't know you then. She knows the Remy you are today, and I think she liked what she saw."

"You make it sound so easy, but you didn't see the hurt in her eyes when I left."

"No, I didn't, but if it has you so torn up about it, you should rectify the matter."

He was right. I did want to fix the wrong I'd made, but the thought of what if it happened again kept me from reaching out to her.

"I need to give us more time."

Eric shook his head in annoyance. "What for?" he asked as if I needed a brain transplant.

"Time for her wound to heal and time for me to make sure I don't hurt her again."

"Don't wait too long. If you do, she'll be healed and leave you in the dust when she finds another man."

If Stella got over me and found someone else before I was whole, it would be my retribution for Damon and Tyler's lives.

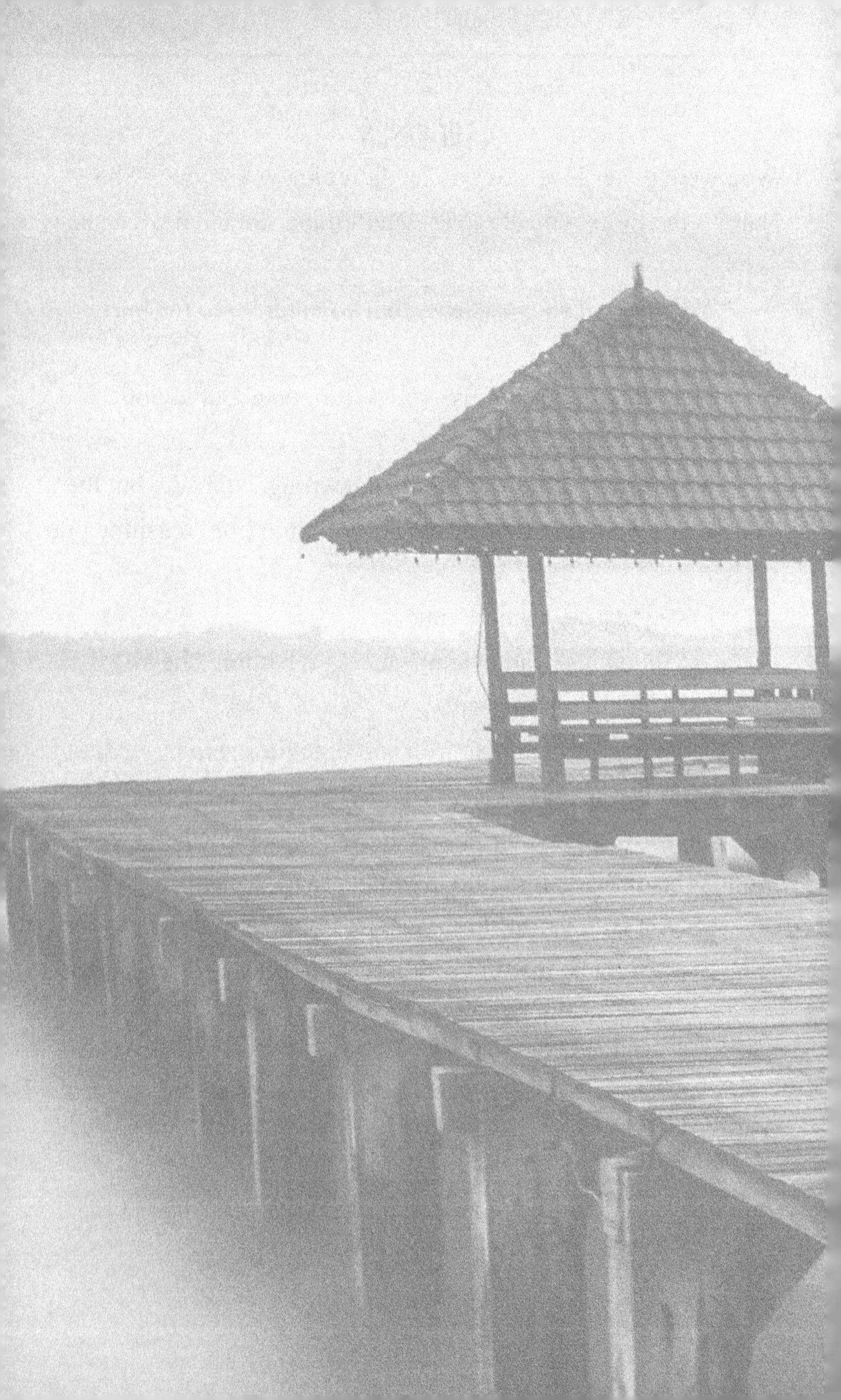

# 21

## STELLA

TURNING MY FACE to the heated wind, I closed my eyes and tried to tamp down the urge to spew my breakfast all over the ground in front of everyone.

"Stella, are you okay?" Lexie called from behind me.

Holding up my hand for her to give me a minute, I tried to nod but instead shook my head.

"Hey, babe," Ryder called out. "Let's go inside and cool off. You've already got some great shots out here. You two can take a break and collect yourselves."

"That's a good idea. We can look over the shots I've already got and talk about what we want to do next. Does that sound okay to you, Stella?"

While I didn't want to go inside, it was better than standing out here with the sun beating down on me. What I really wanted was to go back to my house, crawl into my cool bed, and stay there until the nausea that had plagued me for the last two days subsided.

"I'm coming." I swallowed thickly around the saliva that had worked itself up into my throat and walked slowly to the open door.

Ryder was waiting for me with a cold bottle of water in his hand. "Here," he handed it over. "You look like you could use this."

"Thanks. I'm not feeling too great. I don't know if it was some bad takeout the other day or what, but I can't seem to move past it."

"Why don't you sit down? I'll load these up to my laptop, and bring it to you once I'm done." With her hand between my shoulder blades, Lexie all but pushed me over to the couch.

Leaning back onto the cool leather couch, I placed the water bottle to the nape of my neck to try and cool myself off quicker. I watched as Ryder went to the baby monitor to check on Delilah.

It wasn't long before Lexie came back into the room with her computer in hand. She sat down beside me and then placed the back of her hand to my forehead. "You don't feel hot. Do you think you're getting sick?"

"I don't know. I've felt off for at least a week, and then this nausea that won't subside for the last two days. The only thing I've been able to keep down is crackers and ginger ale."

## THE BOSUN

She bit the inside of her cheek and then glanced over to her husband. "How have you felt off?"

Rolling my head to the side as it rested on the cushion to look at her better, I answered her as best I could. I was dumbfounded by the way I'd been feeling. I was up and down from one minute to the next. "I've been overly emotional. I swear the littlest things make me cry. Yesterday, I cried while I wrote an entire chapter, and it wasn't even sad." My head shook, unable to understand what was going on with me. "My boobs are all of a sudden about ready to spill out of every bra I own."

Her eyes went to my breasts and back up to my face. "I didn't want to say anything, but yeah, they do seem bigger. I thought maybe you're about ready to get your period."

*My period.*

"I...I can't remember when my last one was. I'd have to look at my calendar, but it does seem…" My eyes went wide. "I think I'm late."

What was I going to do if I was pregnant with Remy's baby and how had it not occurred to me until Lexie hinted at it?

"Really?" She sat up straighter—a glimmer in her eyes. "I know you might not be ready, but…" She leaned in closer and whispered, "I do have some pregnancy tests in my bathroom. I brought them this morning and plan to take one tomorrow morning."

"Are you serious?" Could it be possible that Lexie and I might be pregnant at the same time?

"Yes, but don't tell Ryder. I want to surprise him tomorrow night. His mom is going to take Delilah, and we're going to have a little date." She shimmied her shoulders, making me laugh.

"Have fun."

"We always do. So, what do you say we go upstairs, and you take a test, or you can go home, and I'll bring it over to you that way Ryder won't get suspicious?"

It was cute that she wanted to surprise him.

"How could I?"

"Please tell me I don't have to explain the birds and the bees to you," she laughed. "Did you always use protection?"

Not always. There were times when we were too excited and barely made it through the door before he was deep inside of me.

"Not always," I admitted. "It could be possible."

The thought I might be pregnant had butterflies taking flight in my tumultuous stomach.

Jumping up, I started for the door. "I'll meet you over at my house. I'll see you later, Ryder. Have fun tomorrow," I called.

"Bye, Stella. I hope you feel better soon." He waved.

Hurriedly I made my way over to my house and left the door ajar for when Lexie came over. The need to pee suddenly came over me, but I knew I needed to hold it. Otherwise, I'd either have to wait a few hours or chug a lot of water. Wanting to distract myself, I went over to the counter where I'd left

## THE BOSUN

my phone before I went next door to do a photoshoot for my website and headshots. Picking up my phone, I let myself have a few minutes of looking at the pictures of Remy and me that we'd taken during our short time at Pen's place. Most of them were of us in bed with me snuggled up to his side, but there were a few of us while we were out to dinner. In a way, I was sad I didn't have any pictures or many memories of us at my house. It was probably a blessing I didn't, though.

Was it possible I was pregnant? Sure, we'd gone without protection a couple of times, but until now, the thought never occurred to me. What was I going to do if I was? I knew I'd need to tell Remy, even if I wasn't sure he'd want anything to do with me or the baby.

"Knock, knock," Lexie called as she stepped inside and walked over to where I stood with her brows pulled down. "You were like a million miles away. Are you okay?"

"I think so. I was just thinking about Remy. How could I have been stupid enough to have unprotected sex with him?" I asked as I stared down at a picture of us. He had one thick arm wrapped around me. The other was holding the camera as he nuzzled into my neck. We both had the biggest smiles on our faces. Of course, I didn't know he was going to break things off in a matter of days when the picture was taken either. Did he already know what he was about to do to me?

Break my heart.

"You can't beat yourself up about it. Here." She thrust a

box at me. "Go take this, and then we'll talk about what to do once you know if you're pregnant or not."

She was right. There was no sense in going down that rabbit hole if there was no need.

"I'll be right back," I murmured as I stared down at the box in my hand. One little test could change the course of my life forever.

"I'll be right here waiting for you unless you want me to accompany you to the bathroom." The corners of her mouth tipped up. I knew if I needed her to, Lexie would indeed come into the bathroom with me, but I could do this. The idea was both terrifying and exciting. I'd known for a long time I wanted to be a mother, but I thought the chance to carry my own child was slim to zero after all the years of trying with Brock.

I took my stairs two at a time in my rush to take the test. I might not have been sure of how Remy would react if I was, in fact carrying his child, but I would cherish the blessing if I happened to be growing a life inside of me.

After peeing on the stick, I laid it on the box and took it downstairs to wait the longest three minutes of my life. Lexie had her back leaned up against my kitchen counter as she watched me come back into the room.

Gently, I placed the box on the island and stared down at the test, waiting for any sign it was working.

"I can tell you from experience the wait is excruciating. Why don't we sit down while we wait? I set a timer the minute

## THE BOSUN

I heard you coming downstairs."

I hadn't even thought about a timer. My plan was to watch the damn thing until something happened.

"Good idea." I shook my hands out and started to pace around the kitchen. There was no way I could just stand there and watch, but I also couldn't sit down. My body was too amped up.

"You know Ryder and I weren't together when I found out I was pregnant," she said, eyes locked on me.

"What?" I stopped dead in my tracks. I'd thought they'd been together from their very first hookup, but traveling had kept them apart.

"Yeah, it was a whole huge misunderstanding, and then I couldn't get a hold of him. I had to set up this big elaborate way to get into contact with him just to tell him." Lexie went on to tell me everything that had happened to them. Would Remy feel the same way?

The timer went off on Lexie's phone, and all of a sudden, I was too scared to look. I'd appreciated her distracting me while we waited, but now that it was time, I wasn't sure I was ready to be disappointed if the test showed I wasn't pregnant.

Squeezing my eyes shut, I braced my hands on the island top. "I can't look."

The sound of Lexie moving had me squinting one eye open. She had a blinding smile on her face as she came toward me. "Are you sure you don't want to look?"

"Did you by any chance peak at it?" There was no hiding the hope in my voice. I wanted that smile to mean I was, in fact, pregnant.

"I might have." She winked.

"Then tell me already!" I yelled while moving around to look for myself. I couldn't stand the suspense. Lexie backed out of the way as I barreled around the corner.

Picking up the test, I saw two faint blue lines. "Does this mean what I think it does?" I glanced up at her and then back to the stick.

"It does. You're pregnant!" She shrieked in happiness. Grabbing each other by the shoulders, we jumped up and down while laughing and me yelling I was pregnant over and over again.

"I can't believe this," I panted out, still holding onto Lexie for dear life. "We've got to call Pen. She's going to be so upset she missed this."

"FaceTime her," Lexie said as she handed me my phone. What would I do without her?

"I don't even know what time it is where she's at or where she is. It doesn't matter. She'll want to know no matter what." Hitting the button to FaceTime Pen, I was smiling so hard, I thought my face was going to split in two.

"Hello?" she answered, all groggy. Wherever she was, it was barely lit, but from the small amount of light, I could see her hair was a mess, and her eyes were barely open.

## THE BOSUN

"Pen, you're never going to believe what just happened!" I shrieked, unable to hide my happiness.

Her eyes flew open, and I heard a male groan. "What is going on?" Walker said, his voice raspy with sleep.

"I don't know. Stella just called me, and she's yelling. Go back to sleep." She kissed his cheek before she climbed out of bed. Her finger was to her lips as she left the room. There was a click of a door being closed, and then she flicked on a lamp. "What's going on? It's the middle of the night here."

"I'm sorry about the time, but I thought my best friend in the whole wide world would want to know that I'm pregnant." I rolled my lips and pressed down as I waited for her response.

"What? You're pregnant!" All I could do was nod as she squealed. "Oh my god. Are you happy?"

"Beyond happy."

"You've wanted to be a mom for so long!" She clapped and then looked to her left before she spoke quietly. "Is Remy the father?"

I leveled her with an annoyed stare. "You're not missing out on that much of my life. If I had sex with anyone else, you'd know about it."

"Have you told him yet?"

I shook my head. "I literally just took the test a few minutes ago. I told Lexie how I was feeling off, and she made me realize my period was late."

"Hey, Pen," Lexie moved around me and rested her chin on

my shoulder.

"Hey," Pen replied before her face crumpled. "I can't believe I missed it. I'm sorry. I'm the worst best friend in the world. I promise I'll make it up to you when I get back, which is only a couple more weeks. We can go baby clothes shopping, and I'll help you decorate the nursery."

"It's okay. You're not really missing anything. I called you the second I found out, and you'll be here before we know it."

She wiped under her eyes, making my mouth turn down. "When are you going to call him? Or are you going to tell him?"

"Of course, I'm going to tell him. Even if he broke my heart, I'd never do that to him or our baby. They deserve to know each other if he wants to."

"I think you need to find out where he lives and drag his ass back to California," Lexie chimed in.

"What if he doesn't want to have anything to do with me anymore?" I questioned. Not for the first time, I tried to wrap my head around his nightmare and if it was the reason he'd ended things.

"You won't know until you try to reach out to him again. If you show up on his doorstep, he's not going to slam the door in your face," Pen added onto Lexie's idea.

"Let's do a background search on him and find out where he lives. If we can find an address, then you have to go there and tell him. Where's your laptop?" Lexie asked as she looked

## THE BOSUN

around my kitchen.

"It's in my office." Before I could say anything more, she left the room. Leaning closer to my phone, I watched as Pen did the same. "It's been almost two months, and he hasn't reached out to me. If he was regretting his decision to end things surely, he'd have reached out to me by now. He has my number this time," I pointed out.

"How do you feel about him now?" She tilted her head to the side as she asked.

"I miss him, but it doesn't hurt as bad. And I want him in my baby's life."

"But do you want him in *your* life? Do you want him in your bed?"

"Most days, but I don't want to drag him here only for him to leave again. I can't do that to myself again."

"Okay, then you need to go to Florida and find out why he ended things the way he did. If it's because he's a stupid guy, then give him the news and say he can be in the child's life as little or as much as he wants, and leave it up to him."

"She's right," Lexie called as she walked back into the room with my laptop and browser open. "I didn't want you to change your mind, so I already did the search."

"Already? That's fast and scary. I don't want someone to be able to search my home address up that fast."

"One thing at a time. Did you find an address?" Pen asked.

"I did, and I already looked up flight info."

"Okay, you're scary good at this. Have you done it before?"

"No," she laughed and shook her head. "I book plane tickets all the time, but I don't make it a habit to do background checks on people."

"Sure, you don't," Pen laughed. "Did you by any chance already book her a flight?"

Lexie looked at the computer screen and then at me as she bit her lip. "I may have."

"Oh my god, you two are going to be the death of me." Lexie set my laptop down in front of me and rushed to get out of the way as if she was afraid I'd hit her. I blinked a few times at the date and time that was on the page. She had me flying out at the ass crack of dawn tomorrow morning. "Tomorrow? Couldn't you give me a little time to figure out what I want to say?"

"That's what the flight is for," Lexie smirked.

I turned to glare at her but stopped when I saw her hand lightly pressed to her belly. I couldn't believe there was a chance we'd be pregnant at the same time. Seeing her like that instantly thawed me out. "No, I'll be sleeping because I'll have to get up at four in the morning to make my flight."

"You'll figure out what you want to say *after* you hear him out," Pen instructed. "And I want you to call me after you see him. I don't care about the time." She let out a huge yawn, reminding me we'd woken her up.

"I will," I promised. "I'll let you go so you can get back to

## THE BOSUN

sleep."

"As if I'll sleep now. I'm so excited I'm going to be an auntie," she squealed and then looked over her shoulder. "Walker is leaning against the bedroom door, looking at me like I'm crazy, so I should probably go." She pointed at her phone. "Call me tomorrow, so I'll know if I need to go kick his ass when I get back."

"I will," I laughed, knowing she would kick Remy's ass if he broke me again. "Bye." I blew her a kiss before hanging up.

"Now, let's go pick out an outfit that's going to make Remy St. James rue the day he walked away from you."

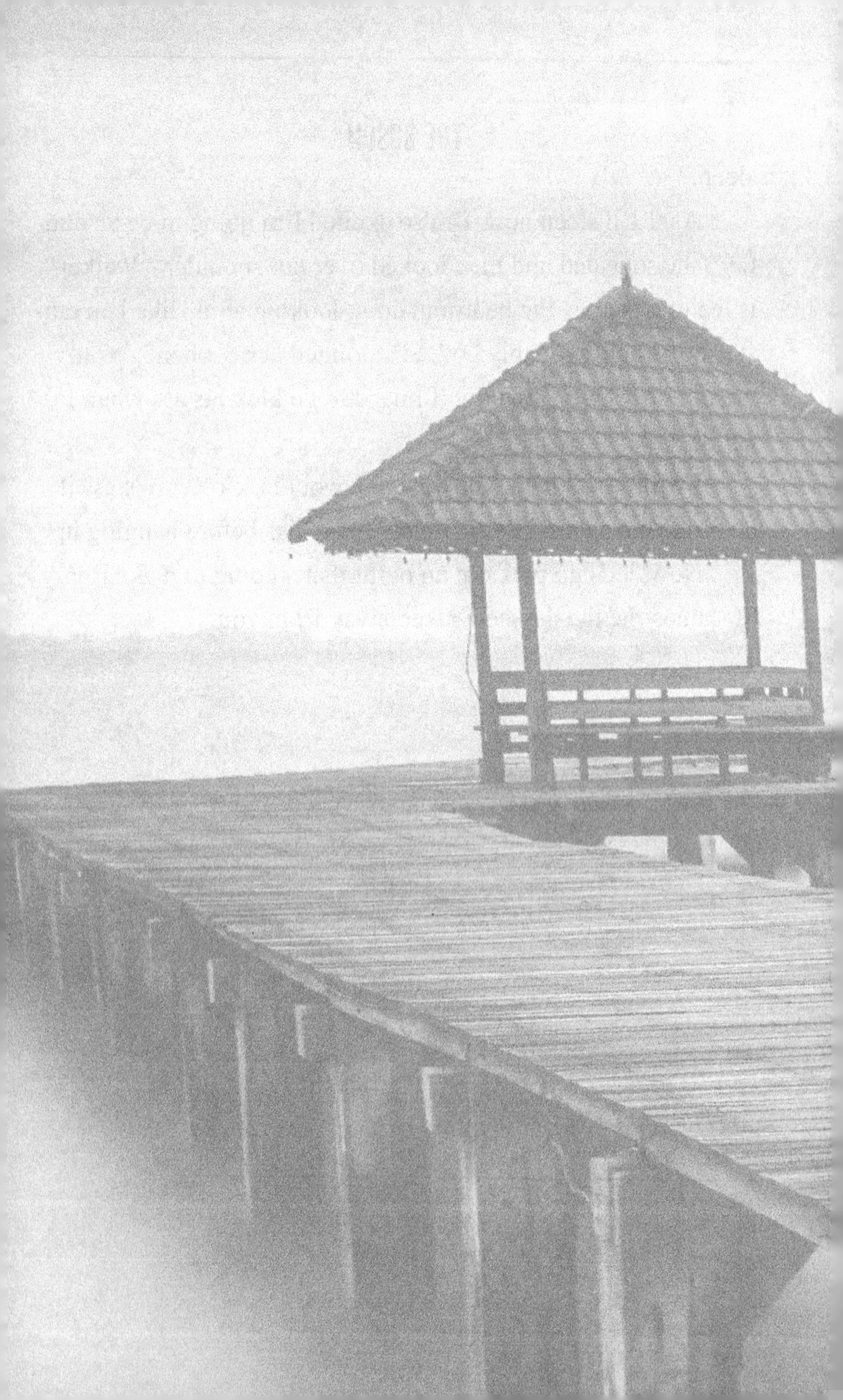

# 22

## REMY

A SOFT KNOCK on my bedroom door had me perking up and sitting up on my bed. "Come in."

My dad cracked the door open and pressed his face into the small opening. "There's someone at the door for you."

"For me?" I questioned. No one ever came by to see me. Ever. At least, not since I was in high school.

"The one and only, and you shouldn't leave them waiting for too long. Otherwise, they might leave."

My brows knitted together, racking my brain on who it could possibly be. Maybe it was one of the guys from the station, but why wouldn't they call before coming over? "Who is it?"

"You'll have to come to the door to find out." The hint of mischievousness in his tone had me up and off my bed in a nanosecond. What was my old man up to?

I thought he might have let whoever it was inside or he would have waited for me at the door, but when I walked by the living room, my dad was reclined back in his chair with a smirk on his face.

When I hesitated to open the door, he yelled. "Hurry up and find out who it is."

Doing as I was told, I slowly opened the front door. Whoever it was stood with her back to the door and her long black hair in a ponytail. For a brief moment, I thought of Stella and how I wished it was her, but she didn't know where I lived, so I knew it couldn't be her.

"Can I help you?" I asked as I swung open the screen door.

The woman turned at my voice, and my knees nearly went out from under me when Stella stood there staring back at me. Her big brown eyes scanned me from head to toe, and once they were done, they were filled with unshed tears.

Unable to move or speak, it seemed, I took in every inch of her body. Her eyes were red-rimmed as if she'd been crying, and her nose was tipped with pink, but she was still the most beautiful woman I'd ever seen. She wore a light blue sundress that showed each and every one of her curves. Her breasts seemed larger than when I last saw those perky globes with dark nipples that I loved to suck on so damn much. Her skin was a beautiful bronze that glowed in the sunlight.

Her hands went to her hips. "Are you only going to stare at

## THE BOSUN

my boobs, or are you going to say something?"

"Stella," I croaked out and had to clear my throat. "What are you doing here?" I wanted to hit myself with the heel of my hand at my stupid question, but before I could take back my words, she spoke.

"I came for two reasons, but before I tell you, is there somewhere we can talk in private?"

She wanted to talk in private? I didn't really want my dad to eavesdrop on our conversation, even though I'd likely tell him all about it later, so I knew we needed to go somewhere else.

"Are you hungry?"

"No." Her face actually looked like it turned a slight shade of green at my question.

"Okay, let me grab my keys, and I'll take us somewhere private to talk." I held up one finger. "I'll be right back."

I sprinted through the house to get to my room. Slipping my feet into a pair of flip-flops, I grabbed my phone and the keys to my truck and ran back, waving to my dad as I went by. I was afraid if I was gone too long, she might leave.

"Let's take my truck." I pointed to the F-150 that I'd had since high school. It was old as dirt, but it ran like a rock star.

Stella followed along beside me. I opened the passenger door for her and waited until she had her seatbelt on before I closed the door and hightailed it around the front to slide in behind the steering wheel.

I thought maybe she'd talk while I drove, but instead, Stella looked out the passenger window with a death grip on her phone. Luckily, where I was taking her wasn't far because I was dying to know why she'd sought me out. Pulling up to the public beach, I turned to look at her.

"Is this okay?"

When she started to open the passenger door, I assumed she was fine with the location I'd chosen. I wasn't fast enough to open her door or help her out, which irritated me. I wanted to say something but held my tongue.

Once her feet hit the sand, Stella kicked off her sandals and held them by their straps with one hand as she headed in a direction where it was less crowded. I let her pick the spot, and once she sat down in the sand, I moved to sit beside her. My pinky finger itched to reach out and touch her silky skin, but I didn't give in to temptation. Instead, I waited until she said whatever she came here to say.

Her gaze stayed on the tide coming in and out. Never once looking at me. "I need to know why you ended things with me. Even if it's awful, I need to hear it."

"That's why you came here?" She could have called or texted, but I hadn't answered those questions when she'd asked before, so maybe she knew I couldn't deny her in person. Even though I hadn't responded to her texts, it still killed me when she stopped contacting me. I knew I'd fucked up royally, only now she was here in the flesh. Now was my chance to tell her

## THE BOSUN

about my dark past. Would she look at me differently after she knew how damaged I was?

"I'm nowhere near good enough for you, and I knew if I stayed, I'd be one of the men in your life who broke you."

"And you don't think you broke me when you ended things?" Her voice was wobbly as she spoke while her eyes were set on the ocean in front of us.

"It wasn't my intention to break you but to save you from me. When I decided to volunteer, I thought I was better, but the night that I fell asleep and had that nightmare, I realized I still had so much more work to do."

"Did you ever think if you explained it to me that I might have understood and given you time? That maybe I could have helped you or at least not cried nonstop for a week straight wondering what the hell I'd done that made you run away from me?"

Wrapping her arms around her legs, Stella rested her cheek on her arms and looked at me for the first time since we'd arrived. Her face was wet with tears. Knowing I'd been the one to cause her heartbreak made it difficult to breathe.

"What was your dream about?" She nibbled on her lower lip as she waited for me to answer.

It was now or never. I knew if I didn't tell her now, I wouldn't get another chance, and Stella would walk out of my life forever.

"You know I was in the military, but you don't know why I

left." This time it was me who couldn't look at her as I spoke. I didn't want to see how she'd take the news. I hated the pity on everyone's faces when they learned of what happened that day. "Growing up, I had a friend named Damon. We were like brothers. We did everything together, much to our parents' dismay at times. If one of us got in trouble, so did the other. I'm not sure when I knew I wanted to be a Marine, but so did Damon. Or at least that's what he always said. Sometimes I feel like I talked him into joining, or he knew he had to enlist since I wasn't going to college. Anyway, we went through boot camp together, were in the same unit, and even deployed together. I thought Damon would be by my side until my dying breath." Closing my eyes, I continued to feel her eyes bore into me as I spoke. "Instead, it was me by his side as he took his last breath. We were ambushed, and Damon being the heroic man he was, threw himself on top of me when a shower of bullets came down on us. He died saving me."

I hadn't realized I was crying until I felt Stella begin to wipe my tears away. When she was done, Stella rested her head on my shoulder and held me while not saying a word. Somehow, she knew exactly what I needed in that moment.

"I felt a tremendous amount of guilt for not saving him. When I left the military, I didn't come home because I thought my dad would be ashamed of me, and I couldn't face Damon's family. Instead, I started working on boats. I'm sure you're wondering where this is all going."

## THE BOSUN

Looking down at the sand, I continued. "After you left, I would go onto your Instagram and look at your pictures. One day I saw my friend Tyler had died while overseas. The guilt was unbearable, but it made me realize I needed to stop hiding from my past. Once the season was over, I came back here and started to see a therapist. I thought I'd made progress, but the dream that night made me realize I wasn't as put together as I thought."

"No one's perfect, Remy," she said quietly. Her arms around me tightened as she spoke. "We've all got baggage, but it's how we deal with it that matters. I wish you would have told me all of this before. We could have talked, and if you needed space to work on yourself, I would have given it to you. It was the not knowing that killed me. I couldn't understand why...I—" She broke off and turned away.

Unsure if she'd want me to touch her after she'd pulled away, I slowly put my arm around her middle. When she didn't tense up, I took that as a good sign and pulled her back to my front. With her between my legs, I rested my chin on top of her head. "I'm sorry I hurt you, Stella. You have to know it was never my intention."

Her body shook as I held it tightly to my chest. Again, I was causing her pain when I didn't mean to. Would I ever be able to take away the hurt I'd inflicted on her?

We continued to sit like that, watching the waves crash and people roaming about until her body relaxed into mine. It was then I remembered she'd mentioned she'd come for two reasons. What the other could be, I couldn't imagine.

Rubbing my hands up and down her arms, I kissed the side of her head. "Are you okay now?"

"For the time being." She sniffed.

"You came for something else. What is it?"

Tensing up, she extricated herself from my hold and moved to sit in front of me. A sense of foreboding filled me. Was she sick and came to tell me goodbye?

"I told you about Brock and me. The troubles we had. How I was unable to get pregnant and him subsequently cheating on me and getting someone pregnant from his office."

Was she back with that douchebag? Had I driven her back into the arms of the man who'd broken her?

"Yesterday, I was doing a photoshoot with Lexie, and I wasn't feeling well. Actually, I've felt off for at least a week. When I'm writing, days kind of blend together, so it's hard to tell. Anyway, Lexie started to ask me questions about my symptoms, and then it all clicked."

What all clicked? Seriously, I was going to feel like such an asshole if she was sick, and I'd left her, providing more stress for her.

"You never said what your thoughts on having children were. Maybe that was because you don't want them or because you didn't want me to feel bad because it wasn't possible with me, or because you're young and it hasn't crossed your mind.

## THE BOSUN

I don't know." She looked down at her painted toes that were wiggling in the sand before her gaze lifted to mine. "I didn't think it was possible, but I'm pregnant. You deserve to know that I'm planning on keeping the baby. Your part in his or her life is up to you." She put her hand into a pocket I hadn't realized was on her dress and pulled out a sheet of paper. "This is a plane ticket to California. Use it or don't, but I hope you do."

My mind was still reeling from finding out she was pregnant. Stella was pregnant with my baby, and I was going to be a father.

"I know this is a lot to take in, so I'll give you time. I'm staying at an Airbnb for the night and then leaving tomorrow. If you want to talk, I'll text you the address."

Every word she was saying registered, but I couldn't speak. Hell, I could barely blink. The reason I hadn't used a condom wasn't because I thought she couldn't get pregnant. Not once had that thought gone through my mind. The problem was nothing penetrated through the thick veil of lust of how much I wanted her that ran through my veins. All I had wanted was to sink into her tight pussy and feel it suck me into its depths.

She stood, her hand hovering over my shoulder as if she was afraid to touch me. "I'm going to go. The heat is starting to get to me, so I'm going to get an Uber."

"Don't go," I called out hoarsely. "I...can I come back to your place so we can talk?" She bit on her lower lip as she nodded down at me. "Thanks, let's get you out of this heat. If I'd known, I never would have brought you here."

"It's okay. I'm learning new things about myself every day lately. What makes my stomach roll, and what makes me want to lose my breakfast. The other day the smell of coffee had me nauseous for hours, and I couldn't figure out why. I guess I won't be visiting my local coffee shop anytime in the near future."

After helping her into my truck, I got inside and turned to her. "You said you took a test yesterday." She nodded, wringing her hands together. "Have you been to the doctor to get it confirmed?"

"Not yet, but I plan to call Lexie's doctor when I get back and make an appointment. If you want, I can send you the confirmation once I have it."

Shifting my truck out of park, I pulled out of the parking lot and onto the street. "It's not that I don't believe you. Now that you told me, it makes sense why I thought your tits look bigger."

Stella crossed her arms over her ample chest, trying to hide her tits, but all it did was enhance them.

"What's the address of the place you're staying?" I asked to get my attention back on the road and not thinking about how I wanted to devour her.

She rattled off an address that wasn't too far from my dad's house. My mind raced with a thousand questions, but none of them spilled from my lips as I drove us. The most pressing

## THE BOSUN

question was, did Stella only want me to be around for our unborn child, or did she want more from me.

The thought of being a father scared the living shit out of me, but the thing that scared me the most was losing Stella again and knowing I'd never have a chance to win her back.

"This is it up on the right," she called when we were only a few houses away. "From what I've seen, you grew up in a nice town. It's very peaceful and quaint."

I wasn't sure about quaint, but it was peaceful. At least most of the time. It saddened me to realize I could have come back here long ago. Maybe I would have sought the counseling I needed then and be the man I wished to be for Stella now, but I knew I couldn't always be second-guessing my choices. If I had come back after leaving the military, I wouldn't have been on Seas the Day, and I wouldn't have met Stella on it. I was learning everything worked out the way it was meant to, and I needed to cherish everything life gave me.

"Don't you find your place on the beach peaceful?" I asked as she unlocked the door to the house she was staying at.

"I do. That's why I bought it, but that doesn't mean I can't find other places peaceful."

"True," I answered. I was really only making small talk.

"Since I'm only here for the day, I don't have anything to eat or drink. I'm sorry. I could get you a glass of tap water if you'd like."

"No, I'm fine. Why don't we sit so we can talk? Now that

I've had time to digest the news that I'm going to be a father, I...well, I want to know how you feel about me. Where do I fit into the picture?"

Stella's legs nearly came out from under her. I wasn't sure if that was a good thing or a bad sign to my question. Her knee bounced as she sat in a chair across from me. "I don't want to force you into anything. You may have moved on since you've been home or don't see a life with me. That's for you to answer. Do I want you in my life as more than the baby's father? Yes, but I understand if that's not something you're ready for, or that's not what you want."

I'd messed up more than I thought if she thought for one second I didn't want her.

Moving around the table, I kneeled in front of her and took her hands in mine. "There's never been one second since the moment I laid eyes on you that I haven't wanted you. It was never about that but about me. I'm sorry I left you with so many questions. I should have replied back to your messages, but I was not in a good place when I ended things. Hell, I'm still not."

Her face fell at my words. Using my finger, I tilted her head back up until our eyes met. "I'm a wreck without you in my life. I'm not sure when it happened or how, but I fell in love with you during our short time together. Each day since I left California, it's been almost unbearable to even get up in the morning, but I fought through it, so I could make myself a

## THE BOSUN

better man for you and unbeknownst to me, our child." I spread my hand over her still-flat stomach in awe that I'd created a life, and it was growing inside of her. "I know I've screwed up in the worst of ways, but I'll do whatever I have to do to make you believe how much you mean to me."

With a trembling lip, she asked brokenly. "How am I to know that if you have another bad dream, you won't pick up and leave again?"

Bringing her hands to my mouth, I kissed the backs of them. "Because I'm promising here and now if I have a bad day, dream, or flashback, I'll talk to you about it. I'll find a therapist in California, who I'll continue to see. What I won't do is leave you again."

"Do you really love me?" she asked with tears welling up in her beautiful brown eyes.

"Why is that so hard to believe? You're a very lovable person, and if you give me a chance, I'd be happy to show you just how easy it is." My hands skimmed up her legs until they reached the hem of her dress. My thumbs rubbed the skin just under the edge until she gave me a subtle nod, giving me the okay to move on. Now that I had the green light, I wasted no time. Pressing her legs apart by moving my body between her legs, I ran my thumbs up the inside of her thighs and didn't stop until I was met with the promised land.

Hooking my thumb into her panties, I moved the fabric to the side with one hand while I ran the tip of my finger through her already damp folds.

With one touch, she was already arching her back and letting out a moan that had my dick straining against my board shorts.

"Fuck, I can smell you from here. I've missed this pussy almost as much as I missed you." Leaning down, I flipped the skirt of her dress up and dove my face between her legs.

"I've missed your mouth." She ground her slick heat into my face as I lapped at her nub. "More," she moaned, "I need you inside of me."

Picking her up out of the chair, I tried to find the bedroom because I knew the second I felt her pussy start to spasm, I'd need to be balls deep inside of her. Instead, I found a table in the hallway that would be the perfect height for her to sit on while I fucked her. "I need to make you come first," I murmured against her lips as she untied my shorts and let them fall to the ground.

My thumb rubbed tight, fast circles on her clit while I nipped at her collarbone and down between her breasts. Stella wound her fingers in my hair and pulled my face to her right breast. Directing me to what she needed. I loved that she had no problem saying what she wanted in or out of bed.

Taking the hint, I pulled the top half of her dress down along with her bra until her succulent tits were bared to me.

My other hand went to her other breast, weighing it in the palm of my hand. If I thought her tits were great before, now

## THE BOSUN

they were spectacular. They were bigger, perkier, and I wanted to spend an entire day worshipping them the way they deserved.

Sucking on the flesh, I rolled the other nipple between my thumb and forefinger, making Stella buck against me. Her body was so much more responsive. It drove me wild, making my movements quicken until she was vibrating against me.

Gripping my straining erection with one hand, I ran it through her slick folds and placed the tip at her entrance. "Are you ready for me?"

"Yes," she moaned as I slammed into her. Her head fell back against the wall. Picking up one leg, I threw it over my shoulder before I gripped her hips for leverage. With each stroke, my pace quickened, our skin slapped together, and Stella's breathy moans nearly brought me over the edge.

Changing up my movements, I started to grind the base of my cock into her clit after I bottomed out inside of her. Stella's nails scraped along the skin of my back and dug in as her walls started to flutter and then take hold of my cock.

Letting go of her hip with one hand, I moved my thumb through her juices until it was coated with her essence and started making slow circles on her bundle of nerves to draw out her release.

"Oh god, Remy!" She sat up straight and shouted against the column of my neck while her entire body shook.

Swiveling my hips, I sunk in as deep as I could go, wrapping my arms around Stella as I erupted inside of her. Not wanting the moment to end, I kept rocking inside of her until I softened and slipped out.

Lifting her in my arms, Stella wrapped her legs around my waist and laid her head on my shoulder as I walked us to the bedroom. I pulled the covers back before I gently placed her down onto the bed and followed in behind her. Stella draped one arm and one leg over my side and nuzzled her face to the crook of my neck.

"I love you, Remy," she said softly before her breaths evened out, and she was fast asleep.

My arms tightened around her, wanting to feel every inch of her body against mine. In that moment, all was right in the world. I knew I was right where I was meant to be. Tomorrow I'd be following her back to California, but I'd travel across the entire globe to be with her.

Tomorrow was the start of a new life with the woman I loved and our unborn child.

# THE BOSUN

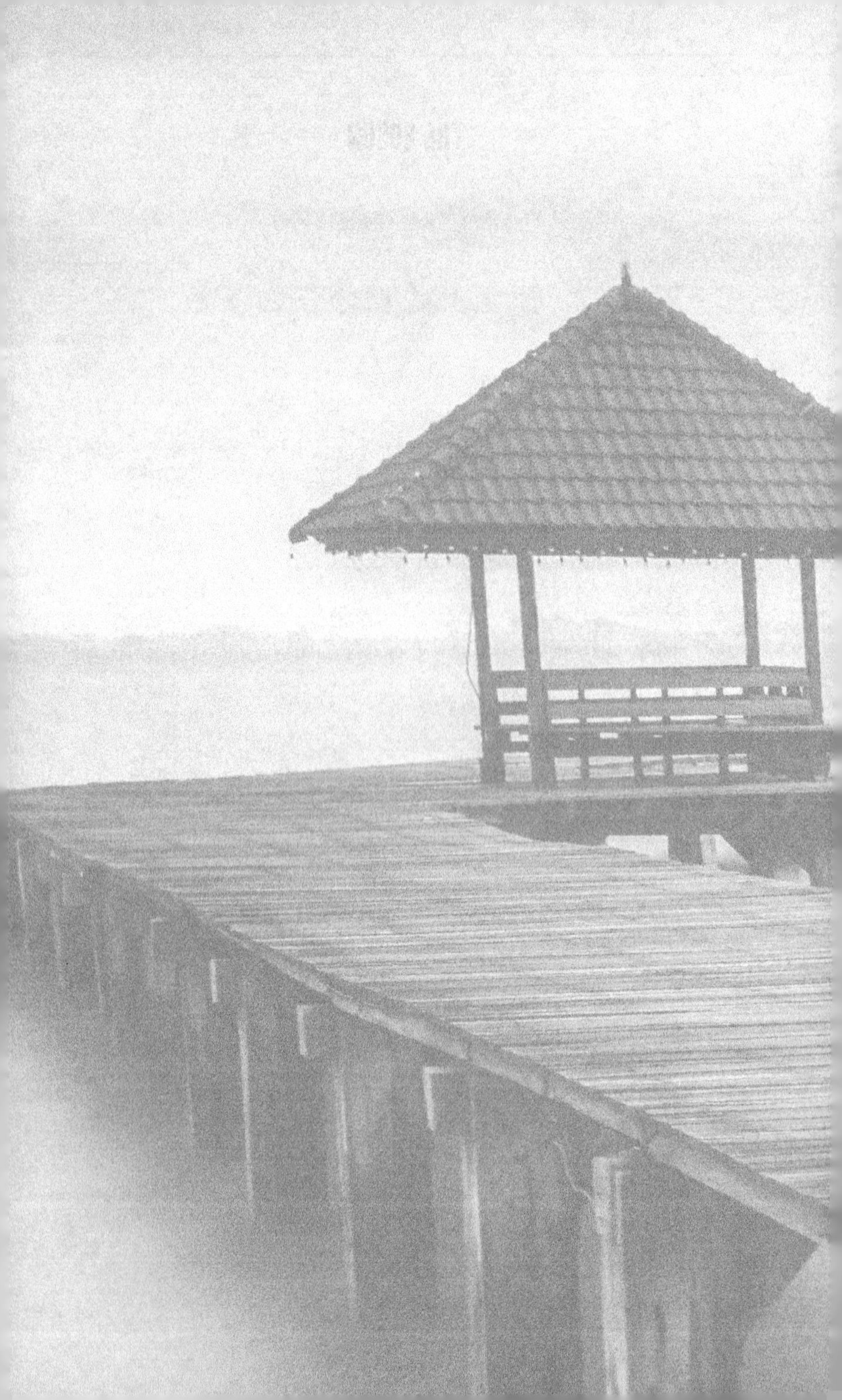

# EPILOGUE

## REMY
## 3 YEARS LATER

SWOOPING MY ALMOST-two-year-old daughter into my arms, I blew a raspberry on her cheek. "Wrong way, Birdie. Mommy's that way," I pointed in the opposite direction she was headed. I was pretty sure I knew where she was going. She wanted to give what was in her hand to her best friend and our neighbor, Ava, Ryder and Lexie's youngest daughter, who was born two days before our Birdie.

"Momma," she squealed and clapped her tiny little hands.

"Yes, let's go surprise Mommy with her birthday present," I said as I set her down and pointed her in the right direction this time. If I wasn't careful, my surprise wasn't going to be a surprise at all.

Stella was out on the deck, putting the pillows on all the

chairs and loungers for when we had guests over later that day. When she heard Birdie pound on the glass door that led outside, she looked up with a wide smile on her beautiful make-up-free face. She had a few more freckles on her nose and cheeks than the day I met her. Each night I liked to kiss each freckle and try to discover new ones.

"Hey, Birdie baby," she picked up our daughter. "What do you have here?"

Wrapping my arm around them, I leaned down and kissed the top of Stella's head. "Happy Birthday, my beautiful Stella."

She looked up at me with her nose scrunched up. "Why are you giving me a present now and not later when everyone will be here?"

"Because this is a special moment just for the three of us. Now hurry up and open it before someone else does it for you." I nodded down to the box Birdie was trying to pry open with her little fingers.

Stella sat down in the chair she'd just placed the cushions in with Birdie on her lap. I tried to be as inconspicuous as possible as I got down on one knee and waited for her to open the box.

"Oh, I like jewelry. Did you help pick it out, Birdie?" she asked as she untied the ribbon. Her hand went to her mouth when she opened the lid, and tears instantly filled her eyes. "Is this what I think it is?"

Taking the ring out of the box, I held her hand while look-

## THE BOSUN

ing up into her glassy brown eyes that were filled with so much love it had my own eyes welling up. "Not a day goes by where I don't thank my lucky stars you boarded that boat and threw caution to the wind. If it wasn't for you and our beautiful daughter, I'd be half the man I am today. I can't wait to watch the sunset each night with you until I take my dying breath. Will you please do me the honor of being my wife?"

"Is this real? Did I fall asleep, and now I'm dreaming?"

"This is as real as it gets when you're already living the dream."

"You're right. My life has been perfect since the moment you stepped on that plane with me. You've been the perfect boyfriend, the best father and son anyone could ask for, and now you'll be a wonderful husband." She sniffed and wiped at the moisture that threatened to spill over.

"Does that mean your answer is a yes?" I asked as I skimmed my thumb over her ring finger.

Birdie tried to pry the sparkling diamond out from between my fingers, making us both laugh.

"Not only is it a yes, but it's a hell yes, I'll marry you. Nothing would make me happier!" Leaning forward, she threw her arms around my neck as she tried not to squish our daughter, who clapped at our happy news.

Cupping the side of her face with one hand, I sucked on her bottom lip before sweeping my tongue inside her waiting mouth. The kiss was short but held a promise for later when our daughter was asleep.

"Later," I whispered against her bee-stung lips, "I can't wait to celebrate with you."

"Why did you plan a party if you knew you were going to ask me to marry you? Now I want to call the whole party off." She stood Birdie on the ground, who went about taking off all the cushions Stella had just put on.

I chuckled as I pulled her up and out of the chair. "It will be a short party, I promise. They all know I was planning on asking you. That's why my dad is flying in today. He's going to watch Birdie for the weekend, so I can take you up to the mountains, and we can sit in front of a fire." I pulled her body to mine and slipped on her engagement ring as I spoke softly into her ear. "There's a no clothing allowed rule for the entire time we're in the cabin."

"Oh, I like the sound of that. I don't even have to worry about what to pack." Leaning up on her tippy toes, Stella pressed her lips to mine for a long minute. "When do we leave?"

Wrapping my arms around her middle, I nuzzled my face into her neck and let the scruff of my jaw tickle her. "Tonight after the party, and before you worry about packing on such little notice, it's all taken care of."

"You're making this the best birthday ever."

"That's the plan. I want to make each day better than the last."

## THE BOSUN

A throat clearing had us looking up to find Lexie standing on our deck with a Cheshire Cat grin on her face. "I'm assuming by all the kissing going on over here, she said yes."

Stella held out her hand, showing off her ring. "Isn't it gorgeous!"

"So gorgeous!" Lexie answered back as they hugged, squealed, and jumped in place. "And don't worry about Birdie. I told Remy's dad if he has any trouble, we're right next door."

Stella sighed in relief. "That does make me feel better. While he's watched her for a couple of hours, two days is a lot to take on."

"Aww, she'll be good for her PawPaw. She adores him, and he adores her." Lexie broke away and started for the stairs. "I just wanted to come over and say congratulations. Maybe when you two get back, you'll have a wedding date picked out."

"Hardly," I laughed. "We've got better things to do than pick a date." Both women turned to look at me with fire in their eyes. "Plus, whatever date Stella wants to get married is fine with me."

"Good save," Lexie laughed. "I'll see you guys tonight for the party." She waved as she ran back over to her house, where Ryder was in the pool with both of their daughters. They were little fish that would spend all day in the pool if you let them.

Wrapping my arms around her from behind, I rested my chin on the top of her head. "We should probably finish getting ready for your party. How about one of us takes Birdie down to the beach? It's going to take forever to get anything done if she's going to follow along and undo everything."

Turning to look over her shoulder at me, she asked. "Are you sure you can do everything if I take her down?"

"If I can survive being at war in Afghanistan and putting out fires, I'm sure I can handle putting up some decorations and making sure everything is without tiny handprints all over it."

Stella smirked up at me. "We'll see about that. You have no idea how easily she can destroy a room when she's determined."

"Don't worry about me. I'll tackle whatever mess she's made. It's your birthday. You shouldn't spend the day cleaning."

"Good luck, hot stuff." She grabbed Birdie by the hand and then slapped me on the ass on the way down the stairs to the beach.

Seriously, how bad could it be?

I shouldn't have asked. Walking back into the house, I immediately smelled something off but couldn't pinpoint what it was. Following my nose, I found myself outside of Birdie's room, afraid to go inside. The smell of poop was strong as I entered the room. I thought maybe she'd gotten into a diaper and left it open, but no, I couldn't be that lucky. Birdie had smeared poop all over one wall and all over her bed.

Did Stella know what I was walking into? If not, how did Birdie get her hands clean from the feces she'd used to paint

## THE BOSUN

her room? I found my answer a minute later when I went to strip her bedding off her bed. A hairbrush for one of her dolls had shit caked into the bristles.

Not wanting to ruin Stella's day, I got the cleaning supplies and went to work while gagging. With each swipe, the rag smeared the horrendously smelling poop making it nearly impossible to clean up, but I manned up and didn't stop until Birdie's room looked brand new. While cleaning Birdie's room took most of my time, I got the house picked up before anyone arrived for the party.

In T-Minus three hours, we would be on our way to the mountains for our own private celebration.

⚓

## STELLA

Leaning over the console of Remy's truck, I kissed his cheek and then rested my head on his shoulder. "Thank you for today. It was absolutely perfect."

Kissing the top of my head, he asked, "You didn't have any idea?"

"Not a single one. I'm shocked Pen and Lexie kept quiet about you proposing." They had asked a lot of questions lately about if and when Remy and I would tie the knot. Truthfully, I'd been happy having him as my partner and the father of my child. I didn't think I needed the piece of paper or the ring on my finger, but that all changed the moment he popped the question. I realized then how much I wanted to become Stella St. James and to be able to claim him as mine with a ring on his finger.

"I swore them to secrecy." He flipped on the windshield wipers as snow started to fall steadily.

"The party was great. I can't believe they let us leave without any hassle, though. I thought for sure it would be late before we got on the road." Sitting up, I turned to look at him.

"They understood," he chuckled while keeping his eyes on the road.

"Yeah, because you told them we had to leave so we could consummate our engagement." I laughed at the absurdity of it.

"It worked, didn't it?"

"I'm glad it did. I like that I got to spend the day on the beach, and tonight I'll be cuddled up to you in front of a fire while it snows."

"Oh, we'll be doing a whole lot more than cuddling. If I have my way, I'll be getting you pregnant with Birdie's brother or sister."

A laugh of surprise escaped me. "Don't you think maybe we should be married before we have another baby? I'm not vain or anything, but I don't want to be a whale when I walk down the aisle either."

Remy chewed on that for a minute. Taking my left hand in

## THE BOSUN

his right, he laced our fingers together and placed them on his thigh. "Do you want a big or a small wedding?"

"Small. Only close friends and family. You?"

"Small as well. Okay, how long do you think it would take you to plan the wedding of your dreams?"

That was hard to answer. I had the big wedding before. A wedding I worked my ass off to pay for, and look where that had gotten me. I didn't need two hundred and fifty people. Only the closest and dearest to my heart.

"I think I'd like to do it on our beach. Lexie would probably let us use some of hers as well. Since it's early December and too cold to wear a dress, maybe we should wait until at least April or May. What do you think?"

Remy grunted a sound of disapproval. "I think six months is a long time, but I'm willing to wait. I want the day to be perfect for you."

"Aww, I want the day to be perfect for you as well. We could always go somewhere warm for the winter and do it there. When we get back, I can ask Lexie and Pen when they're available and work from there."

"A tropical wedding and honeymoon sound good."

A house a few hundred feet away lit up the dark sky with Christmas lights. It was straight out of a picture book. "Look at that house," I pointed it out. "It's so cute."

"I'm glad you like it because that's where we're going. I paid extra for them to put up lights and decorate for the holiday."

"Really?" I jumped in my seat. "You've really outdone yourself." Brushing my lips against the shell of his ear, my hand rubbed against the bulge in his jeans. "I wonder how I can pay you back."

Winding his hand through the strands of my hair, Remy made a fist. "I think you've got the right idea. I wouldn't mind seeing your head bob in the light of the fire."

"If we weren't about ready to pull in, I'd blow you right now, but I guess it will have to wait." I licked up the column of his neck and gently bit the space right below his ear.

"Another time," he husked out as he threw the truck into park. Grabbing my face with both hands, Remy claimed my mouth in a searing kiss that had me panting and wanting to shed both our clothes as quickly as possible. Pulling away, he breathed deeply with heavily lidded eyes, letting me know the kiss affected him just as much as it did me. "Let's grab our stuff and get inside."

Scrambling out of the truck on weak legs, I waited as Remy grabbed our bags out of the back and followed him up the stairs that led to the front door. It was too dark to see much, even with the house decorated with Christmas lights. All I could see was that it was a wood cabin, two stories tall with a wide wrap-around porch.

Unlocking the door, Remy stood to the side and let me enter first. A lamp lit the space along with a roaring fire someone

## THE BOSUN

had already started for us to enjoy.

It was warm, homey, and rustic with wood beams and furniture. There was a furry rug in front of the fireplace that I knew we'd spend a lot of time on while we were here. Wrapping his arms around my waist from behind, Remy rested the side of his head against mine. "I know today is your birthday, but you've made it one of the best days of my life by agreeing to be my wife. Happy Birthday, Stella."

Placing my hands on top of his, I leaned into him. "I don't know how I'm ever going to top today for one of your birthdays. You've made it damn near impossible."

"It's not about topping it. It was never about that. I did all this because I love you. Each day we spend together should be about making it as memorable as possible, don't you think?"

"How did you get so wise?" He shrugged, and I felt the silent laughter vibrate through my back. "Still, you gave me a birthday I won't ever forget. Let me start thanking you." My hands moved from his to reach around and grab his tight ass.

Pulling out of his hold, I walked backward, facing him so he could get a good look. My hands went to the flannel shirt I'd borrowed from his side of the closet and started to slowly unbutton it.

"Are you going to strip for me in the firelight?" He stepped slowly toward me, giving me room to continue my striptease.

My answer was to let the shirt slip off my arms and onto the floor. He took in a sharp breath when I exposed my lacy bra that left no room for imagination. Twirling around, I kicked off my Uggs and shook my ass at him as I shimmied my way out of my leggings.

"Your ass in that thong is downright delectable. I'm going to take you from behind and smack that ass until it's nice and pink for me." He took one predatory step toward me before he had me in his grasp.

Stalking over to the front of the fireplace, he went down onto his knees before he laid me down before him. "I want you to touch yourself over that piece of lace you've got between your thighs and get yourself primed while I strip for you."

Fuck yes. I might have moaned, knowing the heated look I'd see in his eyes when he watched me masturbate.

Taking my index and middle fingers, I moved them over the lacy fabric, loving the way the rough texture felt against my sensitive flesh.

"Just like that," he said as he kicked his shoes off to the side. Undoing the button of his jeans and the zipper, his cock sprung free and bobbed against his shirt. My mouth salivated at the sight before me. "Later, you can wrap your pretty mouth around me and suck me off, but right now, I need to be inside of you."

Gripping his shirt at the nape of his neck, he slowly pulled it off. Was there a class that men took on how to drive your woman wild by taking off your clothes? I didn't know what it was about the move, but it always made me so hot for him.

## THE BOSUN

Kneeling in front of me, he took one breast into his mouth and sucked hard before he let it go with a pop. "Let me see how soaked you are for me." Shoving my thong to the side, he plunged two long digits inside me and pumped twice. "Fuck, you're so hot and wet for me. Turn around and get on your hands and knees."

Doing as I was ordered, I looked over my shoulder at him and watched as he sheathed his length and sunk down to the floor before he ripped my thong off in one smooth motion. When his hands gripped my hips, and I felt the tip of his cock at my entrance, a shiver wracked my body, knowing that pleasure that would soon follow.

I thought he was going to slam into me, but instead, he entered me inch by agonizing inch until he was seated deep inside of me. His thumbs rubbed over the globes of my ass as his fingers dug into the fleshy part of my hips.

"This ass of yours is what dreams are made of." He pulled almost all the way out, and when he slammed back inside, his hand connected with my ass, sending a jolt through me. "The way your pussy contracts around me when I slap your ass makes me rock hard."

Pulling out again and again, he thrust into me with the force of a hurricane and a slap of thunder until my ass stung, and I was begging for him to finish me off.

I went down on my elbows and moved my hand between my legs, but Remy was having none of that. Swatting my hand away, he pulled my arms behind my back and held my hands in one of his as he started to rock inside of me. "Please, I need to come."

"Tonight, all your pleasure comes from me. Do you hear me?"

"Yes," I answered breathlessly when his other hand went between my legs, and the base of his palm started to grind into my clit.

"Good. Now, I want you to come all over my cock. I want to hear you scream my name like I'm your god."

I had no problem screaming his name as he worshipped my body. His hand continued to stimulate my bundle of nerves as the tip of his cock hit the right place in me repeatedly until I was sagging on the floor.

Remy let go of my hands and moved to hold onto my hips as he started to pound inside of me.

When his hot breath became heavy in my ear, and I felt his dick jerk inside, I wanted him all over again.

Laying me down on the rug, Remy spread my legs as he moved between them. Lowering himself onto his stomach, he looked up at me. "I want to lick up all that honey that's dripping out of you for me."

One slow lick from my tight ring up to my oversensitive clit had me bowing off the floor and ready to detonate. It wouldn't take much to have me hurtling over the edge. Lapping at my core and moving up to my nub, one finger slipped inside

## THE BOSUN

and slowly started to pump in and out.

He growled and the vibration, along with the flat of his tongue making slow circles, had me crying out. Flashes of red and white went off behind my eyes as my fingers dug into his broad shoulders. Slowly, he brought me down from my orgasmic haze with caresses to my arms and back.

Moving up my body, he kissed me slow and sweet when he met my lips. Rolling over to the side, he took me with him, wrapping his whole body around me. The heat from the fire and the steady beat of his heart had me in a sleepy trance-like state.

"Sleep for a bit because I plan to keep you up all night," he murmured into the top of my head.

Nuzzling into the crook of his neck, I placed kisses up as high as I could reach. "I love you, Remy St. James. Thank you for making all the dreams I didn't know I had come true."

"Back at you, babe."

It wasn't long until my breaths evened out, and I was out like a light in the arms of my dream man.

We may have intended to wait to get pregnant until we were married, but life had other plans. Or maybe it was the fact that we ran out of condoms after the first day at the cabin, and we couldn't keep our hands off each other or come up for air long enough to track some down. Either way, it didn't matter. Life was a miracle, and we'd been given a blessing. With Remy by my side, I'd take whatever life threw at us.

The way he went out to save the world each and every day at his job and then came home to Birdie and me made me thankful for everything life had given me.

There were still nights Remy woke up from a nightmare, but never again did he run. Instead, he held me tighter through the darkness, and during the light of day, he'd either talk to me or his therapist.

When I set off for Spain, never once did I think I'd find the answer to all my desires on Seas the Day. While Brock may have wrecked me, making my life feel like a tsunami had hit me, I was thankful he'd stepped out on me because if he hadn't, I wouldn't have the man of my dreams in my life nor the father he is to Birdie.

It took the man holding me in his arms to make me at peace with myself. He loved me for me and made me feel cherished every day.

Remy was my light after the storm, and with each passing day with our children and me, I saw the darkness that was still hidden inside of him slowly slip away like the tide.

# THE BOSUN

# ACKNOWLEGEMENTS

**My family**- your support means so much. Thank you for all of your encouragement and giving me the time to do what makes me happy.

**To my girls**: QB Tyler , Carmel Rhodes, Kelsey Cheyenne, Erica Marselas. I love each and every one of you. Thank you for all of your support.

**Wendy**- I don't know what I'd do without you. Thank you for EVERYTHING you do!

Thank you **Kristen Breanne** for making my story into a book.

To all my **author friends,** you know who you are. Thank you for accepting me and making me feel welcome in this amazing community.

To **Wildfire Marketing Solutions and Shauna** , thank you for all your knowledge and for helping me make The Bosun a success!

**Lovers** thank you for always being there.

**Team Harlow's Girls**- thank you for all of your support. Each and everyone of you are so special to me.

## THE BOSUN

To each and every **reader, reviewer,** and **blog** - I would be nowhere without you. Thank you for taking a chance on an unknown author.

# ABOUT HARLOW LAYNE

Harlow Layne is a hopeless romantic who writes sweet and sexy alpha males who will make you swoon.

When Harlow's not writing you'll find her online shopping on Amazon, Facebook, or Instagram, reading, or hanging out with her family and two dogs.

Indie Author. Romance Writer. Reader. Mom. Wife. Dog Lover. Addicted to all things Happily Ever After and Amazon.

# TITLES BY HARLOW

### Fairlane Series - Small Town Romance

With Love, Alex - Women's Fiction, Self Discovery
Hollywood Redemption - Single Parent, Suspense
Unsteady in Love - Second Chance, Military
Kiss Me - Holiday, Insta-Love
Fearless to Love - Insta- Love

### Love is Blind Series- Reverse Age Gap Romance

Intern - Office Romance
The Model - Workplace Romance
The Bosun - Military, First Responder
Coming April 29, 2021
The Rocker - Coming February 17, 2022

### Hidden Oasis Series

Walk the Line - First Responder, Suspense
Secret Admirer - Damsel in Distress, Opposites Attract, Suspense
Til Death Do Us Part - Accidental Marriage, Insta-love

## Worlds

Cocky Suit - RomCom, Office, Interracial
Risk - Forbidden, Sports
Affinity - Part of the Fairlane Series - Accidental Marriage, Enemies-to-Lovers

## Willow Bay Series - Forbidden

You Make It Easy - MM, Second Chance
Away Game - MM, Bully
Basic Chemistry - Student / Teacher - Coming Sept. 2, 2021
First Down - Sister's Best Friend - Coming Fall 2021
Over Time - Student / Teacher
Off Sides - Second Chance, Forbidden

CPSIA information can be obtained
at www.ICGtesting.com
Printed in the USA
LVHW022118130521
687361LV00013B/855